C000063866

After reading English at Oxford, Peter Adamson went on to found the *New Internationalist* magazine in 1970. He has also written and presented BBC television documentaries, and was for fifteen years the author of UNICEF's annual *State of the World's Children* report.

The Tuscan Master is his second novel following *Facing Out to Sea* (Sceptre, 1997). He lives in Oxfordshire and is married with two children.

SCEPTRE

The Tuscan Master

Peter Adamson

SCEPTRE

First published in 2000 by Hodder & Stoughton
A division of Hodder Headline
A Sceptre Paperback

10 9 8 7 6 5 4 3 2 1

A CIP catalogue record for this title is
available from the British Library

ISBN 0 340 69567 6

Printed and bound in Great Britain by
Clays Ltd, St Ives plc

Hodder and Stoughton
A division of Hodder Headline
338 Euston Road
London NW1 3BH

For Naomi and Daniel

1

Tullio let his brush arm fall to his side so that it transferred little touches of paint to his trousers, already stiffened with drying arcs of colour. He closed his eyes, pushing his head back to reach the muscles of his neck, moving the chin slowly from side to side, massaging gristle. The painting was still there, a rectangular orange blur against the soft purple of the brain.

From the window to his left a long fall of light opened a door into the floorboards. On the table, scattered with part-used paint tubes, lay two or three sketches, scraped in charcoal. He summoned himself to look at the canvas: a view of rooftops, streets, alleyways, from which all detail, intrusion, had been excluded leaving only a semi-abstract arrangement of light and shade on the planes and surfaces of the town. He dropped the brush amid the debris on the table. A breeze stirred the curtains. Somewhere outside a shutter was thrown back and a long cry of 'Giulia' fell into the street. He had sought the complexity of the light, its structural interlocking; but at twenty minutes past six on the evening of the fourth day the effect was one of biliousness, as if the work had been created from the palette of ice creams – stracciatella, caffè, nocciola, tartufo, pistacchio – in the gelateria below.

He turned to the table, squeezed out a slug of green, added a cremnitz white and a smear of cobalt, glancing up at the canvas, making a decision he knew to be too quick, too arbitrary; a form of surrender. He stepped forward, wrist poised, and began to paint, working centimetre by centimetre over the block of ochre where the shadows had fallen on the walls of San Lorenzo. A minute passed. The sunlight faded on the floorboards. Around him the silence of the studio waited. The ghosts of artists watched, expressionless.

After a few minutes he threw the brush on the table. The attempt to galvanise the composition, jolt its geometry, had failed, had robbed the canvas of contrast, life. The introduced colour was merely discordant, vulgar, bursting through its own shape, as if a child had dropped a sweet-wrapper into the ice cream. He began to swirl brushes around in the spirit jar, replacing caps on tubes of paint, suddenly needing to be out in the street, to be sitting in the sunlight with a glass of wine in his hand. He wiped a thumb over the glass of his watch, smearing paint. Claudia would not be home for another hour.

At the door of the apartment he turned to look again at the easel, the painting mute under the fading light. Even from the far side of the room its weaknesses sank into him like a slow, heavy fist; the irregular rectangles failing to break into the surface of the canvas, lacking any sense of variously lit planes standing at quiet angles to one another, or any of the conviction of the light, of its hard, searching, truthful passage over brick and stone and stucco.

❖

Tullio made his way through the streets, his world of concentration, of minutest balances, wrongly calibrated, unable to accommodate the immensity of rusticated stonework, the weight of medieval towers, the façades of imposing palazzi, the sky forcing its way down into the narrow street.

He took his table outside the Bar Gerasmo. Wine appeared at his side. He raised a palm in acknowledgement, his reactions slow, subaqueous, surveying the Via Maestra with only a hydraulic awareness of the real world, each scene a canvas waiting to be stilled, composed. He turned away from the street to focus on the velvet beds of the jeweller's windows, the mannequins in the window, the week's offerings from the Teatro Dante. The painting had stolen from the easel, followed him out into the street. Subtle differences tormented: a less obvious approach; a lighter, less literal touch; a more sideways, ironic look; above all, some inspired reaching down from the sky of the imagination, some capturing of the moment without the terrestrial siege, without the long laborious march.

'Ciao, Tullio!'

'Buona sera, Vico.'

He drank wine, aware now of being invaded by the ordinary business of the town, awnings being wound into the walls, metal shutters being dragged over the windows of optician and pharmacist, drinking straws and cigarette butts being swept from under the tables. He set the empty glass back on the wrought iron. Petals drifted by, the remains of the weekend's floral display, their lurid pinks and blues shrunk into dark veins. Artistry was what it came down to, this quality that eluded him, lying beyond his quota of grace. He tilted the chair onto its back legs and gave himself up to the wine, surrounded by harmonies of stone that still held the day's heat, lingering still with his painting. He had managed to avoid looking into the gelateria on the corner, but now he could not avoid seeing how assiduously the late afternoon sunlight followed the subtle contours of the Palazzo Alberti, how patiently it studied the burnt brickwork of the walls, how respectfully it fingered the sober, subtle sandstone, how steadily, reliably, it warmed the peeling, stuccoed façades of bank and pharmacy. For a brief moment he saw the *San Lorenzo* as it had been a week ago, glowing in the ill-lit palace of ambition.

'Tullio, salve!'

'Ciao, Enzo!'

Cyclists and push-chairs weaved a slow way through the growing throng of pedestrians, a collective murmuring jostling between the walls, the spirit of the town released from housework and shops and offices, going abroad into open spaces, communing with itself in streets and alleyways. In front of him a group of old men in pullovers stopped to greet each other with slow, extravagant cries – Ciao! Emilio! Come va? – as if it were not usual to meet like this on the Via Maestra every evening of the week.

He shifted to face the other way, towards Massi's elegant façade, watching a shop girl rearranging the window. For a moment his view was blocked by two middle-aged women in gilded spectacles crossing arm-in-arm towards the sunlight of the piazza where the tide of teenagers was already on the turn, flowing over pools of those who had congregated, sweeping some away, leaving others behind, eroding segregation. It was the hour before dinner, and soon the Via Maestra would empty. But for now it permitted the last of the sunlight to bring the town together, bestowing the certainty of benediction and repose that had been his subject, the evening blessing on its medieval towers and renaissance palaces, its petty politics, its shops and shadowed alleyways, its sons and daughters of all ages. Tullio watched as the girl appeared again among the mannequins, relishing her suppleness against the rigid plastic nudity, pondering the task of reproducing her movement in the stillness of paint, capturing her separateness from the life of the street, from the mute denizens of her window-world. He looked down to rest his eyes for a moment from the glories of the last sunlight, focusing on the little arcs of paint at about mid-calf height. It would have been easy to change his trousers before going into the street.

He was finishing a second glass when a movement from above drew his eye. Shutters were being pushed back on the second floor of the palazzo opposite. A girl leaned out over the street on folded arms, framed in stone, an artless, unobserved look on her face, while in the street below Tullio fell in love as he did a dozen times a week, a dull tug of yearning pulling him towards the window, wings of delight and despair beating over him, lifting him to the girl so that he became the air and light that modelled her uncomposed face and warmed her cheek and stole so chastely over her bare arms. The girl leaned out further, arms pressing down into the sill, the gold chain hanging over the crowds. He was still observing her, in the grip of an acute nostalgia for the present moment, when the boy on the motorino came buzzing bare-headed down the Via Giuseppe Mazzini, raising a hand to the second floor window as he swerved around a push-chair and crossed the Via Maestra.

'Ciao, Mariella!'

'Ciao, Fabrizio!'

Tullio held on to the moment at the window when the face that had been a dried-up lake of boredom swirled and flooded with pleasure and excitement.

He drank the last of his wine and slipped a note under the empty glass. It was a young man's moment. And he was old.

A dozen years earlier, Tullio had also fallen in love with the Palazzo Lanzi, with the ruined sandcastle of its coat of arms, with its smell of the middle ages, its broad, shallow steps rising between whitewashed walls, its line of brass mailboxes worn to a soft gleam, its satisfying stone handrails polished to marble. Bicycles were propped around the walls. On the flagstones, a parcel and a cylinder of propane gas. In the corner, an old sofa and a dying plant.

He began the climb to the first floor, walls and staircase counselling proportion, steadiness, in their even sharing of the last light. The doors on the landing had been left open to clear the heat at the end of the day and the smell of cooking drifted through the building. To his left he glimpsed a work in progress on an easel, an unframed canvas leaning against a wall. The sound of voices from above; two of the other tenants were descending side by side, exchanging smiles and a buona sera. There was no need to turn sideways or press against the walls; there was room for a political rally on the stairs and landings of the Palazzo Lanzi. He turned into the last flight, anticipating the painting.

Claudia had already started dinner. She glanced over her shoulder as he let himself into the apartment, her hands dripping with the juice and seeds of melon. He held the bare tops of her arms, kissing the nape of her neck. She smiled into the gentle darks and lights of the marble surface.

'Is it finished?'

'I think so.'

'Pleased?'

'Not really.'

'I thought you were excited about it?'

He dropped a plastic bag of oil paints on the worktable.

'I was until I painted it.'

An expanse of worn floorboards stretched between the three windows and the high, whitewashed walls. The studio claimed half of the apartment, drip cloths spread under easel and table, separated only by open space from the armchairs and the stone fireplace. He pulled an apron over the paint-smeared trousers.

'We can look at it later.'

'Will you show it?'

'Probably. It's as good as anything else.'

They looked at the painting after they had eaten. The lamps had not been turned on. The walls held on to the last, bluish evening light. He waited for her to speak.

'It's almost there.'

'But not quite.'

He went over to the window, taking an interest in the street, a hand on the piano.

Claudia came to him. Her arm settled around his waist.

'Is it Saturday it starts?'

'Yes. Do you want to come?'

'I promised to help Livia move her things.'

They looked out in silence over acres of pantiled roofs, brooding, burnt, against a last turquoise brightness in the sky. From the window below the sound of a cello meandered upwards, taking over the apartment with a slow, restrained adagio. For about a month now the cello had wandered through the apartments of the Palazzo Lanzi without complaint, the dozen or so tenants looking forward to its slow strains as the eyelids of the day began to droop.

'Can you do the exhibition when you've got the tour?'

'I think so. There's no point in getting there before six.'

She released him with a squeeze and crossed the studio to the kitchen.

'Something very odd happened today.'

He had opened the lid of the piano.

'A young man stopped me on the landing and asked if he could paint my portrait.'

Tullio pondered the paintings stacked against the wall. Tomorrow would have to be spent repainting the frames.

'That's not so odd. Who is he?'

'His name's Giuliano Amedei. He moved in about a month ago. I've passed him on the stairs once or twice. About twenty-five, long black hair. Very skinny. I think he might be the one who plays the cello.'

2

Outside in the piazzetta, fifty or sixty of the leading citizens of San Giovanni Valdarno are eating and drinking in the late afternoon sun that glints on the gold of earrings, necklaces, bracelets and the wings of spectacles as they kiss and compliment, greeting and exclaiming, gossiping and enquiring, circulating among their peers on the Mayor's list. In front of the cellar door a table covered in white cloths proffers prosciutto and salami, skewers of ripe pear and crumbling pecorino, plates of soft figs and sallow, bursting olives. On a table just to one side of the door are tall towers of glasses, mineral waters still and sparkling, fizzy orange drinks in smoky plastic, unlabelled bottles of Verdicchio and Chianti. Over the heads of the crowd a dark red banner – *Mostra di pittura di Tullio d'Attore* – lifts and ripples from the walls of the town.

Inside the cellar door Tullio stands by a small table where a dozen copies of his brochure are fanned out over the polished surface. Behind him in the depths of the cave, twenty two paintings are wired onto iron grids forming a rectangular cage inside the medieval walls. The only other occupants of the cellar are a middle-aged couple from the Romagna and a younger couple who might be German or English and who have been lingering for a long time now in front of a landscape of the Pratomagno. From the ceiling, chromium snakes spit a poisonous halogen light onto the canvases, piling up shadows. Tullio screws up his eyes against the brightness outside where the voices are growing louder, lapping against the town walls as the wine takes hold. Framed in the dark door, a man with patent shoes and one gold tooth has his arms around the waists of two laughing women. Red wine has spilt down the lapels of his linen suit. A summer breeze chases dust and paper in circles, stirs the edges of the tablecloths, lifts the banner on the town walls. Under the table a small boy is feeding a sliver of prosciutto to a dog, which skitters away as an empty plastic bottle bounces onto the stones. Tullio looks at his watch. In a few minutes, as the hour of the evening meal draws near, the guests will begin ducking under the doorway in ones and twos, leaving the peaceful sunlight of the piazza for the violent halogen of the cave, summoning solemnity as they pass from conviviality to culture, as if entering a church.

The young couple are still there in front of *The Pratomagno*, the girl's arms moving to and fro in front of the canvas, stirring bright shadows. He should approach, engage them, ask where they are from, tell them the name of the timeless, lonely tower at the head of the valley off the Talla road. Instead, he picks up a brochure from the outside edge of the fan.

'Tullio d'Attore is without doubt one of the major young artists working in Italy today. His modernity is uncompromising, whilst retaining the resonances of a deftly assimilated tradition . . .'

The church bell begins to toll. In a nearby yard, a dog has been barking for an hour. Outside in the sunlight the river of voices flows on over the day's events: the plans to dig up the medieval main street to bring natural gas into the town; the local florist's son who is lying tenth in the Giro; the merits of the new Supéral in the Via Flaminia; the crack in the concrete lining that has leaked ten thousand quintali of water from the town reservoir; the luck of the ironmonger from Loro Ciuffenna who, in the first week of his retirement, has found a truffle the size of a fist.

'Although profoundly innovative, Tullio d'Attore's work exhibits a definite inclination towards that classicising "rappel a l'ordre" which was so often hearkened towards even by such pioneer modernists as Malevich and Derain . . .'

Tullio raises his eyes to the walls of the cellar, to the show-business of the lights, the bright canvases edged in cheap white wood, newly painted: canvases that have no communion with the lives of those who will creep around these walls, no part in their struggles, no gratification of appetite, offering no aid to worship or focus for secular ideal, no power to assuage fears or vivify dreams, no protection against evil or inspiration towards good, no insight or conviction about the ends of life or the possibilities beyond; an art removed, confined to a rectangle, separated by a freshly painted frame, a brochure, an inclining of the head to one side, a banner lifting and falling on the walls of the town.

Working in the border lands between abstraction and representation, Tullio d'Attore's work reveals the complex influences of his years in London and New York.

They are still there in front of *The Pratomagno*, dark heads against the sky. Two idyllic evenings in the hills, several years ago now; evenings even further away from the harsh halogen that now lights the layers of dull pinks and dead blues in tones and weights that attempt to recreate recessions, depths.

His effects are primarily formal rather than anecdotal, but there is an intense engagement that surpasses mere commentary and enters into the inner life of its subjects.

He turns again to the door. The river flows on uninterrupted. A couple who might have been heading for his cellar are steered away at the last moment by the Mayor's wife. The boy ventures a hand to the dog as the sun spills its last into the piazza.

There is often an ironic tension between the purism of his modernist geometry and the ordinariness of his vernacular sources . . .

The couple in front of the painting have fallen silent. He should move now, out of his dark corner, across the web of iron grilles, tell them about that day at the head of the valley, God's perfume in the air, the musky secrecy of the hills, the stillness of the thirteenth century watchtower, the heat shuddering from the valley floor. He continues to stare at the quotations in the brochure, the newest of which is now ten years old.

In his best work there is both a sly humour and a metaphorical complexity . . .

The silence of the cave is fragmented by the chirruping of a phone inside a jacket.

'Pronto?'

One half of the couple from the Romagna ducks out of the cellar to take the call, smiling apologetically at Tullio, one man of the world to another. His wife has abandoned the paintings and is peering through the bars into damp, archival basements. The younger couple remain in front of *The Pratomagno*, the girl's hair a halogen halo against the dusty pinks and blues. The energy of the telephone voice forces its way back into the cave.

'Ciao, Enzo. Come va?'

He returns the brochure to the table. A photograph of himself – *Tullio d'Attore extends the poetics of visual space* – head slightly to one side, one hand raised absurdly to his chin. And underneath, in bold italic, the item in *L'Impression* that had started it all:

*There are in Italy, fermenting like yeast in the low-rent cellars of
the Via Margutta, two or three artists whose future stature is not
in doubt. One thinks, for example, of Tullio d'Attore . . .*

He looks up again at the couple in front of the landscape. The
telephone voice pre-empts all other possibility.

'No, Enzo, non si può fare, assolutamente no.'

The man steps back into the cellar, returning the phone to his
jacket, only just ahead of the first of the citizens of San Giovanni
Valdarno who, realising the time, have begun moving towards the
cellar in ones and twos, thinking of homes and dinners. Tullio
stands back from the doorway, knowing they will hesitate only for
a moment before beginning on the left, creeping clockwise around
the walls, running the innocuous gauntlet, standing before each
painting for a few respectful seconds, occasionally whispering a
comment or raising a hand or peering more closely, heads slightly
to one side, until the sequence of canvases returns them to the
doorway, to where the artist waits, chin in one palm, elbow in the
other, quietly contemplating the flagstones, where they will smile
and murmur buona sera in a low, encouraging voice, a voice for
the end of visiting hour, a voice for taking leave of the host at the
funeral, a voice for the priest on a Sunday morning, after the
sermon, on the steps of the cathedral. He looks out from under a
bowed brow as they pass into the cellar, observing the beginning of
the clockwise creep that stops sometimes as much as half a minute
before the first canvas, the time reducing as they progress around
the walls, twenty seconds, ten, five, as they near the end; not one
life the least bit different for having passed through the brilliant
grotto; not one who will leave revivified, who will step back into
the town and see the world and himself anew; not one who would
be here at all were it not for a convivial hour in the piazza. His eyes
return to the floor, remembering those who have not passed
unchanged, those who have been moved to tears, those who have

13

been caught and turned around in the middle of their days, those who have seen a fineness, a proportion, to which they might still aspire, those who have been disturbed by art in frames, on walls, an art that will not be ignored, that does not die in the cells of the memory but lives on in the beat of the heart, searching for itself in subways and city streets, in offices at the close of day. But not here. Not in these frames. Not on these walls.

'Il prezzo?'

The young woman has approached the desk, summoning Italian.

'*The Pratomagno?*'

Tullio unnecessarily consulted a list inside a plastic sleeve.

'*Pratomagno . . . Pratomagno.* Ah, eccolo! Two million three hundred thousand.'

He waved away the loose thousands.

'Two million lire.'

The girl grimaced hopefully at her partner, who shook his head slowly.

'Sweetheart, we still haven't got a proper bed, a washing machine.'

Tullio closed his eyes, spread his palms.

'Viaggio di nozze? Honeymoon?'

'Yes. Only three days left.'

'I think I've seen you in Sansepolcro.'

'We're staying there. You know the Fiorentino?'

'My studio's in the same street, just across from Santa Chiara.'

Others were filtering behind them now, pressing to leave the cellar, offering him the tight, funereal smile.

❖

Rather than join the evening frenzy on the autostrada he drives through the industrial sprawl of Terranuova, escaping upwards between the strange eroded-earth balze, blood red with the dampness of the valley and the last of the Tuscan sunlight; the same balze that Masaccio, the local boy, had painted into his backgrounds six centuries before. With the Arno below he turns onto the Sette Ponte, passing through silver olive groves, fields of tired sunflowers, lines of dark, quiet vines, winding across tributaries by narrow Romanesque bridges. After twenty minutes he turns east again, climbing through the forests above the Salutio where the road narrows, weeds eating the weak edges, grass beginning to prick through asphalt, cistus and rock rose surviving in the raw-scraped rockeries as he ascends into the evening, leaving the white road to Monte Lori where years ago he had painted *The Pratomagno*. Not a soul stirs in Talla as he heads out again towards Vezza and Subbiano, crossing the southward-flowing Arno, windows open to the cool air, catching the heavy, paradise scent of broomy hillsides.

Beauty caught at Tullio again between the second and third landings as the deep, melancholy vibrations of the cello filled the stairwell, tremored on the old walls, accompanying him to the top floor of the Palazzo Lanzi.

The hills were still with him as he looked out over the rooftops of the town, at the unchanging outlines of Santa Maria delle Grazie, of the Cathedral and San Lorenzo and the Torre Gherardi and Sant'Antonio Abate. In the palazzo opposite, the blue flicker of a television through the slats of a blind. The strains of the cello grew louder, trembling through the air. He held the curtain back, eyes travelling over the pantiled roofs, the motley of centuries, the texture of time, sweeping over the Via Fraternità, the monastery of the Camaldoli, the Palazzo delle Laudi, the old Palazzo Dotti, the deconsecrated walls of Santa Chiara. In the street below, lamps made intervals in the darkness.

He felt Claudia's arms steal around him from behind.

'You're late, and a bit out of it.'

He placed his painter's hands over hers around his middle and allowed her to sway him from side to side in front of the dark window.

'I'm not out of it.'

'Yes you are. You're floating out there somewhere. How was the exhibition?'

'Two mice and some very discerning lizards.'

He felt her arms tighten around him. The cello had stopped.

'The young man downstairs wants us to go for a drink.'

He turned to face her.

'Tonight?'

'I saw him on the landing again. He asked me about the portrait. I was making a joke of it and he suddenly went all serious and said "I don't know anybody. Will you and your husband come and have a glass of wine tonight?"'

'What did you say?'

'I said I didn't know what time you'd be home. He said to come even if it's late. Apparently he doesn't go to bed 'till dawn.'

'What's he like?'

'A bit wild-eyed. Plays the artist a bit, I imagine. Shall we be good neighbours?'

3

The darkness was deepened by the haloes of candles standing in saucers on the bare wooden floor, casting unaccustomed shadows. And in the middle of the darkness, the artist, smiling as he poured. Candlelight gleamed on jars and brushes, on the varnished edges of the easel, ghostly under its dust-sheet, on the tall shapes of chairs, on the prepared canvases leaning against the walls. He came out of the darkness towards them, holding a glass high in each hand, the eyes shadowed by cheekbones, smiling still. Claudia was the first to speak.

'This is Tullio.'

He stopped, making a kind of strained sideways bow with his head.

'Giuliano.'

He held the wine almost at the level of his eyes, earrings of wine, absurd rubies reflecting the points of light at his feet. Tullio resisted the temptation to reach upwards for the glass.

'Giuliano Amedei.'

He lowered the glasses, proffering them to his guests, cancelling the smile, gesturing towards the centre of the room. Tullio exchanged glances with Claudia as they stepped between bright saucers in the direction of two chairs that appeared to be salvaged car seats bolted onto sections of a beam. Claudia stepped up into the deeply sculpted seat of an Alfa Romeo; Tullio settled into the more sedate breadth of a Mercedes saloon. Darkness pressed up against the window pane.

Giuliano sat cross-legged on the floor, the smile gone, the face drained of colour even in the candlelight. The flames, flustered by his passing, floated evenly again on the dark sea, casting upward shadows of nose and cheekbone, making of his face a sinister Venetian mask. He looked only at Claudia. He had no wine. Tullio, pedestalled, suspected some irritating artistic significance in the arrangement of bodies, some aesthetic practical joke, the low light source disturbing normal relationships. The car seat was comfortable, except that he had nowhere to put his arms, his hands. His eyes grew into the Rembrandt gloom. He raised his glass.

'Welcome to the Palazzo Lanzi. When did you move in?'

'It's been about a month. But I've hardly been out of the door.'

He turned back to Claudia, as if for confirmation.

'And why our little town?'

Claudia was attempting lightness, the clean edges of her shins sculpted by candlelight.

Giuliano shrugged at his surroundings.

'I like old walls. The landlord took my paintings.'

Tullio leaned back into the Mercedes.

'Landini, our modern Medici.'

A silence followed. He looked across at Claudia, who had disappeared into the shadowy space between the wings of the Alfa.

'And before?'

The young man continued to look at Claudia.

'Rome. The Belle Arti. A few months in Crete.'

Tullio set his wine on the side table.

'And did you paint? In Crete?'

The young man looked up from the candlelight, nodding slowly as if the question were of no interest, as if the excitement of receiving visitors had suddenly departed. Tullio reached for his glass. Despite the affected lethargy, there was a trembling aliveness about the young man on the floor, every cell of his being on the edge of its seat in expectation of the next second of his life; and in the sea of that life there was not one drop of boredom.

'Who's selling for you?'

Giuliano looked up suddenly, surprised to be addressed.

'No one.'

From his cross-legged position he rose to his feet in one movement, elongating like an extending mirror, to pour more wine. Tullio's eyes reached for paintings, but the walls of the apartment had retreated behind the candlelight. He drank and caught Claudia's eye across the bright islands at their feet. The conspiratorial smile returned his world to him intact. They were taking a glass of wine with a neighbour, on the second floor of the Palazzo Lanzi, directly underneath their own apartment.

Claudia covered her glass with her hand as Giuliano returned with the bottle.

'You won't have any objection to the portrait.'

The question, statement, was addressed directly to Tullio, who raised his eyebrows, inclining his head towards Claudia, who had assumed her look of amused suspicion.

'Why do you want to paint me?'

He poured for Tullio. The trousers stained with paint. The bare feet bright on the floorboards.

'Yours is the only beauty that's reached me. Since I came here.'

Claudia spoke past him.

'Isn't that a compliment from someone who's just told us he hasn't been out of the door?'

Tullio smiled back at her across the islands of light.

'It wouldn't matter.'

She raised her eyes to the ceiling, cradling her glass, despairing of all artists.

Giuliano had lowered himself to the floor.

'So you'll sit for me?'

Claudia looked down on the young man, his eyes lost in deep oysters of shadow.

'How long would it take?'

'Three sittings, maybe four.'

'For how long?'

'An hour . . . two.'

Claudia hesitated, sipped her wine, glanced just for a second at Tullio.

'It would have to be in the mornings.'

'As you like.'

Tullio lifted himself out of the car seat and waved an arm in the direction of the unframed canvases around the walls of the apartment.

'May I?'

The artist gestured in assent and rose again, turning towards the door. The walls glowed into life as Tullio approached the first picture. Wires had been run loosely around the ceiling, dropping down to battered picture lights.

'It's just these three. Landini took one last week.'

Tullio sipped wine. The car seats had persuaded him that the paintings would be one-shot salvoes, spending whatever they were worth in the first few seconds. Approaching the first canvas he saw at once that he was wrong. The work ached with quality. A portrait of a piano. Oil on wood. A piano in concert. A gleaming grand piano, its verticals emphasised in bold strokes that contrasted with the sensuous, shapely mass of the raised lid that reflected the inner geometry of the instrument. Beyond this inner stillness the painting vibrated with sound; the very air jarred and tremored with light from the pale reds and golds and yellows so that it was impossible not to hear the grandeur of the orchestra, the notes of the piano struck with force and passion. He drank more wine and let his eyes travel down to the suggestion of floorboards of which only the wax shine had been painted. He began breathing again, following the verticals back to the bulk of the piano, only partly defined, sure and subtle and deft; a portrait of stealthy, black, lacquered wood brought to the highest state of reflection; an effect as pure as a single note, its lines taut like the nerves of the music. Holding concentration, he followed the effects outwards as the sound faded away through the yellows and whites to the bare edges of the canvas.

After another minute he stepped sideways to the next work.

The painting between the windows appeared to be a straight-forward representation of the cello. He stepped closer, bowing his head. It had been painted in the manner of a portrait, a portrait that had character and mood and memory, painted with a respect that was almost a love. He bent closer still, examined the innocent shadow on the wall, allowed his eyes to linger on the drifting blues and candle yellows as light and shade passed over the old, uneven plaster. The picture filled him. And he was complete. The canvas was all. Ice slithered beneath the skin of his arms. He was back in the Mauritshuis, moving from Vermeer to Vermeer, dwelling on the daylight as it fell nostalgically across the walls of a room, the creased parchment of a seafarer's map, the soft weave of a tablecloth, the face and figure of a woman standing before a window under a chaste northern light. He returned to the body of the cello, following the reach of a warmer, more southerly light, defining contours with imperceptible changes of weight, aware that he was looking at the product of weeks spent on the high wire of discipline and creativity, of fighting to stay at the edge, resisting all slackening, all temptation to the acceptable, the mediocre. He gave himself to the painting, fought to stay with it, until after several minutes the work began to break down under the cracks and flaws in his own concentration. Behind him in the darkness, the real cello had begun to play.

He crossed to the stack of canvases under the window, pulling them towards him one by one, supporting their growing weight against his thigh. They appeared to be abandoned paintings, waiting to be recycled, despaired of at an early stage, each of them slowly, despairingly crossed, corner to corner, with the broad, muddy wash of the spirit jar.

From the other side of the room, a strained voice called out over the deep vibrations of the music.

'I always play when people look at my paintings.'

Tullio ignored him and moved on to the last work, hanging by a length of electrical flex from a picture rail: a detail of stone steps and painted railings, turning against the whitewashed walls of the Palazzo Lanzi. Not the staircase but its stillness, its fine quietness; a portrait of the familiar stranger who touched him on the shoulder each evening as he climbed the stairs. The notes of the cello had begun to rise, the vibrations filling the room. He moved closer to the canvas, saw the light falling on the fine grain of the stone, revealing its hardness; light slanting onto the uneven white plaster of the wall, exposing the shallowest of craters; light defining the paint-thickened joints of the railing. The cello was becoming more agitated, protesting. Claudia was somewhere to his right. The first cold of night had entered the room. Tullio remained in front of the painting, poised on its edge. The staircase had gone, become geometry in suspense, an abstract composition of whites and quiet greys, its tensions achieved with the economy of a Mondrian. Tullio worked at the painting, nerving himself into it, engaging himself with its embodied permanency, as he might try to outstare a mountain peak.

The cello stopped abruptly. Silence gripped the apartment.

'What do you think? Do I pass the test?'

Tullio turned, straightening his back. The young man was nursing the cello in both arms. A night breeze wandered through the streets, stirring the curtains. Across the street, the sound of washing being wound in. A late motorbike battering its way through the canyon of the Via Mazzini. The ordinary street below, his own apartment above. He raised his empty glass.

'I think they're magnificent.'

Claudia had appeared at his side. She too raised her glass to the figure slumped against the wall as if exhausted by his playing.

'They're wonderful, Giuliano.'

Slowly the young man dropped his head. The candle-burned fingers clawed the face, the fibres of his being rigid, ready to break. After a few seconds the fists tightened and he rose to his feet, striding across the room, panicking the flames of the candles, gripping Claudia, then Tullio, by the shoulders, kissing them on both cheeks.

He stood back, placing both hands together, as if in prayer.

'Does that mean I can do the portrait?'

Tullio and Claudia smiled at each other, and then at Giuliano. The candles steadied at their feet.

Later, when they were climbing the staircase to the top floor, Claudia put out a hand to hold him back. Turning on the dim staircase, she reached up and kissed him softly on the lips.

For some reason, Tullio found himself embarrassed. He spoke to the darkness of Claudia's face.

'I think he's a very fine artist.'

'I know.'

4

The overnight rain had freshened the town, darkening stone and stucco. But now a morning sunlight flashed from the roofs and gutters, hinted of itself in the globules of rain on the plastic chairs, sparkled like mica on the stones of the street, flared on the gilded frame that the restorer Grimaldi was carrying into the Via Mazzini.

Tullio stirred sugar into his coffee and made space for the ring file. Five couples. Four single women. Two single men. Mostly from New England: Boston, Springfield, Northampton, Concorde, Litchfield, West Cornwall. One each from Virginia, Wisconsin, Mississippi. Four from the west coast. He glanced across to the Fiorentino where his party would be breakfasting. Behind him, a few older men were reading newspapers. Coffee and a brioche appeared at his side as he unclipped the brochure from the file. On the cover, a detail from *The Dream of Constantine*. The promise of coffee mingled with printers' ink and the rain-freshened morning. The world renewed.

Tour 16: The Late Medieval and Early Renaissance tour, for many years the most popular on the 'Arte d'Italia' list, is intimately linked to the taste and personality of the respected Tuscan master Tullio d'Attore. The tour is centred on the charming town of Borgo Sansepolcro, birthplace of Piero della Francesca . . .

A middle aged couple wandered hand in hand under the Porta Fiorentina, looking at shops and alleyways and old walls.

Americans in bought-for-holiday clothes, probably in his party. Fine flakes of brioche fell into the fold. A moustache of froth fringed his upper lip. There was also a new photograph, a full length shot of St Mark in his niche at the Orsanmichele. Even in reproduction he marvelled at the seriousness, the sternness, the banishment of the ephemeral with a glance, a portrayal of the new intelligence, tolerant but not impressed. And the drapery, so soft as to belie marble; the cashmere folds of the toga; the creamy poured stone of the coarser cloak. And underneath the folds, the weight of the marble limbs, and the eyes drilled in a single act of genius, allowing the light of Florence to illuminate the mind.

'In twenty years I've done maybe a dozen of these tours, and I have to tell you nothing even comes close.'

Michael Bjornaby, New Paltz, New York.

'Tullio is like no other . . . his love of what he showed us lit up every wonderful thing we saw.'

Barbara May, Twin Lakes, Salisbury, Connecticut.

He looked up from the brochure to see the sunlight claiming back the sandstone of the Palazzo Alberti, a youthful, guileless light evicting the shallow damp. From the Via della Castellina, a car had blundered illegally into the Via Maestra, nosing between the fruit shop and the profumeria, seeking a way out. Tullio frowned, the fumes robbing the morning of it glory.

A second coffee had appeared at his side. The sun had touched the flagstones; the day beginning to warm, awnings being lowered over shop windows. A cycle trickled by. A few more people were emerging from the side streets, turning towards the piazza or the town gate. Tullio breathed in the fineness of the morning, drank the sharpness in the air, tasting its edge of cold on the back of his throat, raising the coffee to his lips. A day not yet grown tired. A mind freshened by an overnight rain. The American couple had disappeared into the hotel.

'Ciao Tullio.'

'Stefano, buon giorno.'

The lawyer from the first floor of the Palazzo Lanzi dropped into a chair and began folding back the pages of *La Nazione*. Tullio glanced at him. Giuliano's neighbour. Living on the other side of the wall from the bare studio where Claudia would now be sitting. The lawyer reached blindly for one of Tullio's cigarettes, lit it without his eyes leaving the newspaper. The piano. The cello. The pale geometry of the stairs. No guide to his painting of the warm and the living.

Tullio looked up to see an old man making his way between the tables, his morning dissolving as his eye caught the felt trilby and the stiff new jeans. The brochure fell to the flagstones as he found a soft pencil from his shirt pocket and began sketching over the list of names, reworking the stiff crease of the jeans on legs that were old and bowed, the felt sweat marks darkening the silk hat-band, scribbling a note in the margin to include the gnarled olive hands and the worn ring sunk into the flesh. The old man stopped for breath, prolonging the moment. Tullio redrew the knee in a corner of the page, already knowing that he would not make the bold, unliteral leap; that he would fall short, slithering and scrabbling into the abyss of the ordinary, obliterating his aim with his own earnestness, lacking the sureness of touch, the elegance of means. He had never painted Claudia.

Stefano's coffee and brioche arrived as he turned the newspaper inside out.

'New tour, Tullio?'

'Just in.'

'So where to today?'

'Just the Museo this morning. Monterchi this afternoon.'

The lawyer began reading again. The old man had disappeared inside. Tullio picked up the brochure from underneath the table.

'People say we're mad doing the same tour three times in five years. But they haven't done Tullio's tour.'

Moira Donahue, Ann Arbor, Michigan.

'When you understand what you're seeing, every moment is fascinating. And with Tullio, you understand what you're seeing.'

Percy Ernst Matjasczek, Norfolk, Virginia.

All of the names were from last year's tours. There had been Christmas cards from the Russos and from Percy Matjasczek and he had standing invitations from the Donahues, and Stan and Barbara May.

'Okay. Ciao, Tullio.'

'Ciao, Stefano.'

Stefano carried his newspaper off towards the Porta Fiorentina as the old man in the jeans emerged from the bar with a bag of brioche. Tullio's eyes followed him towards the piazza. But the moment had gone. The first faint sourness had touched the edges of the day.

He turned the brochure over. Gianfranco Borda was accompanying to Agrigento as well as Pompeii and Ercolano. A new name, an academic from Iowa, had Bernini's Rome. Another American had taken over Venice from Carlo. He closed the file and was about to leave when a movement caught his eye. The petite, middle-aged woman from the shoe shop had stepped out into the sun to sweep the street in front of the doorway. Tenderness carried him towards her as she moved up and down in high red heels, loving the carefulness of her professional attire, the over articulation of the spectacles, the deliberateness of the make-up exposed by the raw morning light, the sheen of her legs through the little dust that rose around her, the sunlight making a fairy-tale of the bright shoes. He was late now, but he began sketching again, transfixed by the economical rhythm of broom and body, moving in counterpoint, up and down, to and fro, along the flagstones of the Via Maestra. And behind her the shop window, with its pedestals of perfect shoes.

❖

'Your face is stilted.'

Claudia relaxed the muscles of her face, her neck.

'Let the shoulders go as well.'

She allowed her spine to curve so that it touched the back of the dining chair, staring past him at the bare wall. The apartment was larger and less romantic by day. Emptier. Almost unfurnished. Damp stained the plaster at the edges of the window. He had neither canvas nor sketch pad.

'And the mouth.'

Claudia moistened her lips. Did she normally keep her mouth closed, or were her lips usually apart? He waited for her, sitting astride his chair, supporting his cheekbone on the heel of his hand. She closed her lips, tightening her mouth imperceptibly.

'I don't want you to compose yourself. I want you to get rid of that idea you've got about how people sit for portraits.'

Claudia breathed in deeply and tried to relax. The art of sitting naturally seemed to have vanished. It was an unnatural thing to be doing, sitting on an dining chair in the middle of a room with nowhere to put her hands. She had sat before. For one or two of Tullio's friends, years ago. But their looking, had been circumspect, mild, alcohol-free. Restlessness was all she remembered.

The mind milling elsewhere. Not this brink of mutual awareness. She blinked elaborately.

'Don't go lifting your chin again.'

She bowed her head a little, focusing on a button on his chest. Brushes had been wiped on the thighs of the black trousers. The feet bare. The shirt frayed at the sleeves and collar. The hands resting on the back of the chair, the fine black hairs against the dead white of the wrists. She had been shocked when he opened the door. He was malnourished, ill.

'You're frowning.'

The painting of the cello hovered in the margins of her vision. The piano on the opposite wall. The quality undimmed. A faint shadow of disloyalty falling across her thoughts. A shadow without substance. Tullio admired his painting. Giuliano walked over to the window, ignoring her.

'Can I move?'

'I'd rather you didn't.'

She raised a sardonic eyebrow. Everything about him suggested a stereotype. The pale Caravaggio beauty. The dark bruises of the eyes. The bare feet and untouched hair. The threatening extravagance of personality. The balancing act on the verge of an inner world. But there was no suspecting the thinness of him, the starvation.

He returned to sit astride the chair. For a moment she caught his eye, and as quickly looked away. Two or three misshapen coat-hangers in the darkness of the wardrobe. A pair of sneakers thrown into a corner. He rested his chin on the chair-back, the look touching her face as tangibly as the palm of a hand. She concentrated on the wall. Each moment intensified the stillness, sharpened the edge of awareness. She swallowed drily. A car horn sounded three times down in the street, breaking the crystal of silence.

❖

Tullio in his paint-stained trousers walked slightly ahead of his group, leading the sixteen Americans between glass-fronted shops built into medieval towers and renaissance palazzi, turning the corner into the Via Matteotti, passing the Torre Gherardi and the warm sandstone façade of the Cathedral, passing under the town gate into a cobbled street and a dappled, leafy park where the group gathered around him under the statue of the town's most famous son. The high, excited, caffeine-edged voices fell silent as he held up one arm under the trees. The painter in his painter's gown looked down, the shadow of his palette on the path.

'Signore e signori, you've all had a long journey. So I'm going to save my long and tedious introduction until this evening. Instead, we're going to start straightaway with just a fresco by our local artist.'

A moped stitched its way along the Via Niccolò Aggiunti. Tullio paused until the needling faded away beyond the walls of the town.

'But I should tell you that our local fresco is a work that the greatest galleries in the world – the Uffizi, the Met, the Louvre, the National, the Fine Arts, the Getty – would cut each other's throats for, pay any price to hang on their walls.'

The banker from Virginia, dressed a little too warmly for the day, had begun taking earnest notes. The medical doctor from Toulane was pointing out a pied wagtail to his wife. Most of the party stood attentively in the pleasant garden, listening to the rise and fall of their guide's voice, enjoying being abroad and on holiday, the sunlight falling through the beech leaves, dappling the gravel, warming bare arms. His eyes came to rest on Alice May-Nyall from Maryland whose face was alive with anticipation.

'In fact it's one of probably only about half a dozen great masterpieces of European art that can still be seen in the villages or small towns where they were painted.'

Tullio nodded to the proprietor of the restaurant standing in his doorway. One or two of the group also turned.

'Piero della Francesca was a leading citizen, a town councillor for thirty years, a well known figure in the streets we've just walked through . . .'

Squirrels launched themselves through frail branches. Chaffinches blew like leaves over the bare earth and the broken sunlight.

'. . . He never married, and in later life he lived in the house he had built for himself and his brothers, the house you see opposite . . .'

Heads turn in unison under the beech trees. The Virginian's pen raced. The woman from Litchfield had turned away and was checking her make-up under the trees. At the intersection of the gravel paths, Mrs Lindbergh was panning slowly upwards from Tullio to the stone figure of Piero della Francesca.

A few minutes later he led them back across the road, passing in front of Pasquale's, where one of his own paintings stood in the window. He glanced at the study of a baroque balcony on the corner of the Via Giordano Bruno. Effete. Precious.

In the Museo, Lucca gave him his change and waived the party through. The custodian smiled up from her knitting, quickly transferring her look to the Americans. The polished floor squeaked as he led the group across to the *Misericordia Polyptych*, though there was not one who had not already stolen a glance at the famous fresco on the north wall. Gold leaf burned on the panels as he described the altarpiece's troubled history; the crude sawing up of the panels in the seventeenth century; the eventual reassembly; the tentative reordering of the panels in the 1950s.

The woman from Litchfield raised a hand.

'Mr d'Attore, this is probably a really silly question but why is the Madonna's face ever so slightly green?'

A stir of laughter fell away into the emptiness of the council chamber.

'Tullio, Mrs Guige. Tullio everybody. And there are no silly questions. She's slightly green because the undercoat is beginning to show through. It's terra verde, the green earth that painters used under their flesh colours. There's a book that's survived from the Middle Ages, a kind of painter's manual that tells artists how they should go about painting flesh tones. It says you should always put down an undercoat of terra verde and then build up the flesh colour over it in layers of egg tempera until the green is almost but not quite covered. If you almost but not quite cover the green, it makes the flesh look more like flesh. The trouble is, after five centuries, the top layers aren't what they were. So more of the green's showing through.'

'They mixed the paint with egg?'

'Yes.'

'White or yolk?'

More laughter in the council chamber.

'Do you have a dishwasher Mrs Guige?'

'Gracie. Yes I do.'

'And what won't it get off once it's dried on?'

'Egg yolk?'

More laughter as he turned the group towards the north wall of the council chamber, a murmur following behind him.

'You're drifting away. Just slightly towards me.'

Easier, now that he was sketching, broken bits of charcoal scattered on the floorboards. The face all hollows. The skin an ostrich-egg white. An occasional shudder passing through his frame. The beginnings of a cold.

She looked past him, focused on an area of blank wall above the bed, where the plaster was turning damp. The light streamed in

33

from behind, making chasms of dust in the room. An itch on the side of her nose. A moth panicking against the window pane. She began organising the slides for her mid-week lecture, bringing them up one by one on the white wall behind the bed. The wide shot of the tympanum at Vézelay. The apostles being sent out into the world, charged with the power of the outsize hand. Christ's robes swirling like stone fingerprints. The signs of the Zodiac. The labours of the months. The medieval Picassos on the lintel. A warm breeze blew in through the window, failing to dislodge the heavy scent of linseed and turpentine. If she closed her eyes she might be in her own apartment, sitting for Tullio, who would be with *The Resurrection*, growing enthusiastic with people from Iowa and Mississippi. Just before she had come downstairs a young couple had appeared at the top of the staircase. English. On honeymoon. Come to thank Tullio for a painting he had apparently left at their hotel. Afterwards she had picked up the new brochure from the table, fought back unexpected tears as she had read the centre spread.

'Think about something else.'

She brought up another slide. The Autun version. The terrors of the damned. The joy of the saved. Signed by Gislebertus after all those years. Not true that the craftsmen of the Middle Ages had no individual pride, no sense of themselves as artists. Someday they would go together, to Vézelay, to Autun, to Fontenay and Cluny and Conques and Moissac, where she could be Tullio's guide. The moth had settled itself against a beam.

'Could we have the window open?'

'In a minute.'

Giuliano coughed. The long fingers and the fragile wrists. The whiteness of a body that breathes only stale air, sees no sunlight, eats no fruit, takes no exercise. On the floor, a plastic water bottle, split down the middle, cradling various thicknesses of charcoal.

'You're looking down.'

She raised her head a fraction. The bed pushed against the wall. A blue nylon sleeping bag fallen to the floor. The edge of the car seats, old and tatty in the daylight. Art books piled on the floorboards. Boldoni. Severini. The Macchiaioli. Would Tullio be living like this if he were on his own? Would he be doing the tours? Or giving everything to his painting? Not eating. Or washing his clothes. Beside these bare floorboards their own apartment was luxurious. And would the painting be any different? Impossible to know.

'Don't frown.'

She settled herself and focused again on the bare plaster, the sun returning as she began bringing up slides. The south doorway of Moissac. Earlier still. St John's apocalypse in stone. The same subject in the porch of St Benoît-sur-Loire. Then back to the capitals of Vézelay. The originals in the museum, at the top of the stone spiral. The naïve beauty of the flight into Egypt. The stone Judas hanging broken-necked from his tree. The pouring of the stone grapes. The spiral stair into the sunshine. Tomorrow night he would be away. She imagined him for a moment, returning to his hotel, walking alone through the dark streets of Rome. She pictured his sad, unobserved face as he turned the key on an ill-lit landing. A chill tightened inwards from the surface of her arms as she realised that her picture of Tullio was of a man who was sad, acknowledged to herself that the sediment of worry about him was becoming hard, permanent, instead of being washed away in the ebb and flow of their lives.

'Now you're holding your breath.'

The room cooled and darkened under a passing cloud, the brightness fading from Giuliano's shirt, dispiriting the morning.

❖

Light streamed into the Sala della Risurrezione as they gathered in front of the broad polished bench and began examining the great fresco rising above them into the vaulting of the north wall. Soon the murmuring and shuffling had stopped; a true silence had descended on the council chamber for the first time.

Tullio allowed them their minute, then began quietly.

'This of course is what we have come to see. The subject is one you can see on dozens of walls and altarpieces. After the crucifixion, the authorities suspect that Christ's followers might steal the body and tell the crowd he's risen from the dead. So they send soldiers to guard the tomb. But the guards fall asleep. And as they sleep, Christ rises. It's a familiar episode in art, in painting, though in fact there's no mention of it anywhere in the New Testament.'

The banker's pen is poised. The woman from Litchfield is trying to suppress a sneeze. The couple from the West Coast are holding hands. Only the athletic Bostonian appeared uninterested, already wandering off to see what might be in the next room.

'All artists at this time worked to commission. They weren't like artists today, painting what they felt like painting and hoping someone would come along and buy. They painted to order. And the order here was for a conventional resurrection scene. A tomb. Christ rising with the flag. Four soldiers who have fallen asleep. It was probably chosen because the town's name, Sansepolcro, means holy sepulchre.'

He turned to the painting again and allowed a few more moments.

'But like all great artists, Piero rises above the commission. Look first at the soldiers below the tomb, at their sleeping faces and their sleeping bodies. Imagine falling asleep yourself, unintentionally, perhaps in the chair in front of the fire after a good meal. Your friends, family, are sitting around, trying not to look. Eventually you wake up, a little bit confused, a little bit embarrassed. Because you fell asleep. Because of the way you probably looked when you were asleep. The muscles of the face slack, the head lolled to one side like the soldier on the left, mouth dropping open like the soldier with the helmet. Maybe a little spittle at the corner of your mouth. And you're a little alarmed because you know that while you were asleep you couldn't compose your face into the you that you wanted to be seen. You were not in control of the self you were presenting to the world.'

The group is entering into the painting now, everything else forgotten, the long flight, the novelty of another country, the bizarre plumbing arrangements, the new friends.

'And there's also that uneasy, primeval feeling that while you were asleep you were vulnerable, defenceless; that anyone could do anything to you, cut your throat, maybe, especially if it was exposed by your head falling backwards, like the soldier on the right.'

Three or four other visitors had gathered quietly at the edges of the group.

'Piero has brought in all of these things, all of these conscious and subconscious feelings about falling asleep. And he's used them to create an image of human vulnerability, a portrait of human weakness, a study in lack of control.'

All eyes are on the sleeping soldiers. The camera has stopped. The banker's pen is still. There is no sound in the council chamber.

'Now let your eyes rise up to the figure of Christ.'

He allowed another thirty seconds to pass.

'For almost the first time we see Christ not as some refined, unearthly figure but as a man, as a Tuscan peasant. If you sit for a few minutes outside the bar in the Via Maestra this lunchtime, you'll see him walk by. Piero didn't want a refined, ethereal Christ here. What he wanted was strength. Strength of body and strength of feature. Strength of mind and strength of purpose. An image of Christ that would contrast totally with the image of human weakness below. So he created this Christ of uprights, of strong verticals to set against the slackness of line in the soldiers below. Look at the verticals of the flagstaff, the long straight nose, the tendons and shadows in the neck continuing the line of the beard, running into the strong vertical down the very centre of the body, through the middle of the breast and between the ribs. Look at the leg, upright and powerful, poised to push out of the tomb. See how firmly the foreshortened foot rests on the stone edge. These straights, these strengths, this unwavering and absolute control of composition, are what create the inevitability, the invincibility, of this rising, the irresistibility of this advance into the world.'

Another pause.

'Now look again at the scene below. At the weak slope of the lance, the loose angle of the helmet on the soldier whose head lolls above the parapet on that long, vulnerable, exposed neck. See how it contrasts with the upright flag, the fixed horizontal halo of Christ's divinity. And look how the painting mocks the elaborately armoured knee of the soldier, contrasting it with the powerful dome of Christ's knee covered only in a pink cloth – but a cloth that is buttressed by its falls and folds into an image of stability and endurance. Look at the slack facial muscles and bulging orbs of the eyelids of the sleeping soldier resting his head on the tomb, the artist's self-portrait . . .

'. . . and then at the dark implacable circles of Christ's wide-open, wide-apart eyes . . . the dread, unstoppable symmetry of Christ's face.'

He paused again. Every member of the party was looking up at the wall of the council chamber. He told himself to stop. Some of his audience had risen into the painting, become tensely engaged with it on a level of taut awareness that could no longer be helped by words. He moved around to the back of the group and looked into the eyes that allowed of no self-deception, giving himself up to the artistry and authority of the great fresco of the *Resurrection of Christ*.

5

The eighteen-seater shouldered its way onto the superstrada and began building towards a hundred kilometres an hour, a glass cage of cold air shuddering through the morning heat of the Tiber valley. Tullio signed the driver's docket and made his way back towards the first empty seat.

'May I?'

'Please.'

'It's Mrs Usher isn't it?'

'Carole.'

The middle aged woman from New England moved closer to the window, a gesture, occupying less of her own seat. Arms rose and fell in front of them as the Californians pulled on sweaters, defending themselves against the air conditioning. Tullio inclined his head towards the paperback that lay open on Carole Usher's knee, an abridged version of Harding's *Art of the Early Renaissance*.

'A wonderful book. Mine's falling apart.'

She closed the book, smoothed a hand over the detail of the Brancacci Chapel.

'Some of it's kinda tough going though. Why do these guys have to say polychrome when all they mean is coloured?'

Tullio smiled.

'Can I ask you something about yesterday?'

'Please.'

'That fresco. What if you're not a Christian?'

Tullio frowned. Carole Usher was looking at the seat-back, as if at a screen.

'I could see those eyes in front of me the whole day long. Staring at me out of the dark in my room last night. Not scary or anything. Just looking at me. I got to thinking about it. If it's about, you know, human weakness, the power of Christ's truth . . . well, what if all that doesn't mean much to you? What if you're a Moslem or a Buddhist? Or if you're just . . . nothing?'

The coach entered a tunnel, displaced air and tyre noise rebounding from the walls, suspending conversation. He saw the fresco rising sternly out of the darkness, the eyes challenging him with himself. And Claudia sitting before a window, chin held high, the light modelling the line of her jaw. Day returned with a whoosh.

'What I mean is, is it still a masterpiece if you're Jewish?'

Tullio focused himself.

'I don't think . . . I think if you can accept that coloured pigment soaked into plaster can represent the figure of Christ, then you can accept that the figure of Christ can represent . . . the power of a great truth . . . or a great sustaining ideal.'

Carole Usher was still staring at the seat-back.

'So it can be a great work of art, a masterpiece, whatever God you believe in?'

'I think so. A painting that's only a religious painting confronts you with someone else's truths. *The Resurrection* does more than that. It confronts you with your own truths. It doesn't matter who you are or what you believe. Anybody's evasions, self-deceptions, would quail before it.'

A figure leaned over from the seat behind, pulling at the headrest.

'Carole, would you mind if I borrowed Mr d'Attore, for a minute or two?'

'Not so long as I get him back, Frank.'

Tullio stood up in the aisle, swapping seats with the wife of the man who had interrupted, a man of about his own age wearing a lemon sports shirt.

'Frank Nelson, by the way. Chicago. Sorry to butt in. I should have told you ahead of time. I'm with "Arte d'Italia". Vice-president for marketing actually.'

Tullio frowned, prepared to be prickly. Frank Nelson raised his hand.

'No, I know, don't trouble, I'm not one of your airline ghost riders. Ellen's been wanting to take this tour for years.'

Tullio relaxed. Frank Nelson leaned towards him, whispering elaborately out of the side of his mouth.

'And I got a great discount.'

Tullio smiled and looked past his companion across the aisle to the opposite window where the vineyards of Pierantònio were marching over the low hills.

'Plus. Plus. I was kind of interested to see for myself what the big secret was. Yesterday was great, by the way. Normally I'm not too big on frescoes. But yesterday was . . . great.'

The dull purples of Monte Acuto and Monte Corona were clearly visible to the west now, the sun warming denuded slopes as the coach moved into the outside lane and Tullio waited for the man from 'Arte' to begin, wishing the glass of the window were not tinted.

'But I do have a little business to discuss, if this is a good time?'

Tullio nodded, knowing what was coming

'Tullio, I know we've written you about this, but Michael thought, as long as Ellen and I were taking the trip, I should take it up with you face to face.'

Tullio pressed his lips together. He had not replied to any of the letters from Chicago earlier in the year.

'Look, I'm at the grubby end of this operation and I'm not about to give you any bullshit. Where I'm coming from is we're turning away close to one hundred fifty clients a year who're willing to sign up for two thousand four hundred and twenty eight dollars plus tax to do the tour. And that's without a nickel on promotion by the way.'

Tullio's eyes had drifted back to the window. They were passing below the hilltop town of Montone now, on the left hand side of the Tiber valley, birthplace of Braccio Fortebraccio, one of the first to dream of uniting Italy.

'Ordinarily of course we'd just up the number of tours, push a few more buttons, hire someone from some college somewhere. But in this case we have ourselves a supply side problem. Because what they want, what they want, is Tullio's tour.'

The American glanced sideways at his companion as the coach pulled out again.

'You see Mr Nelson . . .'

'Frank.'

'Frank. I'm a painter. This was just a way of earning some extra . . .'

Frank Nelson nodded with too much sympathy as the coach settled down again in the inside lane.

'I guess it's tough making a buck?'

A small smile, a slight lifting of the hands in his lap.

'I was thinking we should have some of your work in Chicago.'

Tullio gave him one of Claudia's smiles, sardonic, good humoured. Frank Nelson shook his head vigorously and spread his hands.

'Tullio, where I'm headed is pretty simple. 'Arte's' uppin' the ante. Same as now for the four you're doin'. Double for every new unit.'

'Your other guides won't be very happy about that.'

'Screw them, Tullio. No one's knocking on their door. We don't even have any advertising costs. We could fill this tour three times over without even putting it in the brochure. If all our experts were like you, by the way, we wouldn't need a marketing director.'

Tullio fell quiet. Perugia was there in the distance now, its Etruscan, Roman, Medieval, Renaissance walls besieged by industrial estates and shopping centres. Ellen Nelson twisted in her seat to see if the conversation was finished. Out of the corner of his eye he saw his companion close his eyelids, giving a slight shake of the head. Tullio let his head fall back against the high seat-back. The currents of the argument ran too deep to share with a stranger on a coach to Rome.

Frank Nelson made a sudden, decisive gesture with his hands.

'Tullio, here's the deal. You do four tours now. We could fill twelve. So you take eight. That would still be only eight times ten days a year. That's not even three months. Your take-home triples. And you're still a painter.'

Frank Nelson had written out the sum on the 'Arte d'Italia' brochure and was doing the addition.

'There's the bottom line, Tullio.'

Tullio had already done the calculations. Almost as much as Claudia earned. He looked through his reflection in the tinted window. Factories and warehouses crowded the coach as it passed the exits for Ponte Felcino and Ponte Valleceppi, beginning the long, slow swerve around Perugia. Would she still be downstairs? The head slightly raised. The soft lips closed. The face turned towards the easel. The artist glancing up at her from time to time as the light streamed in through the window. He shook his head.

'It's not that simple. I can't seem to paint much between tours. I can't seem to settle to it.'

Frank Nelson let the point go, sensing that there were better openings to come. Tullio took the 'Arte' brochure from him for no particular reason.

'Besides, I don't want to get stale. I love the tours. That's the secret, if there is one.'

Frank Nelson raised both hands, moving to more confident ground, palms facing the seat-back.

'Believe me we're on-side there. You said it last season and we respect your feelings about that all the way. As a matter of fact Michael and I spoke about it the other day and we think we've figured something out. How about you work up a new tour, something separate? Michael says what about a little restructuring, split the tour, one on the late medieval and the other on the early Renaissance?'

Tullio shook his head.

'That would destroy the whole idea. It's about seeing the ground being broken, the struggle beginning, what it was all about. You'll see what I mean this week.'

'Right. I mean I don't know anything about it. You slice the cake any which way you want. Michael said to lay it on the table and let you pick it up. He also said to mention a Florence tour and a speciality tour on Piero della Francesca. Just to run them by you is all.'

'I thought all the demand was for this tour?'

'Tullio, let's be clear about this. The demand is for you. If you were doing a Florence tour everybody who's ever been with you would sign up tomorrow. We could book it solid with a two-bit mail shot.'

The ceramics factories of Deruta were rushing by on either side, urns and jars and decorated vases of every size, acres of painted tiles, armies of Davids and Venuses and Neptunes and discus throwers. The Piero tour would almost write itself. Radiating out from Sansepolcro to Florence, Arezzo, Monterchi, Perugia, Urbino, Rimini for the Malatesta Temple. Florence he could do eclectically, or, much better, a tour on the shining hour, those first four decades of the quattrocento; the hour of Brunelleschi and

Donatello, of Ghiberti and della Quercia, of Masaccio and Angelico and Michelozzo. Frank Nelson remained silent as the coach disentangled itself from the suburbs, heading south towards Rome.

❖

Giuliano placed her under the morning light. He had not shaved. A pair of speakers had appeared on either side of the chair.

'Can't you come in the afternoons?'

'I work in the afternoons.'

The music began as he returned to his seat and pulled a sketch pad onto his knee. Another sonata for piano and cello. She changed her position slightly, shifting her weight in the chair. A warning frown as he scrabbled for charcoal. A small rip in the paint-stained trousers, exposing a pale centimetre of thigh.

She took in what details she could of the room. The wire hanging from the picture rail. A dusty glass of water by the bed. Giuliano's eyes jumping from subject to sketch, the sudden movements at odds with the slow winding of the sonata.

'Ease the shoulders.'

Tullio would be having dinner with Palmiro and Lelli. She would be alone, unless Livia called. He would be halfway to Rome by now, talking about frescoes and mosaics. She had been with him once or twice, when there had been a spare seat. To Orvieto. Lucca. Florence. She was used to lectures, her own and other people's. But to hear Tullio in front of an altarpiece, a fresco, a sculpture, was different. It was to hear of unscholarly things, of the reaching out to the moment that contained all moments, of the struggle for perfection and proportion, of the struggle that was not only about art. It was to hear of human aspiration and longing, the

47

touching of the hands across the centuries, the uniting instant, the sense of deep belonging to the human race, the ending for a prolonged instant of the loneliness of the inmost life. It was to hear of the things that her colleagues feared, pulling away their gowns lest they fall into the quicksand on either side of the scholarly path, following beaten paths across well-worn contours, confining themselves to the bleak ridge-way of the verifiable. She should have gone with him to Rome, to hear him on the Torriti apse mosaics, the Cavallinis.

'Anyway, the light likes you.'

She glanced at him as the music swelled, resonating on the floorboards. Hypnotic, the delicate strength of the two instruments, the fineness of their dalliance, expressing in sound the searchingness of the glances, the drawing out of whatever he saw, the deftness of the fingers, the beauty of him as he worked.

She returned to her lecture, bringing up slides on the wall: the carved capitals at Vézelay; the palm trees; the pagan heads; the crudely drilled foliage. Next up, the wonderful carving of the mystic mill of the Crucifixion, grinding the hard husks of the Old Testament into the fine flour of a new truth. She paused the slide show, seeing that all of the imagery of her calling had become a symbol of a symbol, that religion itself had become a symbol of secular love, the love that was the truth into which they were born again in each other, the inward love through which they reached out into the world, milled out their truths, their gospels. But now there were things that were not being talked of, a wall of silence being built around the unspoken sadnesses, silently, day by day, partitioning off parts of him, places that became the more taboo with time, building a wall that would become a part of them, taken for granted, hardly noticed at all, a wall that, once built, would be breachable only by the unthinkable, by assault and destruction; or it would never be breached at all, so that only a part of themselves was contiguous, open plan, until they could no longer see each other whole, note the origins of act and word. Until they no longer understood.

Giuliano had moved around behind her. She watched his shadow passing over the floorboards, felt his warmth at her back. Without warning he grabbed the top of the chair with both hands and levered it against his body, changing her angle to the light. He came around again, swinging one leg over his chair, settling down, chin wedged into knuckles, his look reaching into her face, her eyes, her cheeks, her mouth. The light from the window nagged at the edges of her eyes.

The sketch pad had fallen to the floor. The music had stopped. The last slow notes hung in the dusty silence of the room.

'Can you hold eye contact?'

She turned her head to look into Giuliano's eyes.

For ten seconds the ordinary physical act of looking sufficed. But in two more seconds ordinariness had withdrawn. She held on to his look, alarmed at the running out of assuredness, the sudden and precipitous transparency in depths that were normally opaque, protected. Pride preserved the mask of looking, maintained the suspended, mutual staring through the windows of the self, the confronting of the full force of his person-ness, intensifying a relationship without knowing what there was to intensify. Ten more seconds and the cliff edge was beginning to break. Her jaw tensed as she closed up the fibres of herself, resisting the power of him, resisting invasion. The space outside her grew infinite; the look became as intimate as making love.

He lifted his face from his fist, breathing in with exaggerated impatience, the voice scalding with scorn.

'Can't we do it without all that determination?'

With an effort she closed herself off, returned his look without seeing, dissolving his features into a lifeless abstract, ignoring the person-ness, the energy, the structured, delicate face, the eyelashes fine as a child's. He returned his cheekbone to the heel of his hand.

'Now you've just gone somewhere else altogether.'

She summoned herself again, concentrating, distracting herself by trying to identify noises in the street: the faint hum of the bakery fans; the sound of voices outside Santa Chiara; a three-wheeler labouring up the slight incline; the stop-start organ playing of the weekly choir practice. She could feel the touch of his look on her face, the faint tingling of the flesh around her mouth, the rising of the blood, a hollowness in her stomach. Her neck ached and she sought to put more energy into her eyes, flexing invisible muscle.

Giuliano stood up suddenly, banging the back of the chair.

'I can't do this if you're going to go steeling yourself up like that.'

Claudia stood up, no longer the sitter for a painting. The licence had expired.

'I won't do it at all Giuliano if you can't allow yourself the occasional lapse into politeness.'

Giuliano's head dropped. When he looked up again it was in abject apology, as if he had suddenly woken into the world. Claudia leaned her neck back on her shoulders.

'I'm going to take a break now. And you're going to offer me coffee.'

He raised his head, startled, as if he had just heard of coffee. Claudia walked to the window, describing circles with her head and neck until she felt slightly dizzy. From the kitchen came the sound of cups clashing. She turned to see Giuliano rummaging in a drawer, picking up cups and glasses to find two that were usable. Awkward; dissonant with his surroundings, unless he was sitting with an easel, a sketch pad. He ought always to be there. Nowhere else. The bare feet gave a nakedness to his thinness under the loose shirt. She turned away, making herself ignore him, pushing the window all the way up, resting her hands on the iron rail. Her own apartment caught more of the breeze. And it was pleasanter to be able to look out over the roof tops. Down in the street the woman from the ground floor was wheeling her bicycle slowly towards the piazza. The three-wheeler, loaded with watermelons, had stopped outside the ortofrutta. From the kitchen came the sound of a match, the small explosion of igniting gas. She half turned again into the room. Giuliano was bending low over the sink. She looked across at the canvases on the wall.

'Have you done any other portraits?'

'No. I don't do them. I don't like portraits.'

Claudia refused herself the obvious response and looked down into the street. Tullio's friend Grimaldi was lighting a cigarette outside his workshop, pushing the packet into the front pocket of his apron. The paintings were almost as real to the imagination as to the eye. Even looking at them for the first time she had known what Tullio would be thinking, felt the force of his admiration, the shadow of his disappointment. It was months since he had shown any enthusiasm for anything he'd painted. Even longer since he had sold anything. Only on his tour days was the burden temporarily lifted, the day taken with ardour, the steps two at a time. What was stopping her breaching the wall of silence, walking into the half-built room. What's this, Tullio? Building your own house to live in? Under our own roof?

'Coffee!'

Giuliano drew the kitchen door wider with a bare foot, concentrating on bearing two cups, an expression on his face that suggested he had performed a miracle. She joined him at his work table, avoiding the oily surface. He set down the saucerless cups.

'It won't come off. I varnish it between paintings.'

Claudia looked down at the thick undulating laminates of oil paint imprisoned in layers of varnish.

'Tullio knows artists who'd exhibit that.'

The artist ran a hand over the uneven sea-bed of the table.

'Can I come up and see his work?'

Claudia hesitated, stirring in sugar.

'Most of it's out on exhibition. Come up next week when he brings it back.'

Giuliano looked disappointed, staring at the sheen of the table, both hands around his cup.

Claudia sipped the instant coffee, barely warm. The urge to run a comb through his hair grew. The loose shirt hardly stirred with his breathing. She waited for him to speak, but he seemed content with silence. Half a minute passed.

'So do you make a living from painting?'

He looked up, as if surprised to find her still in the apartment.

'No. I've never sold anything.'

'So how do you live?'

'I've got a bursary. It's supposed to be for six months. I'm making it last a year. Maybe two.'

'Is that why you're so thin?'

Giuliano seemed to consider the question.

'Probably. I don't really eat until I have to. I eat once a day, usually in the afternoon. I don't go out. I sleep a lot.'

'And you pay the rent with paintings?'

Giuliano tried to nod while sipping coffee and spilt a little on the table. She handed him a tissue from a box.

'How did Landini find you?'

'He saw my stuff at the Belle Arti. There's a show every year. He wanted the two I had there. Four from whatever I do here.'

'For the year?'

Giuliano nodded again, deflated, unrecognisable from the peremptory figure of a few minutes before.

'I don't suppose you've thought about getting a part time job or anything like that?'

'Painting's my job.'

'So why don't you exhibit?'

Giuliano showed signs of agitation.

'I can't.'

'Whyever not?'

'I can't. You don't understand.'

'Understand what?'

'What it's like.'

'What what's like?'

He gestured as if with a brush, the face contorted.

'Some days I can't. I just can't. I go back to bed. I daren't get up. I can spend days like that, starting a painting. When I start I . . . When it's finished . . . it's like there's more of me there on the easel than there is inside. Surely it's obvious. Surely you can see I can't just haul it off somewhere. Show it to someone who'll look at it like it's . . .'

Giuliano was scowling, imagining himself into his pain. Claudia hesitated, listening to the stretching and squeaking of the ropes that moored him to the normal. Was it the imitation of a cliché or the source? Either way, it was not to be indulged.

'So get an agent to do it, if you can't face the selling part.'

'I won't. I can't. You're deliberately not understanding.'

He had stood up, almost angry now.

'You're deliberately not explaining.'

He turned on her.

'Why should I explain?'

Claudia drank her coffee calmly. From the beginning, they had seemed to fall into this fractious intimacy. He turned back halfway across the room.

'Sometimes I couldn't even submit at the Belle Arti. Most of the time I just couldn't put pieces in. It took six fucking years.'

'You don't like criticism?'

'No. Absolutely not. I don't care what people think. I don't need criticism. It stops me painting. I can't paint for days. I just can't.'

Claudia had not quite finished her coffee but Giuliano gathered up the cups, pushing through into the kitchen, standing over the sink. She ran a finger over the sea of varnish. To be with him was to live in his magnetic field, to feel the uncontained charge of his aliveness. Were the talent and the temperament intimately connected; or was the one an excuse for the other? His voice came back from the tiles on the wall.

'It was terrible that first night. Showing you the paintings.'

'So why did you?'

'Because I'd seen you on the staircase.'

He walked quickly over to the window and stood looking down into the street, tugging on the iron rail. Claudia spoke to his back.

'Have you shown them to anyone else?'

'No one. No one at all.'

She crossed the floorboards towards the window.

'Giuliano. This is silly. How are you going to live?'

He turned to look at her, impatient again. She sighed and turned back towards the dining chair.

'Shall we start again? I have to be away by twelve.'

Giuliano seemed to take several seconds to understand.

'No, that's fine for today. It's fine, really. For today.'

The thought of the portrait seemed to have cheered him again. He came towards her in the centre of the room, holding out his hands for hers. Instinctively she lifted her hands to be taken. The eyes held each other again.

'It's going to be wonderful. I had no idea.'

Claudia withdrew her hands.

'Are you sure this will only take three sessions? You don't seem to have made much progress. In fact you haven't started.'

'Oh, but I have. I've almost finished.'

Claudia raised her eyebrows and walked to the door. When she looked back the artist was on his hands and knees, making chalk marks on the floorboards, fixing the position of the chair.

❖

Tullio's voice and neck were tired from the visits to the mosaics in Trastevere. A siesta in the cool of the hotel would be preferable to rushing around in the mad heat of the city. He dropped the timetable on the dresser and stood in front of the window, looking out over residential streets and hidden courtyards, breathing in the smell of Rome. Eventually he lay on the bed, forcing off his shoes. The city that had once excited him seemed now to alienate, to bully, to rape the senses, each thrusting, competitive stimulus oblivious to all claims other than its own. Claudia would be eating alone.

The offer from 'Arte' occupied the room, propped itself on the marble-topped dressing table, came in with the dim Roman light at the window, tugged at a loose edge of wallpaper. There were other occupants: the painting of the old man in the jeans, that was going nowhere; the prospect of a weekend spent ferrying back twenty-two canvases from the cellar in San Giovanni; the four hundred thousand lire owed Pasquale for paint and canvases; Claudia sitting for Giuliano under the light of the window, an intimate painter's quiet between them. All floated amorphously in the frame of the ceiling moulding as he stared, engaging nothing, every concern unaddressed, every thought slack-toned. He closed his eyes. Tour seventeen. The shining hour. The Orsanmichele. The Bargello. The bronze doors standing open. The statue in the garden under the trees. The notes of the cello rising into the Old Sacristy. The young man who seemed to look out at him from a more comprehensive world. My husband the tour guide. The *Maestà* and the ruined Fonte Gaia. The coloured purples of Monte Acuto in the morning sun. I'm giving him an hour. One thinks, for example, of Tullio d'Attore.

He awoke at half past five, the lunchtime wine hanging just inside his skull.

❖

Claudia stood by the open window listening to the cello. In the darkness below, people were making their way between the pools of lamplight to the Via Maestra. Perhaps she would go out herself. Once up and down to the piazza. A coffee at the Gerasmo if Sauro was there. Or maybe an ice cream. And an early night. She looked up to the rooftops. A different sonata, the notes as lucid as moonlight. Delicate. Sure. Languishing in the depths of its own solitude. How old was he? Twenty five? Twenty six? Ten years between them. Where would he be at forty? Famous, if Tullio was right. Dead, if he continued to act out the cliché. The cello had picked up again, making determined progress, finding a new vigour. She left the window and poured herself a glass of wine. Should she go down and offer to sit for an hour? Tullio would be out somewhere in Trastevere with Palmiro and Lelli. Or drinking with the pair of them back at the apartment. Or walking alone through the streets behind the Piazza del Popolo. The sad face on the ill-lit landing. She returned to the sofa and switched on the lamp. The cello was coming through its ordeal, strenuous in its beauty, pushing her towards tears.

She picked up the phone. The notes of the cello ignored the ringing of a telephone in an empty apartment in Rome. She replaced the receiver and carried her glass back to the window. Probably he didn't work in the evenings anyway.

She sipped her wine and nursed the bruises of the day.

6

There were more galleries now in the Via Margutta. Almost all of them spare, whitewashed, violently lit. Tullio stepped into the Galleria Anastasia. Spiky lights on white walls. A natural jute carpet down the centre of a bare floor. A bored glance from a girl reading a magazine at a glass table. He walked between the exhibits: butted boards of bleached pine in different lengths, full of age and wear, held together by battens, roughly carpentered. Thousands of blue-steel nails had been driven into the soft, yellowing wood, more densely towards the middle, an approximate circle, a bruise of steel. Five on each side, and an eleventh on the narrow end wall; almost impossible to tell apart, numbered rather than titled. The girl ignored him as he stepped out again into the warmth of the evening. Ahead of him the traffic and the crowds heading towards the Piazza del Popolo. He turned back into the Via Margutta. Another gallery across the road; the lights of a bar ahead. He crossed and stepped up into the Solus.

The walls had been darkened, narrowing the focus, directing the eye to the five or six pale purple pedestals arranged in a line down the centre of the room, each lit by a single overhead light. He walked deeper into the gallery. In front of him, on the first pedestal, two short, brutal sections of a steel girder had been spot-welded into a crude cross. On the scoured and bolted surfaces, pitted with a fine rust, he discovered a brilliantly enamelled beetle on legs of filigree gold, as if by a jeweller. The other four sculptures followed the same idea, with a different arrangement of the truncated girders and a variety of gem-like insects, butter-flies, crickets, millipedes, scorpions, a praying mantis, each glimmering in its own overhead light.

A minute later he left the gallery and walked towards the lights of the bar. The street was almost empty, lonely enough for passers-by to murmur a buona sera. Another gallery displayed a dozen African masks arranged on what looked like a duvet. Somewhere above a piano was playing. A stranger passed, footsteps receding into stone. A parchment lamp in an upstairs window, arousing longing. There had been times when he had known that he was an artist; times when he had experienced and felt and imagined with an intensity that reached back to the common source; times of such fine engagement; times when he had been caught unawares, confronted by something so elusive as to be beyond any other expression; times when he had shared a glimpse of something which all art is merely a failed attempt to reach, something in the face of which even great art was but heroic failure. He stopped outside a gallery offering a suite of coat-hanger sculptures inserted into heavy marble bases. Two scooters buzzed past, side by side. Searchlights played in the sky above the river. If he was an artist, then the failure lay elsewhere; in the deeper registers of character; in some flaw that inhibited, or refused to serve; in laziness, perhaps; in the lack of sustained intensity, the ease with which he allowed himself to be seduced by . . . ease. Or in the weakness for distraction, for any offered escape from the effort of summoning nerve and will, of bringing the fibres of his being to the edge of aliveness, the state of tension, that was required to paint. That was the problem. He needed more of the tension that he successfully avoided. He needed turning out from the calm backwater into a more turbulent stream.

He ignored the bar and pressed on down the street, stopping for a moment to peer into a newly opened gallery where a collection of battered and rusting radiators hung like canvases on the whitewashed walls. In the window, a fluorescent pink poster for the final year exhibition by students of the Belle Arti directed him towards the deconsecrated church of San Michele.

Plant-pots huddled in doorways. Basil and thyme among the geraniums, their faint scents mingling with the aromas of roasting meats. He slowed his pace, pushed his hands into his pockets. Perhaps it was a propensity to fight with half-clenched fists; the setting out each day to conquer arduous peaks and always, by mid-morning, contenting himself with a stroll in the foothills, never nerving himself to the challenge, telling himself that easier slopes could lead to the same summit, that there was always another day. Or perhaps the cast of mind was too obvious, unsubtle enough for the nuances of intellect or feeling which divide the banal and the breathtaking. Or perhaps the motivation was at fault; perhaps he was driven not by art at all but merely by the wish to be an artist, to lay claim to laurels of unmeasured greatness. He crossed a small piazza, still following the fluorescent signs. The offer from 'Arte' would give them a holiday. Claudia had mentioned something about a few days in France. Burgundy, perhaps. It was the obvious thing to do, to be alone with Claudia. There were times now when he seemed to be on his own, even when they were together. He could manage eight tours and still paint. Time was not the problem. Painting was the problem.

The disused church of San Michele was set back a little from the street, creating its own three-sided piazza where a few students sat on artist's boxes drinking beer. He passed through a vestibule of leather-padded doors and entered into a pale pink world: pink the walls and niches, the balustrades and baroque mouldings, the side chapels and plaster saints; pink the stone steps to the altar, the carved confessional boxes, the angels and the over-nourished putti over the sacristy doors. Down the length of the nave canvases stood in loose lines of makeshift easels. In one aisle, structures of junk and chicken-wire defended niches where once the saints had stood. It was almost seven thirty and only a few visitors wandered up and down between the easels; mostly art students, a few tourists, curious Romans. There were the usual figure studies in red chalk; sketches in charcoal; a few youthful oils that barely concealed their debts to promiscuous early enthusiasms. But as he neared the centre of the church the figure studies gave way to more impatient creations, greedy strivings after premature effects, aggressive forays into the shallow hinterland of the imagination, harsh and hurried in execution, dry of thought and awash in self-love. He stopped halfway down the south aisle in front of a large canvas that appeared to be completely bare. Stepping closer, he saw that the canvas was in fact untreated linen, except for a fine wire mesh tacked to the outside of the frame; in the bottom of the mesh were a dozen or so unshelled peanuts. On the wall, set into spaces edged by plaster mouldings that had once held Depositions and Crucifixions, he found a polystyrene panel in which lumps of coal had been embedded. Next door, in a side chapel, a youth was staring intently at something that had been placed on the pink stone of the altar. He stepped up between pink railings. The object of the young man's scrutiny was a canteen of cutlery, probably nineteenth century; oak inlaid with rosewood; the soft velvet slots filled with disposable knives, forks, spoons, in serried ranks of translucent white plastic. He stepped down from the side chapel and made his way into the transept where a few young people were staring at a plastic disposable razor hanging from a medieval chain. Next to it, resting on the pegs of an easel, he found a dense collage of interleaved and overlapping condoms in transparent colours, the whole ensemble varnished and mounted in a gilt ormolu frame. Beside it stood a work after Alberto Burri in which two or three delicate items of female underwear had been placed under the cling-film before the blow-torch had been applied. On the floor by his feet he found a large wooden chest, an old fashioned cassapanca for storing bed-linen, filled now with blown hens' eggs and light bulbs in what seemed to be equal proportions.

❖

By ten o'clock the three friends were settled down in Quartucci's third floor apartment above the upholsterer's shop in the Via dei Carbonari and about to open a fourth bottle to go with the three they had already consumed at the restaurant. Palmiro put a hand on Tullio's shoulder as he came in from the galley kitchen. He was still handsome at forty-two, dark-grained silver hair cropped short to the lined face.

'At least you're still painting, Tullio.'

'Not for much longer.'

'Come on, you're not giving up again?'

'Why not? You gave up. You too Lelli.'

They drank in the silence of a friendship that had been formed at the Belle Arti and had survived the two decades since. Palmiro Quartucci, after a few unrecognised years as a conceptual artist, had gradually eased himself into art criticism. Lelli Ugolini, a year younger, had once painted bizarre psychedelic still lifes but now taught part-time and reviewed new exhibitions for *La Stampa* and, at more length, for *Quadri e Sculture* and specialist journals in France and Germany.

Palmiro poured more wine. Tullio took the glass and sank back into the chair. The lights of a car passed over the ceiling like one of Lelli's yawns. Conversation had lapsed to the point where it had become inappropriate to speak, displaced by a silence heavy with thoughts that the energy of day-time had kept at bay. The alcohol in the bloodstream, the indulgent soul-winding of the jazz, had conjured a moment whose significance bore down on all three. Each knew where the others' thoughts had flown, not alighting on any particular but suspended in the exquisite and generalised misery of contemplating who and where they were, what they had once been and hoped to be, the fraudulent claims of maturity, the unacceptability of middle-age.

When the music paused between tracks, Palmiro spoke as if the silence had never been.

'Anyway, you're doing okay with the tours aren't you?'

Tullio turned an aggressive look towards him.

'It may have escaped your notice for the last twenty years, Quartucci, but I have this slight preference for being thought of as an artist.'

'So keep painting your trouser leg, no one will know'

'Fuck off.'

Since his divorce, Palmiro had drifted back into the seedy bachelorhood of younger days. Weeks of newspapers and un-washed cups of instant coffee covered the surfaces of the room. One half of the glass-topped table was a crystallised lake of spilt red wine. Only one bulb still functioned in an overhead light that glowed unpleasantly, its marbled bowl a cemetery of dead and dying insects. In the semi-darkness the red lights of a graphic equaliser followed the mournful journeyings of Roy Hargrove's *September in the Rain*. Lelli pushed the wine towards Tullio, who poured another half glass and moved the bottle on.

'How come it's taken me twenty years to find out something that was obvious to you in two?'

Lelli swallowed the wine he had been holding in his mouth.

'That's the wine talking, Tullio. You've done some good stuff.'

'I don't want any bullshit reassurance.'

'You're pissed.'

'Could you say that again more clearly?'

Lelli closed his eyes.

'The thing is. Quiet. That's what it is. Your work. Quiet. It's like . . . all that old stuff was painted for a world where there was zippo to look at, no visual im'gery, no competition. You could afford to do . . . quiet stuff. When there was no competition. But now it's there all the time. Visual stuff. All the time. And it gets more and more sensational. I mean some of it's really striking. That Benetton poster in Bologna? The whole of one side of the piazza? Art's got to respond, Tullio. It's got to respond. It's got to get out there and command some attention. The noise is rising all around you and you're still whispering.'

Tullio replied in a distant voice, as if the point were not worthy of his full attention.

'That's undiluted horse shit, Lelli. Art's not about shouting louder than everyone else. If you were a priest, God forbid, you'd be arguing the job of the church was to compete with rock concerts.'

Another long silence followed, broken by Palmiro.

'Is everything all right with Claudia?'

Both critics were divorced, rendering Tullio self-conscious about the astonishing longevity of his marriage. As if it showed a lack of solidarity, as if he were somehow letting them down.

'Everything's fine with Claudia. She's still keeping me isn't she?'

Quartucci poured more wine.

'Don't be bitter, be grateful. Anyway, remember Jules Renard. "Being an artist is the only profession where no one considers you ridiculous if you earn no money".'

'Jules Renard probably had a private income.'

Lelli opened his eyes.

'Or a wife.'

Tullio gave him one finger and fell into his own reverie. Roy Hargrove had moved on to a drawn out version of *Alone Together*. Claudia would be asleep. He should be asleep. His party would be waiting for him in the lobby at eight.

'What I miss is the feeling of reciprocity.'

Lelli sipped his wine, evidently pleased with himself for having negotiated the sentence thus far.

'I mean when our fathers switched on the light or flushed the loo they knew that some other poor bugger was shovelling coal or crawling about in a sewer so they could do it, didn't they? Didn't they? I mean they knew that?'

Tullio was away on his own, back with his parents, looking at a masterpiece in his mind, an early memory, the dirt floor of a barn, a glistening hill of yellow corn cobs, his mother stripping the stalks, a fertile figure in a Millet landscape, while his sisters stuffed the leaves into the mattresses and the dark figure of his father strode back and forth, sweeping up armfuls of stalks to the billowing bonfires in the fields.

Palmiro reached for the bottle. Lelli came forward in the chair, changing the fist into an admonitory finger.

'But they knew that they'd spent the whole fucking day in the fields so that the guy shovelling coal and the guy shovelling shit would have something on the table when they got home.'

Palmiro poured, and exchanged a long-suffering look with Tullio.

'I mean when my old man bought something he needed, he bought it with money he'd got by doing something that somebody else needed. Do you see my point?'

'We saw it about ten minutes ago, Lelli.'

'So you see . . .'

Lelli was refusing to have his hard-won grip loosened.

'. . . They felt . . . alongside other people.'

He collapsed back and stared up at the ceiling, savouring the significance of the phrase. Tullio's eyes closed. Palmiro was leafing through an old supplement. Lelli spoke to the ceiling.

'Alongside other people. Not above them. Not apart from them. Alongside. That's what we've lost. Hence the ennui my friends. No one needs any damn thing that we do.'

Palmiro threw the magazine onto the sticky table.

'So piss off back to Puglia. Go and grub about in the soil if that's how you feel about it. You're like the guy who left his money to an art gallery if it could be proved that the people wanted pictures. If we all felt like you we'd all be busy reciprocating away in the dark ages.'

Tullio had fallen gently asleep in the armchair.

There followed a long silence in which Lelli also threatened to drift away. Palmiro fingered his glass and looked across at the slackening muscles of Tullio's face.

'I think we should do something.'

Lelli's eyes opened again. He looked at the sleeping figure in the chair, the head fallen to one side, the mouth slack.

'About Tullio?'

'Yeah, he's low.'

'He was low last time.'

'Not this low.'

Tullio's gentle snores filled the room. Lelli's eyes closed again.

'We could do a couple of rediscovery pieces. Tullio d'Attore twenty years on.'

Lelli's eyes opened to the ceiling.

'Not easy. He's right off the map.'

He stole a glance at Tullio.

'And you have to ask yourself what there is to rediscover.'

He had spoken in almost a whisper, and now raised his eyebrows significantly at Palmiro.

'Come on, Lelli, you've rediscovered a respectable amount of excrement in your time.'

Lelli lifted his head from the back of the armchair.

'Well that's funny, I seem to remember you rediscovering Sergio Collini who as we all know should never have been uncovered in the first place.'

'That was just a little favour to Riccardo, as we all know.'

'And we all know why too.'

'So now we do a little favour for Tullio.'

Lelli stared at the ceiling, working his way round to the idea. Eventually he shrugged.

'I'll do a piece if you will.'

Palmiro poured a little more wine and held the glass up to the dim bowl of light.

'It's too obvious. If it's just the two of us everybody will know its a back-scratcher.'

Lelli pushed out his lower lip in concentration.

'Tommaso owes me one for that piece I did last year on his girlfriend's wretched little show in Ostia.'

'Tommaso owes me, too. Twice in fact. And Fabrizio, too, come to think of it.'

'We'd need something to hang it on.'

Palmiro waved a hand dismissively.

'Anything. Something is always twenty years after whatever it was that happened twenty years ago.'

Lelli raised a finger in the air, becoming enthusiastic.

'Salvatore would probably do something if I asked him.'

'Oh yes, I'd quite forgotten Salvatore. Salvatore would do anything if you asked him.'

'You're becoming very cheap you know Palmiro.'

Palmiro ignored the remark and began scribbling something in the margin of the newspaper.

'If we had four or five pieces we'd be there.'

He passed over the newspaper. Lelli looked at the list, then at the sleeping figure in the soft chair.

'It's a pity we can't buy shares in him.'

'We could always buy a few paintings.'

❖

Claudia came to him in front of the window.

'How was the sitting?'

'Okay. He didn't do anything. Just looked at me for an hour, snapping at me to sit naturally, concentrate, look at him, do this, do that. In the end I snapped back and made him give me coffee. Then he said that was it for the day.'

'Didn't he even do a sketch?'

'Nothing. How was Rome?'

'Filthy, noisy, stinking, like . . .'

'Rome?'

'Exactly.'

'Good group?'

'Great. There's a guy from Brooklyn who's a bit of a pain in the ass, as he would say. But the rest are great. How did the new lecture go?'

'It was good, I think. Except I really needed to go on a bit further.'

'And Eduardo wouldn't like it.'

'Eduardo would start waving his arms about and we'd end up in the same situation as last year. He goes on and on about Romanesque and Gothic being only "frontiers of convenience" but if I so much as mention a pointed arch in front of my lot he starts running up and down barking. What did you do last night?'

'I saw Lelli. Palmiro.'

'And got drunk.'

'And got drunk.'

'They OK?'

'Lelli's fine. Pal's life gets seedier.'

'So you didn't envy them the single life?'

'No-oooo . . .'

'We could always get a divorce.'

'I'd only have to ask you to marry me again.'

'So ask me now and miss out the difficult part.'

'Will you marry me?'

'I'll think about it.'

7

The candles had gone, the saucers piled on top of each other in a corner of the room. Apart from the tinge of orange from the street light there was only the lamp clamped to the easel, its flex trailing down to the floorboards. Tullio glanced at the back of the stretched canvas, the format landscape not portrait. Giuliano approached carrying wine, his face expressionless.

'I saw you this morning.'

'Where?'

'Going up the steps into the Museo Civico, with a crowd of people. They looked like Americans.'

'My new tour party. So you do go out?'

'Only to Pasquale's, to pick up paint.'

Giuliano was still holding the wine, but showed no sign of producing any glasses. Tullio watched as Claudia crossed to the kitchen and opened the left hand drawer, taking out glasses, checking to see if they were clean. She called over her shoulder.

'Did you just finish it this afternoon?'

Giuliano poured wine, filling the glass too full.

'I finished it two days ago.'

'Giuliano!'

He poured for Claudia, remaining in front of her, staring into her face as if Tullio were not in the room. She turned away. He filled Tullio's glass and retreated to the kitchen, snapping on the picture lights.

Tullio glanced around the walls. Paintings he had seen only

once leapt towards him with the force of recognition, as if seen many times in reproduction. Giuliano remained in the kitchen, facing the wall, doing nothing.

They passed on either side of the easel, coming together again in front of the painting. Silence stewed the day's residual heat.

Tullio took in the side-by-side portraits, forcing himself to look first at the one on the right. Claudia. Claudia composed for the world, the fibres of herself pulled together, giving away nothing; a hint of defiance in the eyes, of resistance to invasion; an exhibition of realism, down to the perfect luminosity of the jade pendant, down to the slightest change of light on each individual hair; the finish almost Ingres, the surface as hard as a Bronzino. He carried his attention across the ragged ribbon of untouched canvas to the second portrait, already knowing what he would find. Claudia painted freely, spontaneously, each brush-stroke flowing from the inspired imagination, released from the literal and the mundane, energy pouring from the fusion of heart and eye and hand. Claudia as he knew her. He closed his eyes for a moment, saw the portrait still, felt her release his hand. He looked again. No sentimentality. No surface flattery. If anything his wife had been aged beyond her thirty six years; every line, every asymmetry of feature, every variation and blemish subtly recorded, relished, wondered at, loved. There was no other word. He drew in a deep breath. Some unfathomable dimension of talent, of art, of being, had revealed the depth of the beauty, in the person that she was, in the eyes set dark and deep, in the slight turn of the head, the mouth that was both ironic and forgiving, in the face that offered no resistance to the searching and the knowing.

The cello spiked his concentration, striking up in the corner of the room, a nervous, edgy andante, energetic and tense. He blinked and began to explore the work, determined on a degree of detachment, summoning the years of looking at paintings. Claudia had withdrawn to the window.

Images of loved portraits, of Velázquez's *Juan de Pareja*, of Cézanne's *Seated Peasant*, came to mind. Like them, it was a portrait of a particular psychological moment, giving the impression that the moment might pass. Like them, it was a painting whose surface appeared supremely still, uneventful, but whose depths held the trembling moment in suspension, filling the stillness with the movement of the inner life. Like them it revealed its subject with a painful intimacy, so that the watcher might know the depths without knowing the surface, the residual effect without the drip of a lifetime's events. Like them it was a portrait of the essential; the racial pride and hurt of Velázquez's Mulatto; the ingrained working-class pain of Cézanne's labourer; the long, subtle history of womanhood in Claudia's utter womanliness, poised now for change, coming into its strength. Like them there was a power about it, something that came from the depths of creativity, from the vibrant edge. The wine burst intensely across his palate, breaking up dryness.

Tullio's focus began to fragment. Air escaped through his teeth. He glanced across the room at Giuliano whose playing had become more aggressive, the bow bouncing off the strings as if he were attacking the music, drawing out its pain. Rather than look at Claudia he turned again to the painting, trying to regroup. But the nerve had snapped, expended, and after a few moments more he relinquished the struggle. Ordinariness returned, and with it a quantum of calm. He took a last look at the painting, both paintings, divided by the strip of bare canvas; a diptych missing its arched and gilded frame.

The cello stopped abruptly, unable to complete the arduous journey. Giuliano leaned back against the wall, looking at them through half closed eyes, his face a subtle writhing of concern. Eventually he opened his eyes.

Claudia broke the silence.

'If it was of somebody else I'd say it was wonderful.'

'What does that mean. You can't be wonderful?'

He had almost snapped at her in his agitation.

'Don't be obtuse Giuliano. I mean I can't quite separate seeing it as a painting and seeing it as a painting of me.'

'Why bother?'

The artist let his head sink back against the wall in disgust. Tullio refilled his glass, registering the familiarity. He walked around the easel into the centre of the room. Giuliano's eyes remained closed.

'Congratulations is too frothy a word.'

Giuliano's eyes opened wide, inviting Tullio to continue.

'I think it's magnificent.'

The face relaxed, the shoulders dropped back to the wall. He closed his eyes for five seconds, then looked up at Tullio.

'Then I want you to have it.'

Claudia had arrived at Tullio's side.

'No, Tullio! He can't!'

Giuliano's head had fallen to his chest, his fingers nervously searching out the strings of the cello. But he spoke calmly.

'You must have it. Nothing else will do.'

Tullio looked down on the young man on the floor.

'Then I'd like to buy it.'

The eyes widened in threatened anger.

'That would be worse than anything. I want you to have it. Take it now.'

Tullio made a last throw.

'Don't you want to exhibit it?'

The young man slowly looked up into Tullio's eyes.

'I don't exhibit. I paint.'

❖

Tullio stood in the centre of the room with no memory of climbing the stairs. Claudia was spooning coffee into the machine, talking in a normal voice.

'It's a bit odd, having a portrait of yourself in the living room.'

He lowered the canvas slowly until the bottom edge rested evenly across the toes of his shoes. She was lifting down cups, turning on lights under the kitchen cupboards.

'Do you think he'd be upset if we gave it to my mother?'

'I think he might be.'

'The spare room then.'

She closed the fridge, setting it vibrating gently. Around him half a dozen of his own canvases looked down from the walls.

'I'll put it here. I want to show the *Santorini* anyway.'

He lifted the seascape down from between the two windows. She came towards him.

'I'm still not sure about it in here. What about the hall?'

Tullio scrabbled in the drawer of his worktable.

'You'd be on top of it.'

'Come and have your coffee.'

He twisted eye-hooks into the frame, slipped gold wire through the rings, guessed at the amount of slack. She watched him over the top of her cup.

'Do we know anybody with their own portrait in the living room?'

He lifted the painting into the gap left by the *Santorini*. She stretched out a hand. He joined her on the sofa, letting his head be persuaded back onto the softness. After a few moments he opened his eyes. The painting would need to be lowered slightly to be happy in the space.

'What do you really think of it? '

Tullio summoned himself to keep life normal.

'I think it's extraordinary. I don't think I've ever . . .'

He turned away, towards the portrait, though his eyes were closed. Claudia placed her hand over his.

'Tullio, there's no wall between your feelings for me and your feelings about the painting. They're pouring into each other.'

'It's more than that.'

'You really do think he's a fine artist, don't you?'

'Oh, I know he is.'

Claudia leant against him, turning his face away from the portrait with the tips of her fingers.

8

The nude fibreglass mannequins were suitably lifeless, though their facelessness had none of the embryonic quality he had been looking for; none of the plastic anonymity, the bland neutrality of individuals one would never know. He sipped water from the glass. The window was wide open but no breeze blew in over the rooftops of the town, only the faint notes of the piano from the music school.

He let the brush fall from the canvas. The problem was the girl. The silk skirt and blouse refused to float and cling, to reveal the limbs they hid. And he had failed to suggest the view through a shop window, to identify plate glass with picture glass. There was no depth of field. The reflected light into which he had painted echoes of street-life insisted on occupying the same plane as the girl herself. The brush swivelled gently between his fingertips. The smell of oil paint and furniture polish hung in the warmth of the afternoon. The colours on the palette waited. Silence stood like a judge over the canvas.

Eventually he dropped the brush onto the ledge of the easel. The afternoon was not the best time for painting anyway. Especially in the middle of a tour. A breeze stirred the curtains, freshening the air, but none of it reached his brain where the cells were dying, the head heavy with too much warm summer blood. Tiredness drew his eyes back into his skull, though he had slept well. It was too late for coffee, too early for wine. He pushed the sofa out of a strip of sunlight and picked up the *Giornale dell'Arte*.

He had read two paragraphs when he let his head sink back. Claudia looked down at him from high on the wall. Claudia revealed, identified for all eyes and all times, as long as oil and canvas last and people have eyes to see. The strike of talent. The scorn for the terrestrial march. The refusal to live in the sublunary world. The nerving of the self, the will to paint, to live. There was no separation of painter and personality, no escape from one into the other. Dullness occluded life as well as art. The artist lived as he painted. Style was character. Claudia must know it, feel it. To be in the same palazzo was to feel his presence. To be in the same room was to be more alive. He turned away from the portrait. Why had he not told Lelli, Palmiro, about Giuliano?

When he opened his eyes again he was looking at the trilogy above the fireplace. The frames were wrong, competing. Claudia chose better frames for his pictures. He stared at the canvases, his breathing shallow, the muscles of his face slack, knowing as well now as then what it was he had sought to achieve. He had sought his own style in which to attempt Cézanne's gentle reaching out to the landscape, to Provence, to its earth and stones, its trees and skies; to discover in paint his own sense of joy, of homage, of steady, mature delight in his own land. His eyes moved from painting to painting over the mantelpiece. The summer that year had been flawless. And on walks for whose beauty he had wept he had painted the yellow innocence of the broom, the deep mystical greens of the hills, the pale purples of the fading light, the grasses bright in the last of the sunlight, the delicate dog rose strewn over the heat-heavy land.

He tried to relax his neck, resting his head against the back of the sofa. Mannequins moving. The card players at their game. A life measured in unsold canvases, stacked deeper and deeper against the walls. The girl gliding across the shop window. The *Santorini* hanging in the Chicago office. The bristles of his neck settled into the velour. The magazine slipped to the floor. I saw you this morning. My husband the artist. Don't be obtuse, Giuliano. The smell of sleep, of bedclothes. I'm giving him an hour. He opened his eyes again as the notes of the cello drifted up from below, the vibrations penetrating the apartment with the heat. In front of him still, the Casentino trilogy. And in a moment of certainty, he took the full measure of the gulf between the work over the fireplace and his beloved Cézanne. It was the difference between waking and sleeping, between living and the half-life. He closed his eyes again to see the house on the Marne, the subtle patchworks of Mont Sainte-Victoire, the house of promise through the tangled trees. Cézanne, Cézanne, who had painted not landscape but the steady spirit of the places he had loved; not the beauty but the effect of the beauty on the heart; not the moment but the recollection of the moment. What it had meant. What it was about. Painting not just the external but the external in such a way as to recreate the internal; reading the inner sense, the fleeting moment. The cello had stopped. He looked anew at the paintings above the mantelpiece. Whatever message there might be remained on the canvas, not in the invisible spaces of the heart; in the end, paintings only of landscape. He was wide awake now, heart beating quickly though he remained still.

He awoke as the instrument began to play again, the deep notes carrying from the apartment below. His eyes were drawn irresistibly to the portrait. To his right the curtains glowed, diffusing a sudden release of spilt sun onto the floorboards, illuminating his absence. He summoned himself to return, the muscles aching down one side of his neck. He hesitated over where to start, hovering over infinite possibility, contemplating the meaninglessness of one brush stroke over another as the cello cut through the slow heat of the afternoon. Anything would do. Nothing would do. Only art could decide. And no decisions came. After five minutes he began stirring the brush around in the spirit jar. Bottom left to top right, top left to bottom right, stroking the dripping bristles across the surface, watching the spirit run down, the colour of watered Brunello, dissolving the flesh of the mannequins, the silk of the blouse, until the whole canvas wept.

❖

An hour before his usual time he dropped into a chair outside the Bar Gerasmo. The day had not yet begun to cool.

'Troppo caldo, Tullio.'

Arturo took the seat beside him, leaning back, balancing. A clean apron rose smooth as licked ice cream over his stomach. Tullio took one of his cigarettes. The Via Maestra was empty apart from a few shoppers. Music drifted from the gelateria. Lazarini stood idle in his doorway. Outside the pharmacy, a delivery van coasted to a stop, its rear doors open. Toby and Gala Millner had strolled in under the Porta Fiorentina; a pleasant, intelligent pair from Syracuse, predisposed towards everything. He followed their progress past the first two bars, watched them pick up a *Herald Tribune*. He had sometimes been tempted to finish his tours with a visit to his studio, where, over a glass or two of wine, sentiment would no doubt have spilled over into one or two sales. 'Arte' would not mind. Frank Nelson had even suggested as much. He had promised him a reply weeks ago.

The Millners were approaching the Gerasmo, crossing the street into the shade, hesitating as they neared the tables. He gestured to the vacant seats. Arturo disappeared to bring drinks menus. Gala Millner began fanning herself with a street map of the town.

'We've been up to have another look. At *The Resurrection*.'

Tullio smiled. Toby Millner took off his sunglasses, screwed up his eyes.

'Someone told us some English writer said it was the greatest painting in the world.'

'Huxley. *Along the Road*. Some time in the twenties I think. There was a chapter on the best picture. I believe he had one on the best sculpture as well. The Apollo of Veii, I believe it was. He must have seen art as a kind of Olympics.'

Wine arrived. Carole Millner raised her glass, looking over her sunglasses into Tullio's eyes.

'Our chance to say thank you, Tullio.'

'Niente.'

Toby Millner had also picked up his glass.

'I see now why we had to make our reservations ahead of time.'

He waived down their appreciation, sipped his wine, looked away down the Via Maestra.

'Does it ever strike you as odd that all of it's religious?'

Tullio turned to Gala Millner, inviting her to continue.

'I mean most of us aren't religious are we? At least, that's not why we're here.'

Toby Millner sipped his drink, admiring two handsome, middle-aged women walking past the profumeria.

'So what are you getting at, sweetheart?'

'Only that everything we've seen has been either Christ or Mary or John the Baptist or Apostles or Saints or Devils or church fathers. I mean that's all painting was until the fifteenth century. Wasn't it?'

Tullio thought for a moment, sipped his wine.

'Just about, yes.'

'Well, what I'm trying to say is, wouldn't they be just blown away if they could see people coming from all over the world and chopping it all off from religion? Coming for some other reason?'

'But sweetheart . . .'

'So what is it that we get from all these Madonnas and children, annunciations, crucifixions . . . what's that other one, Christ being taken down from the cross . . .'

'The Deposition.'

'Depositions, if we're not religious? Would they have understood why people come to see them?'

Tullio looked at her.

'Why have you come to see them?'

Gala Millner took a deep breath.

'I don't know. Some of them are just so beautiful. And old of course. I mean they're history. They give you a sense of the past, I mean a real sense of the past, a sense of being connected, that you can't get anyplace else. Not just with facts. With individuals. With their sense of being alive I suppose. You feel they were alive like you are alive now . . .'

Toby Millner was looking on in amusement.

'Darlin', I'm not gonna be alive too much longer if we don't go eat soon.'

'And sometimes I think it's just the pleasure of recognition; seeing things that you've seen, in books and posters. Just the pleasure of connecting when you see the real thing.'

'Sweetheart . . .'

'And the lady from Carolina? The one in the purple track suit? She told me she came for the consolation. Her husband died last fall. That's why she wants to look at paintings. Do you think that's silly?'

'C'mon, Gala, give the guy a break.'

Tullio waved down their attempts to pay, watched them disappear into the Fiorentino.

❖

Claudia was practising at the piano when he arrived home, frowning at the score. He started dinner, preparing artichokes on the marble surface.

She stood up in disgust at her performance and came to join him in the kitchen. He took a glass from the cupboard and poured her a glass of wine.

'Aren't you having one?'

'No, I had a couple in the bar.'

'Bad day?'

'Not great.'

'Where were you this morning?'

'Just up the road at the Madonna. I got myself attacked by a feminist.'

'Good. Just what you need. What for?'

'Apparently it's all political. A way of making women conform to what men want them to be.'

'All true.'

'Claudia, this was the *Madonna del Parto*!'

She smiled and lifted herself onto the kitchen stool.

'I thought you liked it when they argued?'

'I do. Everybody was arguing today. We had lunch at Enzo's. A woman from Chicago told one of the men that he couldn't make up his mind which Madonna he wanted, the modest virgin with the buttoned-up bodice or the rock-star with the metal bra and the leather knickers.'

'I like this lady. Why don't you invite her tomorrow night?'

Tullio looked blank.

'You hadn't forgotten?'

'Eduardo?'

'And Valentina, and Sauro.'

'Tomorrow? Shit, I'd forgotten all about it.'

'You'll be back by eight?'

Tullio nodded.

'We'll be out of Florence by five.'

'Well don't be going to Arturo's with them when you get back. You can put up with Eduardo for a couple of hours.'

A few minutes before eight the evening recital began. Claudia slipped an arm around his waist and drew him to the window. An evening purple stared back at them from across the town. A few clouds preserved the last tinges of the day.

'Do you know what this is?'

'Brahms?'

Claudia nodded slowly, listening.

'He's playing the piano part in his head.'

'That's why we have the long pauses?'

'Mmm. I thought I might surprise him tomorrow night. I've got the sheet music.'

She walked over to the piano. Tullio, changing his mind, poured himself a glass, glancing up at the portrait as the cello reached deep into the sonata. Claudia caught the look.

'Let's not have that up there for tomorrow night.'

'No, leave it. I want them to see it.'

'I met him on the stairs just now.'

'You could ask him up tomorrow evening as well.'

Claudia grimaced.

'Can you imagine? Anyway, I expect we'll be talking shop.'

'I can't wait.'

'He asked me if I'd sit for him again.'

Tullio remained silent as the cello penetrated the old walls.

'Only he wants to do a nude study this time. What do you think?'

9

Tullio pulled himself up the metal steps at the front of the coach, arriving in an ordered upper world of ranks and rows, newly familiar faces, the sickly throb of diesel, the virgin expectations of the day.

'Posso?'

'Please.'

He lowered himself into the vacant seat as the coach pulled away from under the old walls.

'First time to Florence?'

'Yes. I've always wanted to go. I suppose everybody has.'

'And what do you do when you're not going to Florence for the day?'

'I'm with Channel Thirteen, Boston.'

'Public television?'

'Yes. Documentaries mostly. You've lived in the States?'

'New York mostly.'

Tullio leaned back into the seat as the coach made the turn onto the Arezzo road, following the morning traffic through the out-skirts of the town. He had wanted to escape while Claudia was still asleep, but she had wandered through into the studio wearing only a silk gown.

'I was just thinking, yesterday, that it's actually very like television. What you were saying about art and history and landscape gardening.'

Tullio looked up at Teresa Guardia. Perhaps thirty-five, forty.

Eyes too large and experienced for the girlish body. Limbs gathered together neatly, naked and composed under the fine American cotton. Are you posing this morning, was all he had said, his voice light, turning the pages of the brochure for the Festival delle Nazioni.

'About art historians being a bit like landscape gardeners, shaping the contours of the past, about the past really being today's creation.'

'That's very good. Did I really say that?'

'Yes you did. You said that the past, how we see it and all, isn't like some old vase or something that's been dug up intact and all. About it being more like fragments of the vase? Or maybe a lot of different vases? That historians try to put together in different ways?'

Tullio patted his pockets.

'Un attimo. I'd better write all this down.'

Teresa Guardia had pushed her tongue into her cheek to contain a smile, pressing on through his teasing.

'Television's very like that. People think they're seeing things as they are. As if they're looking down one end of a glass tube and the other end is roaming around all over the place, poking into people's lives just as they are, other countries, cultures . . .'

A tall figure leaned over them, lifting himself up on the back of Tullio's seat.

'I hope you're not going to monopolise him all the way to Florence, Teresa?'

Teresa Guardia did not look round.

'Butt out, Guy. He's mine till the coffee stop.'

Tullio smiled and looked out of the window as Anghiari came up on the hill. They would be taking the Libbia pass, passing the Istituto where Claudia taught two afternoons a week. She had said nothing. Only that she would give him an hour. Yawning. Picking up the morning paper. A silence between them over coffee.

Teresa Guardia threw Tullio a rueful smile, sympathising, wondering whether to go on, her bare arms and legs glowing with the first touch of the Italian sun. He caught her look.

'Sorry. The glass tube?'

She nodded, concentrating again.

'Whereas in fact there's an entire industry between the two ends – deciding what to put into the tube, what's important and what's not, cutting and shaping it all so it looks just natural, like it's just what's there at the other end.'

Tullio watched the Tuscan countryside go by, glad to be listening to Teresa Guardia talking about television, glad to be going to Florence with his Americans, to be spared time alone in the apartment.

❖

Claudia stood naked on the floorboards, light flooding in through the tall windows. Too much light. Exploring every pore. She wore no make up, fearing the contrast with an un-made-up body. She closed her eyes for a second. The day was warming up and the smell of baking bread from the panificio layered itself with the sunlight and the faint, permanent mustiness of the Palazzo Lanzi. She had washed her hair, painted her toenails with a transparent gloss, applied an all-over body lotion. The carillon had finished, the bells of the Badia settling into a steady tolling of the hour. She had drunk too much coffee, could feel its edginess on the surface of her skin. Tullio had left half an hour ago. They had hardly spoken. He had enquired if she were going downstairs, affecting a mild interest, consulting the programme for the music festival in Castello. In another apartment, a radio played.

She turned half sideways in front of the long mirror, lifting her chin, pulling in the stomach, observing herself. The buttocks too slack and heavy. The stomach a little too full. The skin beginning to lose the sleek of youth. She pulled her shoulders back, lifted her chin. A word was all she had wanted. But no. He could not bring himself to be so bourgeois, so unbohemian. She had only his silences.

An hour was all it would be. A class at two. A lecture at three. A dinner party to prepare. He would be on the autostrada by now, getting to know the new group, chatting to one of the party, growing enthusiastic. She began to dress, pleased that he had taken his silence to Florence for the day.

She paused in her underwear and turned again to the mirror, looking boldly into her own eyes. He stared back at her. The uncombed hair. The delicate face. The eyes arrogant. Would she be able to undress in front of him, without self-consciousness, posing for an hour in the middle of the bare floor, thinking of other things? She unhooked her bra, still looking in the mirror. Behind her the unmade bed; the silver frame; her mother, satisfied, proud. The bra fell to the floor. She looked into her own eyes. The mundane danced with the daring. The salad to pick up at the last moment. The breasts lifted slightly as she breathed. The wine to put in the fridge. The ripple of ribs still visible. Pasta from Gino's. Eduardo to remind about the music. She slipped off her panties, threw them onto the bed. Nakedness confronted her. A tingling of the flesh. A hollowness in her stomach. The lecture notes to remember. The sheet music to look through again. The picture looking back at her, real and therefore not real. She tried the contraposto, putting her weight on the right leg, trunk turning to the right, only the toe of the left foot touching the floor. Easy looking into one's own eyes, confronting one's own threat, one's own secrets. Where would this body, this face, be in ten more years? And twenty, and forty? This unreal painting, framed in a wardrobe door? Already the young men no longer looked at her on Saturday evenings in the Via Maestra.

She dressed quickly and left the bedroom.

There was too much light in the living room, too. She would have liked wooden blinds for the mornings. On the end wall the portrait seemed to float in the light. Could she live with it year after year, unchanging as she herself grew old? She pulled dead flowers from the vase. Tullio's painting, the *Santorini*, had left a thin white shadow on the wall, a second mount. The two versions of herself looked down on her, though it was the version on the left that occupied the room. It would be difficult to be more revealed than that, was all he had said. She looked around the room at Tullio's own work. The Casentino paintings. The *San Lorenzo*, not yet framed. All the walls needed painting. He had said he thought he might be able to manage that. The programme for the Festival delle Nazioni was still on the table.

She jumped as the phone rang in the corner of the studio.

'Claudia? Vittorio.'

'Oh, ciao, Vittorio. Tullio left half an hour ago. He's in Florence for the day.'

'Tell him the shop's empty for a month starting the twenty-fourth. He's welcome to it if he wants to put some pictures up. It'll cost him a glass of wine, and tell him I don't mean Arturo's.'

'Thanks, Vittorio. He'll be pleased.'

❖

'. . . by Angelico and his assistants in the late 1430s and early 1440s. One in every cell, fifty in all. In a minute we can wander round on our own, but let's spend a moment together on the figure down here on the right.'

Sixteen people were gathered in cell number seven, bare apart from the fresco on one wall. Tullio kept his voice low, eliciting quiet, focusing his party. Behind him the heat of sixteen bodies made itself felt. Perfumes and deodorants mingled the present with the past.

'It's a portrait of St Dominic, the founder of the order, and a contemporary of St Francis. But forget dates and names now. Forget the hectic morning. Forget the traffic and that slight Florentine headache. Let your eyes come to rest here on the gentle blue-grey of the cloak, the harmony of the cream under-robe, the stillness of the monk, the patience of the gesture.'

The shuffling of feet had stopped.

'I think Angelico painted this. It has his heart's trademark – the sense of outer perfection reflecting the inner, the immaculate lovingness of the technique, the way the light models the volume of that spherical, tonsured head. The tenderness of the conception . . .'

Tullio told himself to shut up for a moment and let people see.

'Nowadays we tend to think of piety as something cold and external. But not here. Not for Fra Angelico. He painted piety all his life. He made the subject his own. But his piety is warm and internal. It has humility, tenderness, humour. It's the joy of piety that he paints.'

He checked himself again.

'And what he's painted here in this corner is more than just a portrait of Dominic. In this restrained light, in this subdued colour, in this graceful, ordered drapery, this calm, refined face, in the patience of this pose – he's painted not just a monk but the idea of a monk. He's painted a portrait of that great ideal that inspired thousands in the middle ages – an ideal that still calls men and women today. In these calm harmonies, he's painted a state of mind, an image of the ordered, contemplative life, the subduing of the individual ego to the ideal of obedience and order under the

Rule, the alternative to disorder, arbitrariness, uncertainty. Painted as well the virtues of calm and order and balance and proportion that the minds of men and women can aspire to in all ages, even today. In quiet folds and patient gestures he's asserted the dignity of humility, of surrendering the self. And in this corner of a quiet cell he's painted a portrait of an idea that held western civilisation together for a thousand years.'

The heat inside the cell was becoming unbreathable. Tullio allowed a minute to elapse, then stood up to face the group.

'Let's meet at the gate at about one. Don't worry about seeing everything there is to see. The danger isn't missing something. The danger is that you end up not really looking at anything.'

The sixteen members of the tour party ducked one by one out into the corridor, dispersing along the corridor, filtering into the other cells.

❖

His pallor shocked her. His eyes dead. The skin on the cheekbones tight and dull.

'I didn't expect you.'

She let her impatience show.

'Giuliano, you only asked me yesterday.'

She followed him into the room. The window still closed, the air stale. The light noticeably less than in her own apartment; a greyness to it that was dispiriting.

Giuliano had returned straightaway to his easel, leaving her in the centre of the floor. For a few moments she listened to the rough scraping of charcoal on paper. The head bent, the dull hair falling forwards. He appeared to be working on something else.

'I only have an hour.'

'No one only has an hour.'

After a few moments he looked up from his sketch pad, raised his eyebrows elaborately, insolently, as if surprised to see her still there.

'Aren't you going to get undressed?'

'No Giuliano, I'm not. Does that mean you don't want to bother?'

She had half turned to the door. He was staring hard at the sketch pad. She could not see whatever it was he was working on. The hands were still, the hair black against the forearm, the colour of a corpse. He glanced towards her.

'Tullio wouldn't like it?'

Claudia's anger flared.

'It's nothing to do with Tullio.'

He turned to her again, his eyes sunken, dead.

'Then why?'

'Because I — I myself — don't want to.'

With hardly a change in his expression Giuliano flung the piece of charcoal hard at the glass of the window.

'I suppose that's what I get for burying myself in the provinces.'

Claudia turned and left the apartment.

Twenty metres away the Florentine traffic was racing six abreast around the Piazza San Marco, but the room was quiet, still, as he approached the largest of the altarpieces on the west wall. Half a dozen of his party were already gathered in the small vestibule, next to the biglietteria.

It was a painting he had taken some years to love. The elaborate, gilded frame intruded into the composition, medieval ways of defining space clashing with the new perspective of the Renaissance; angels floating on magic carpet clouds, absurd to modern eyes; the garden stilted and stylised, like the landscape beyond; the clumsy confusion of cross and ladder with the carved arches of the triptych; the bright, insouciant colours, the limpid reds and mauves scattered in promiscuous profusion, at odds with the sombreness of the subject. But he had found himself returning to the work, winding himself into its finely tuned struggle. Each robe and tunic, each obligatory figure and posture, had received the monk's total attention, as though there were nothing else in the painting, as though there were nothing else in the world. It was an obsessiveness that did not amount to any marvel of composition or harmony; it was too bright, too involved with its individual parts. Yet across the centre of all this limpid colour, this loving perfection, these rigid verticals of cross and ladder and city walls, lay the loose, slack figure of the dead Christ, hanging limply from the hands of his followers, pulling together the whole flamboyant scene by its contrast, by the dead colour, the dead lines, the dead weight, sagging across all that was vertical and vibrant. Being careful not to trigger the alarm, he leaned forward to inspect the delicate scourging of Christ's dead flesh, the light falling on the torso and neck, the genius of the slightly parted lips and the tiniest glimpse of teeth, the extraordinary veining on the hand reaching down. Tullio held his breath, knowing that he stood in the presence of one who had struggled mightily for his perfection, never weakening in his desire to hold in his hands the silver thread of art. And for a few moments, in front of the *Deposition from the Cross*, he held on to the struggle in his own mind as a timeless essence, the struggle of art, in all its limitless possibilities of form and expression.

Outside the tour group waited, eager for the afternoon.

He surveyed the room. The gilded frames of predellas and altarpieces, the glorious innocence of Angelico's colours, on every wall. How many figures had he painted, including all the serried ranks of haloed saints, the gorgeous-winged angels, the treasuries of kings and shepherds, the Last Judgments and the Maestà, the Depositions and the Assumptions of the Virgin? A thousand? Two thousand? All of them carefully dressed, draped in fluted shadows of pinks and reds and blues.

❖

Claudia was working on her notes, spread out over the coffee table in front of the fireplace, when Giuliano called through the open door.

'Claudia?'

She looked up at him, unsmiling, over the top of her reading glasses. He stepped inside in his bare feet, his body a rag of repentance.

'Claudia, I'm sorry.'

Claudia took off the glasses, unwrapping them from her face in a swift movement, a lecturer's gesture, keeping her place in the book with the flat of one hand.

'Giuliano. Rudeness followed by an apology is okay once. As a habit, it's unattractive.'

'I'm sorry.'

Her eyes remained fixed on him, expecting excuse, explanation. Giuliano looked back at her in silence. She attempted to stare him out, not wishing to offer too easy an accommodation. He began looking around the apartment, apparently fascinated by the domestic detail. She sighed, a conventional ending to the impasse, and began gathering up papers from the table. A boy. A talented boy. Struggling only for himself.

'I suppose I'd better offer you coffee.'

He crept forward into the open space of the studio, looking at the walls, at Tullio's canvases, at his own painting edged by its pale shadow. Claudia glanced back at him from the kitchen. The hands were held together in front of the unnaturally thin body; a deliberately weak, apologetic posture, sincerity in doubt. The light from the three tall windows flooded the worktable, the empty space before the easel. He had turned to examine the three landscapes over the fireplace.

'Do you like your husband's paintings?'

'Most of them.'

'Do you think he has talent?'

'Yes, I do.'

'Remarkable talent?'

Claudia looked down into the shadowy marble of the kitchen surface.

'Who knows these things.'

'I do. I know I have remarkable talent.'

She remained in the kitchen, waiting for the coffee.

'Will you pose for me again?'

'Dressed. And I won't even talk about anything else.'

He had dropped onto the sofa.

'Does art have no claim?'

'On my body? None at all.'

They sat at opposite ends of the sofa, Giuliano drinking coffee with both hands as if it were a bowl of soup, sipping continuously, looking at her. She picked up her glasses.

'What are you reading?'

Claudia turned the book sideways so that he could read the spine.

'Can I stay while you read? '

'Stay?'

'I could bring my sketch pad.'

A minute later he crept back into the room, making an elaborate show of not interrupting her reading. He settled into the far corner of the sofa, a sketch pad on his knee.

She consulted the index and looked up the page.

'Probably built by the Lombards in the eighth century on the site of an earlier church '

The knowledge of his looking intervened between eye and page, his nearness distancing her from the text. She reached for her pencil. An involuntary glance. A mock innocence. Playing with her attempt at sternness.

'The capitals of the upper church, like those of nearby Gropina, are carved with an almost pagan freedom . . .'

She took off the glasses.

'Giuliano this is ridiculous. I can't possibly concentrate with you looking at me like that. You're not doing anything.'

'Painting is mostly looking.'

'You look terrible. What have you had to eat today?'

He began sketching, the shirt pocket pregnant with charcoal.

'Nothing yet.'

'And what will you have, later?'

'Chocolate I expect.'

The work with the charcoal had become more careful. A thin smile at some effect he had succeeded in achieving. A series of quick glances at the lower part of her face.

'Do you know what happens when a body becomes malnourished?'

He carried on drawing, in the delicate grip of what he was doing. She twirled the reading glasses between thumb and forefinger.

'If it can't get the calories it needs from food, it looks to the fat stores.'

Giuliano selected a new stick of charcoal from his shirt pocket, held it towards her, evidently pleased with himself.

'I make these myself. From spindle twigs. You must have seen them.'

'But in your case there aren't any fat stores. So where do you think it gets the calories from?'

'The berries are orange and magenta. Exotic, Asian colours. You must have seen them.'

Giuliano had begun filling in background, something unimportant, the charcoal loose in his fingers.

'The tricky bit is knowing just the moment to take them out of the fire; after they've turned to charcoal but before they turn to ash. You don't need calories to paint.'

She dropped the book on the table.

'Giuliano, three quarters of the calories are just to keep you alive, the organs functioning, the blood warm, the heart beating. You'd need them even if you never got out of bed.'

Giuliano was frowning at something now, picking something off the pad with a fingernail. Claudia persisted.

'So? Where do you think they come from?'

'What?'

'The calories.'

He settled back into the sofa, the pad braced against the knees, the flat of the charcoal scraping softly across the texture of the paper. A glance up at his subject, uninterested in the interrogation. Claudia sank back on the sofa, watched him observing her legs, her body.

'It gets them by breaking down protein instead. Raiding other parts of the body, the organs, the muscles, just to get calories. Nutritionists say it's like chopping up antiques for firewood.'

'I thought you were reading?'

'Including the heart muscles. It's not particular.'

'Could you keep your mouth still now?'

❖

Tullio had decided not to have lunch with his party. He found a hole-in-the-wall place in the streets beyond the Piazza della Santissima Annunziata, carrying a Peroni and a panino to a revolving stool. A steady flow of people passed in front of the window. Tourists. Students. Office workers. Clerics. Lovers. Behind him the world was full of the clash of cups and saucers, orders being called, the hiss of escaping steam, customers ordering and talking above the din, his skull unable to keep out the noise. The smell of coffee and focaccia bread drifted past him out into the street.

The Deposition was still with him, conflicting with the noise. And the Annunciation at the head of the stairs. And the portrait of the surrendered ego, the achieved serenity, the putting of trust in another. He drank from the plastic cup and looked out across the street. A minibus from Belgium had turned the wrong way into Santissima Annunziata. A tour guide raised a stick tipped by the scarlet leaf of a Canadian maple. The two lovers were strolling hand in hand towards the Accademia. He should be at the Caffè San Marco, answering questions, listening to what they'd found in the monks' cells, building up anticipation for the Baptistry doors, the Orsanmichele. He made room for a young man in a black T-shirt approaching the stool next to him, leaning a new portfolio against the wall. Drawings, probably. Anatomical studies from the masters' notebooks. Sketches from a life-class. He glanced at his watch. She would be on her way to work. The young man next to him took out a felt tip pen and began drawing on a paper napkin. The noise in the bar forced him to his feet. There would be time for coffee with the group. He would dabble with painting a bit in the winter months, stop using master quality oils, leave the struggle to the young man on the stool.

10

The coach hauled itself in under the walls of Sansepolcro twenty minutes ahead of schedule, hissing to a stop outside the Porta Fiorentina. Tullio made his way forward amid a lifting down of hats and bags, a stretching of limbs, a pulling off of sweaters in readiness for the afternoon warmth.

By the time he had signed the driver's slip most of the party had already passed under the walls of the town and were meandering into the Via Maestra. He caught up with them outside the Bar Gerasmo as chairs were being shuffled, a space being made for him. He glanced at his watch and perched himself in what he hoped was a temporary pose at the corner of the group. Tall-stemmed glasses of wine were appearing, prosecchi, cold beers, elaborate fruit drinks garlanded with mint and grapes. Grace Lederer and her husband were fussing with a cat; next to them were Toni Yamaguchi from Michigan and Hans and Annie Kluivert from Pennsylvania, with Geraldine Fisher and her daughter whose name eluded him. On the other side of the table, facing the Via Maestra, sat Mario and Pia Battistuta from California, Ferdinand Liversedge and Eric Boyd from New York, and Sol Thomas, the heavily built widower from Texas who began every intervention with the words "Here's a dumb question for you, Tullio". Half a dozen others whose names he did not know sat with their backs to the street. The bells of the Badia were sounding six o'clock.

Annie Kluivert took off her sunglasses.

'You still mad with us Tullio?'

Laughter round the tables. Tullio frowning, refusing to be mollified. A ritual. Taking his group into the Galleria dell'Accademia to see an obscure and rather harrowing thirteenth-century pietà by Giovanni da Milano; pretending to be annoyed because they insisted on spending most of the time with Michelangelo's David: High Renaissance, and not on the itinerary.

'So what's up for tomorrow?'

'Siena.'

'No, Siena's Thursday.'

'Yes, tomorrow.'

'Today's Wednesday?'

On Tullio's right, Sol Thomas raised a hand for quiet, bringing it down slowly on the painted iron-work of the table to more laughter and cries of 'Go to it Sol'.

'Okay Tullio, here's a dumb question for you. Your big wheels. Giotto. Masaccio. The monk Angelico. If they're such all-time heavy-hitters, how come you have all this *de*bate about who did what bits on which wall? '

A slow cheer around the table. Tullio sat back. He had taken an instant liking to the quantity surveyor from Houston. More laughter as Sol Thomas let his mouth drop open in a way that he had, implying that the point was obvious, opening his hand, appealing to common sense.

'I mean, you'd think you'd be able to tell if something's done by some all-time genius or some dime-a-dozen assistant no one's ever even heard of?'

Tullio drank wine, trying to relax as the day cooled and the evening crowds began to flow along the Via Maestra. On the wall across the street a new poster had appeared, a nude woman crouching over a lute, advertising the Festival delle Nazioni di Musica da Camera.

'That question's so dumb Sol, I might need a little notice.'

More good humoured jeers. Hands reaching for potato chips.

Grapes being lifted from the edges of tall glasses. The Kluiverts lighting furtive cigarettes, turning to blow the smoke away from the tables in that way Americans had. Toni Yamaguchi pushing back her chair, stepping back to include the whole party in the view-finder. The Texan's hand coming down again on the table top. The poster had not been there in the morning.

'What I'm getting at is . . . maybe it all comes down to we need superstars . . . and maybe it exaggerates things that little bit, that's all, makes us widen the gap between these guys.'

Tullio leaned back on two legs of his chair. The group of older men in pullovers had begun to move off towards the piazza, heading for the Bar della Torre to sit in the last of the day's warmth. He raised his own hand.

'Part of it might be that, Sol. But part of it's genuine. Part of it's because once a really great innovator – say Giotto – makes the big breakthrough, the lunge of genius, then sometimes there are others around who are inspired by it and can probably imitate it pretty well, even though they might not have been capable of making the breakthrough themselves.'

A neighbour from the Palazzo Lanzi squeezed Tullio's shoulder as he passed by. Arturo had appeared in his doorway, fascinated by Tullio speaking English. The poster was hidden now behind a group of teenagers. Sol Thomas emptied half the peanuts from the glass bowl into his fist and considered Tullio's answer.

'So that means you can't appreciate the genius just from looking at the painting? You have to know the history? That they were the first guys to do it?'

Tullio paused for a moment, wary of falling in with Sol Thomas's little propositions. He caught Arturo's eye for another round. Across the street from the bar he could see the half dozen nude mannequins, the plate glass window reflecting the steady flow of the early evening passeggiata.

'To appreciate that they were great innovators, yes.'

Sol chewed slowly on the peanuts. Swifts played in the blue strip between the eaves.

'So suppose one of these guys makes a breakthrough, making volume with light, making things look three dimensional, whatever. And supposing someone else comes right along and copies the idea but does it a whole lot better. Which one gets to be the superstar?'

Tullio raced through those who had breached the walls, the Giottos and Masaccios, and the ones who had poured through the gap. Arturo's wife appeared, collecting glasses.

'It doesn't seem to work out like that, Sol. Those who come afterwards don't usually do it better than those who make the breakthrough. Probably because the genius isn't compartmentalised. It's not confined just to the breakthrough part.'

Sol Thomas swallowed and looked at the rest of the peanuts in the glass dish, reluctantly leaving them for others at the table.

'But from where I'm sitting that brings us right back where we started. If the genius isn't only in the breakthrough, if it's in the actual painting, how come even the experts can't decide whether something's by Giotto, whoever . . . or someone you've never heard of. Surely it should be obvious?'

Tullio smiled as another cheer went round the table.

'What if you're the one who's preoccupied with the individual, Sol? What if both worked on the same wall? Or even on the same figures? With the master intervening all the time, showing how it should be done?'

Annie Kluivert, who was in the habit of firing from the hip, leaned forward now, removing her cigarette.

'Besides, that's just the way it crumbles, Sol. It's the old "who was the second guy on the moon" thing.'

The silence following the non sequitur gave Tullio a chance to glance at his watch, breathing in deeply, straightening his back, pushing with the heels of his hands on the edge of the table. Sol

Thomas ignored the body language, poured the rest of the peanuts from the dish into his hand, turning to him again.

'Well then here's another dumb one. These breakthroughs. They all seem to be about making things look more real, more like you really see things. Right?'

Tullio sank back into the group, head on one side, non-committal. The Texan continued, his other hand measuring out the points evenly onto the table.

'You know, working out how to do the whole shebang in perspective, making folks look like they're occupying space, getting stuff to look solid, letting light do the work instead of painting black lines round everything. I mean it's all about making things look like people see them. Instead of, you know, odd, stylised, Byzantine, whatever. Right?'

Tullio waited warily. Sol Thomas was appealing to the whole table now.

'Well, my question's this. How come making things look real was great art then when it isn't now? I mean, today, if somebody paints something that looks like it is, no one gives a shit. To be art it's got to not look like it is. It's got to have both eyes on the same side of the nose, or legs growing out of armpits, or it's got to not look like anything at all.'

Another glass of wine appeared in front of Tullio amid a murmur of agreement. He looked at his watch.

'Making things look real was only ever a part of it, Sol. The real purpose was always something else. To tell a story, inspire belief, maybe. To teach. To move people. To frighten them, whatever. Or maybe to express an ideal, a state of mind, a yearning, a striving, an inner sense of order, of the perfection that might be possible. Or some conviction. Some human need that couldn't be expressed in any other way. Making things look like they appear to the eye was only ever a means for achieving something else. I mean after the fourteen hundreds lots of artists could make things look real in the sense that they knew how to deal with light and they knew how to handle the laws of perspective. But it didn't make them great artists. It's what they did with it that counts. Look at *The Resurrection*. It's perfectly possible to imagine the scene being painted just as realistically without having any of the power.'

Grace Lederer leaned forward into the conversation.

'So you're saying the perspective thing wasn't such a great breakthrough after all?'

'No-oooo. It was a great breakthrough. And it was part of a much wider story of the Renaissance, of making sense of the world from a human perspective instead of leaving it all to the clergy. It was part of the struggle to impose order on the world from a human point of view, to get to grips with a world where humans were at the centre. It was part of one of the greatest changes there's ever been – the struggle to begin investigating and taking control of the world instead of just accepting it. It was important. But it was never the only purpose of painting.'

Grace Lederer rotated the stem of her glass on the table.

'I suppose if it were, then photography would have pulled the plug.'

Tullio leaned forward into the group again.

'But it didn't. In fact some people would say that it's helped to get rid of the distraction of realism, of preoccupation with surface and representation, and allowed artists to concentrate on other things.'

'What other things Tullio?'

It was Sol Thomas who had fired the question. Tullio drew in a long breath.

'I don't know, Sol. To communicate something that's deeply felt. To communicate it even to total strangers. Things that can't be communicated any other way. Maybe not even those you're closest to. Uniting. Any communication tells you you're not alone, but art . . . art can communicate that you're not alone even at the deepest level of your soul. Only art can do that. Art and love . . .'

Annie Kluivert took over as Tullio began to struggle.

'Besides Sol, art has to move on like everything else. You can't just discover how to make things look real and then just keep on doing it for five hundred years. Art has got to move on, it's got to be relevant.'

Sol Thomas raised his hand from the empty peanut bowl, his large head weighing her words. Tullio already knew what was coming.

'I hear what you're sayin' Annie, but now you tell me this. If art has to stay relevant and all, then how come we all haul our asses all the way to Florence Italy to see stuff done five hundred years ago when none of us would cross the street to see what they're doin' now?'

'I do, I see everything that comes to . . .'

Tullio stood up abruptly, raising both palms, apologising.

❖

Claudia, in the kitchen area, threw him a sarcastic look as he glanced around before entering the apartment. Candles reflected in wine glasses. Schubert glimmering on the CD player. The wall lights dimmed. Eduardo Mignini, Claudia's head of department, standing below the portrait, glass in hand, ignoring Tullio's arrival, apparently continuing a conversation with Claudia.

'It's magnificent, Claudia. It's you, and it's magnificent.'

Tullio kissed Valentina Mignini, standing alone by the tall window. A sympathetic smile. A complicit look. Valentina, too, looked towards the portrait, almost whispering.

'What do you think if it yourself, Tullio?'

'I can't tell you how good I think it is.'

In the kitchen he bowed his head in contrition. Claudia rinsed her hands under the tap and lifted her head to be kissed, holding wet hands out by her sides.

'Traffic bad on the autostrada?'

'It didn't get really bad until about halfway down the Via Maestra.'

'By the smell of it I'd say it came to a complete stop.'

She dried her hands, turning towards him, kissing him again, gently. He held her for a moment by the shoulders, breathing her in, his thumbs making circles on the silk of her blouse.

'I'll have a glass now, please.'

Tullio opened another bottle and began filling glasses. Eduardo remained under the portrait.

'So, Tullio, holding someone else's light under a bushel are we?'

He carried the wine to the window. Claudia had joined Valentina Mignini, taking her gently by the arm, turning her away from the portrait.

'We're not keeping it there. I can't live with this.'

Eduardo turned towards her, boldly examining the real Claudia.

'Would you like me to keep it for you?'

A buzzer croaked on the wall, the battery weak. Tullio released the street-lock, not bothering with the intercom. Valentina had crossed to the landscapes over the stone fireplace. The last notes of the concerto were dying away. Eduardo remained in the middle of the room, addressing Claudia.

'You realise it's a marvellous portrait?'

'I just wish it wasn't of me.'

Tullio selected some slow jazz and slid the volume up a fraction.

'And of course it's very much more than a portrait . . .'

A loud wailing buona sera echoed from the stairwell, followed by the sounds of tired steps reaching the top landing, bringing with them the substantial figure of Sauro Rubellini, his face flushed with exertion and pleasure, arms spread wide, a bottle in each hand.

Before the kissing and handshaking were finished, Sauro's eyes had followed Eduardo's to the portrait.

'My God, that's not one of yours is it Tullio?'

Tullio took the bottle of wine.

'No. The young man downstairs. He moved in about a month ago.'

'Didn't take him long to find his subject did it? Another of Landini's finds?'

'Yes. Only this time I think he might really have found something.'

Sauro slipped his jacket off onto the back of a chair and joined Eduardo under the painting. Claudia came between them.

'Come away from it both of you, please. I can't stand it.'

Sauro turned to her.

'He lives downstairs?'

'Right below us. You'll be hearing from him any moment. He plays the cello before dinner.'

Eduardo turned his back on Sauro, addressing Claudia.

'Well or badly?'

'Well, I think. He plays with a lot of emotion.'

'And what does he play?'

'Brahms. Always Brahms.'

'Is that why you wanted the music?'

Eduardo smiled, raising his hands to receive hers. Claudia touched the offered hands briefly before turning towards the kitchen. Eduardo followed her, leaving Valentina by the fading light of the window. Sauro took Tullio's arm, steered him to stand again before the portrait.

'What's his name?'

'Amedei. Giuliano Amedei.'

'Young?'

'Mid-twenties.'

'And you've seen other stuff?'

'Yes, he's got two or three things on his walls.'

'Portraits?'

'Not of people no. But portraits in a way . . .'

'Where's he from?'

'I don't know. He trained in Rome, at the Belle Arti.'

'You know what I find remarkable is that it's a painting about painting as well as about Claudia. The one on the right seems to be saying "look, this is what a photograph can do, only perhaps not quite as well as a painting", and the one on the left is saying "and this is what a painting can do that a photograph can't do at all". It's a sort of commentary on the photographic plate and the artist's canvas, if you see what I mean?'

Tullio had scarcely looked again at the portrait on the left. He considered it now as Sauro enthused.

'Most people would have cheated wouldn't they? Made a cliché of it. The mask juxtaposed with the inner self. But he hasn't cheated. The first face is a real face. Composed. But a real face. He hasn't set up the contrast to favour the real portrait. He hasn't needed to. The real thing is so extraordinary.'

The jazz meandered across the room, mingling with the smell of the roast, overcoming linseed and turpentine; satisfying, reassuring smells. Tullio refilled Sauro's glass.

'He's painting another one.'

'Of Claudia?'

'Yes. He seems to have found his Gioconda.'

Sauro drank deeply of the wine, closed his eyes in satisfaction.

'Well I can't quarrel with his taste. But where does he go after this?'

Tullio turned towards the window.

'I don't know. He's only just started.'

'You don't do portraits yourself?'

'No. Too difficult I expect.'

'Nonsense. How many tours are you doing?'

Conversation ceased as the notes of the cello penetrated the apartment, tuning up, calling for silence. After a frozen moment, the tableau began to move; Sauro and Valentina to the window; Tullio to switch off the jazz; Claudia to the piano, followed by Eduardo, as the cello began to play.

Claudia edged the stool closer. Eduardo had placed a hand on her shoulder. He leaned over her, turning pages.

'The thirty eight in E minor, I think you'll find.'

Tullio remained in the centre of the room as Claudia began, almost silently at first, sounding the slow, soft chords that were all that were required of the piano at the opening of the E minor Sonata.

The cello stopped. Looks were exchanged. Claudia's hands waited above the keys. The palazzo had fallen quiet.

Slowly, hesitantly, the cello began again from the beginning. Claudia came in quietly, punctuating the deep strains with soft chords, until the tempo picked up, the piano quickening its climb, ending the first passage in an exposed rill. The cello stopped again. Silence.

After a few moments the deep notes resumed, the cello playing cautiously, until it was the piano's turn to lead, advancing the melody in single, clear, unmistakable notes. The strings hesitated, stopped again to listen. Claudia played on alone, picking up the opening five note motif, carrying the piece forward until the cello realised what was happening and rejoined the sonata with an eager, joyful sadness.

From inside the room, Tullio's eyes came to rest on Claudia, her head tipped slightly towards the window, towards the last of the light, towards the strains of the cello, her slim arms bare over the keys, the music running through her fingers, swaying slowly as she played, winding herself into the notes of the cello as they carved through the floorboards, through the open windows, through the generations of the Palazzo Lanzi, filling the apartments with sound. He turned to look at the portrait on the wall, closed his eyes, stormed by intimacy, by real things that could not be seen or said, things that touch but cannot be touched, the colours and tones of the inner life, unities and separations, things of great moment, things he should paint, mighty and vulnerable. An involuntary prayer, not to be alone.

Eduardo leaned closer to Claudia, preparing to turn the page. By the window, Valentina and Sauro had bowed their heads. Tullio listened as he sometimes saw, knowing that heightened sense of the moment, of the ordinary made miraculous, hearing the lucid notes of the piano, giving articulation, backbone, to music that he had begun to think of as too indulgently beautiful, too sunk into itself, as the instruments climbed together, now piano now cello straying from the path, the other always seeking, leading back into familiar ways. He saw Sauro and Valentina exchanging smiles, listening intently as the two instruments danced within each other, separating and coming together, now the cello growing stronger, insisting on its vibrant melancholy, now languishing in the depths, almost ceasing under the weight of its own sorrow, until the piano, reaching out, leads it delicately by the hand towards the light, offering excitement, tension, recharging with life. Tullio opened his eyes again to the portrait, transfixed by hopefulness and vivacity, listening to the piano bringing out the more structured beauty of the sonata, leading it to its slow, quiet, satisfied conclusion.

He turned to Claudia at the piano. Her hands remained above the keys. At her side, Eduardo, entranced, eyes delicately closed, lips slightly parted. At the window, Sauro and Valentina, not moving, sculpted into the silence until the last imperceptible strain had gone. A suspended moment, broken at length by the un-mistakable sound of hands being clapped together in another apartment, slow, single claps, like the first large spots of rain, merging into spatters of applause as more hands joined from the windows below and opposite, Sauro clapping loudest as they converged on the window, clapping as they looked down into the street, calling and laughing to the occupants of other apartments, other palazzi, to neighbours silhouetted against windows, to the half dozen people who had gathered in the street below.

Tullio's eyes followed Claudia to the kitchen as the commotion faded. She paused over the salad bowls, her back to the room, hands resting on the edges of the sink, head bowed. He was about to go to her when she turned around, smiling, a salad bowl in either hand.

Tullio herded to table, relit a candle, poured wine, reinstated the jazz. Eduardo took one end, facing the portrait. Plates of antipasti appeared. Claudia took her seat. Darkness had stolen into the rooms, bringing an intimacy, five against a doubtful world, gathered in the complex patterns of candlelight, picture light, lamplight on whitewashed walls, the hints and reflections in dark windows, in plates and glasses, in the depths of wine, in the waxed floorboards and the gleaming black ramparts of the piano. Silence had returned to the street outside.

Eduardo waited for the talk of porcini and melanzane to die away.

'So, tell me, Sauro, Claudia, have you had a chance to read my piece on Piero?'

Sauro exchanged the briefest of glances with Claudia, and did the gallant thing.

'In *Art in America*? I was going to congratulate you on it.'

Eduardo pouted, fork poised, rocked his head from side to side, closing his eyes slowly: it was not, of course, a major piece of work. Sauro was obliged to continue.

'I was interested in what you had to say about *The Flagellation* being really about policy-making, some sort of emblem . . .'

'. . . of administrative ethics, yes. Possibly even a critique, I think I might have said.'

Sauro speared a cube of melon, hoping he had done enough.

'Anything else strike you? '

A pause. Sauro again into the breach.

'Well, the idea about the general good and the generous lawn . . .'

'Guston and Marilyn Lavin? Yes, I thought I improved on that. Claudia?'

'Not my period Eduardo. Quite a coup though, I should have thought, *Art in America*.'

Eduardo nodded. It was no more than his due. He reached for his wine.

'You read it though?'

'Of course.'

Claudia glanced for an instant at Sauro as she took up the burden.

'Interesting how often Cézanne comes into discussions on Piero.'

'Yes, well, I thought I'd better say something about it, after Pope-Hennessy. He's quite wrong, of course. The only real point about the sodality between Piero and Cézanne is that they both recognise that all painting is really all about revealing terms and conditions of visibility.'

Silence fell for a moment until, microseconds before a change of subject would have been possible, Eduardo gave it another push.

'"Containment and grandeur" I was rather pleased with as well.'

He looked up at Sauro, who held a forkful of prosciutto above his plate.

'Yes, I thought they could perhaps have used that for the title. But I wasn't quite sure what you meant about them both being phases of the same focal charge?'

Eduardo looked up from his plate, shaking his head. If it were not self-evident he could hardly be expected to explain. He looked at Tullio for the first time.

'You've read it Tullio?'

Tullio nodded. In the silence, Sauro took to helping Claudia clear away the plates of antipasti. Eduardo spread both his hands.

'So do give us the benefit of the artist's perspective.'

Tullio wandered from the table, began looking through a tower of compact discs. Glasses were being refilled, chairs pushed back.

'There were parts of it I had difficulty with.'

Eduardo's eyes followed him warily.

'Really? I rather thought I'd written it for the layman.'

A warning glance from Claudia in the kitchen. Tullio hesitated, drinking wine.

'The bit about Piero's figures being permanently aware of the gravitational verities at their feet, for example. For a while I thought it must just mean his figures had weight.'

He saw Sauro turn his face rapidly away, sensed Claudia looking at him. Eduardo raised his look from Tullio to the wall above, hands behind his neck, balancing his chair on two legs.

'My God it's magnificent, Claudia. I can't keep my eyes off it.'

Claudia returned with more plates.

'It's going to my mother's. First thing tomorrow.'

Sauro followed her, carrying the steaming bowl of pasta. Valentina made space on the table and smiled at Tullio.

'So where were you today?'

'Florence all day. San Marco. The Accademia. The Orsanmichele. The Bargello.'

Eduardo cut through whatever his wife had been about to say.

'Yes, do tell us, Tullio, how are our culture collecting cousins?'

He was looking around the room, the issue not requiring all his attention. Sauro, taking his seat again, tried to restore blandness.

'Yes, what sort of people are they, Tullio?'

Tullio watched the pasta being heaped onto his plate.

'Mostly middle class professionals, I suppose. A lot of business people. Lawyers. Civil servants. Doctors. A few artists. Academics.

Teachers. TV people. Accountants. Social workers. Technical people. This week we've got two statisticians and a quantity surveyor.'

Eduardo made a show of choking on his wine.

'One struggles to reconstruct what a quantity surveyor might make of the divine Angelico. An estimate of the weight of gold leaf perhaps? Or the lapis lazuli?'

Claudia entered the conversation gently as she lifted more pasta from the bowl onto Eduardo's plate, temporarily eclipsing him from Tullio's view.

'Would you rather they all go on holiday to the Caribbean, Eduardo?'

'From my point of view, Claudia, more or less anywhere would be preferable.'

'Oh come on, I would have thought you'd be pleased that people wanted to spend their holidays looking at art.'

'One would be pleased, Claudia, one must be, if one could think for one moment that the motivation were genuine. But most of them, one suspects, are merely gathering ammunition for their nasty little wars of one-up-manship on long winter evenings in New England drawing-rooms.'

Tullio rested a fork wound with pasta on the edge of his plate.

'Most of them come for better reasons than that.'

Others seemed ready to comment, but Eduardo held up both hands to command the table.

'And do tell us what they are, Tullio, these better reasons?'

Sauro, twirling his pasta, tried to help out.

'That composer. Forget his name now. Died recently. Always said people listen to music because they're searching for something to feed their souls.'

Eduardo indulged in one of his deeper chuckles.

'So Botticelli is a type of pasta now, is he Sauro? Michelangelo I suppose is the main course? And what's to follow? Something sweet. Filippino Lippi? Pinturicchio? Perugino?'

Claudia interrupted, gesturing to Tullio to refill the glasses.

'That's not really fair, Eduardo. It's obvious people come because they feel a need for something.'

Eduardo drank his wine dismissively.

'And they've got some vague idea that it might be culture?'

Claudia had stopped giving warning glances.

'Yes, it might be culture. That's the idea we tend to put about isn't it? That culture meets a higher need? An almost, if not quite, spiritual need?'

Eduardo sighed patiently.

'And it's true, Claudia, it's true. But if what Tullio says is right and these people are at all serious, then one might ask why they take so little trouble to inform themselves even marginally. I mean, these people being herded round the Palazzo Ducale, or gawping up at the copy of the David – why do I have this inescapable feeling that they'd gawp like that at a garden gnome if someone told them it was art. Fair or not fair?'

'Not fair.'

Tullio left the sentence bare, looking around the table to see who might be in need of wine.

'You're not going to pretend they have the faintest idea they know what they're looking at? So long as they can take their snaps and say how awesome everything is.'

Tullio forestalled Claudia.

'Some of them do. I've got people whose copies of Harding are as well thumbed as mine.'

'Ah, Harding!'

Eduardo pronounced the word with a harsh 'h', drank his wine, as if trying to rid his mouth of the taste. Tullio spoke quietly.

'Yes. Harding. Because he's one of the few experts who takes the trouble to be intelligible. And it's still a brilliant work. How do you think they should prepare themselves – by reading about focal charges and gravitational verities?'

Claudia stood.

Eduardo stared over the top of Tullio's head.

'I'm sorry, Claudia, but that portrait just commands. It just commands. I think I might really have to sit somewhere else.'

'More salad anybody?'

Eduardo turned sideways in his chair, briefly surveying the other pictures in the room: the Casentino landscapes over the fireplace, the small still life on the wall to the right of the piano, the two semi-architectural pieces to the right of the tall windows. Eventually his eyes returned to the dining table.

'No, don't get me wrong, Tullio. I understand why you do the tours. I respect the necessity. But don't ask me to buy the virtue thank you very much.'

Sauro intervened optimistically.

'You know Harding's coming?'

'Coming where?'

Claudia brought bowls of spinach to the table.

'I've kept forgetting to tell you. He's giving the Montefeltro lecture.'

Tullio turned to her, dropping his fork on the plate.

'Harding's coming to Urbino?'

Eduardo had closed his eyes. Tullio ignored him, questioning Claudia.

'When?'

'The nineteenth I think. Don't worry, we'll be there.'

Eduardo, bored, touched Claudia's arm.

'I caught your last ten minutes on Wednesday. I meant to be there for the whole thing but Gramaci called one of his meetings. Awfully good, I must say. Especially your rise of Cluny. But then I've always thought there was an element of sheer luck about Cluny. I mean just look at the line up: Odo, Mayeul, Odilo, Hugh. A kind of episcopal Inter Milan . . .'

Sauro began talking about a cycling holiday in the Veneto. Tullio looked down to the table to where Claudia was trapped in candlelight. The glint of glass, porcelain, steel, seemed arranged for the glow of her skin, the gentle, perfect line of cheek and jaw, the soft folds of the sleeve, harbouring shadows.

Cluny seemed to have run its course. Eduardo had risen to stretch his legs, wandering over to the fireplace, glancing at the three landscapes. After a few seconds he came back to the table, looking again at the portrait over Tullio's head.

'My God, Claudia, what did you say his name was?'

Claudia pushed the salad bowl towards Sauro.

'Giuliano. Giuliano Amedei.'

'And where does he exhibit?'

'He doesn't exhibit. He paints.'

'So how does he live?'

'Only just, I think is the answer. He's got some kind of a bursary. He doesn't eat anything. Hardly ever goes out. I've never actually seen him in shoes. He's very thin. In fact I think he's clinically malnourished.'

Sauro raised both hands from the table.

'So why doesn't he exhibit? God knows what he'd get for work like that.'

'He says he can't, or won't. He can't bring himself to submit his work. Not to anybody. He gets agitated if you even talk about it. Refuses. Snaps your head off.'

Claudia made a swooping, grabbing motion with her fingers.

'So what does he do for paint, canvas?'

'I don't know. I imagine Landini pays his bills at Pasquale's.'

Valentina Mignini was also looking up at the portrait.

'I really think he's good.'

Eduardo glanced sarcastically at his wife and turned to Claudia.

'How old did you say he was?'

'About twenty-five, I think.'

Eduardo leaned forward with his elbows on the table in an informal pose.

'Even setting aside my predisposition towards the subject, I'd say he shows the most enormous promise.'

Claudia looked at him through the candlelight.

'Tullio thinks so too.'

11

Claudia sat upright, two metres from the curtainless window, aware on her left side of the burgeoning daylight and the dark energy of Giuliano Amedei crouched on the floorboards.

'Keep looking in the mirror.'

He had known what he wanted before she had arrived, placed her on the straight-backed chair at ninety degrees to the light, to himself. The wardrobe had been manoeuvred to the middle of the room, the full length mirror positioned so that he could observe her either in profile, directly, or from the front, through the glass.

'Can you keep your lips just slightly apart?'

Crystals of dried wine glinted in the depths of glasses that were standing where they had been left, almost a week ago when she and Tullio had last visited. The light came in behind him, including artist and sitter in the same shaft of sun. The only portraits in profile she could bring to mind were Piero's: the Duke from the left side; Battista from the right; Sigismondo Malatesta; and the famous one by Pollaiolo she had never liked. In the mirror she followed the slender white wrist and its charcoal extension.

Giuliano shuffled back against the wall, the sketch pad against his knees, the heavy sill of the window jutting into the back of his neck, the faintest smile on his lips, the artist's eyes permanently narrowed at the corners. The only movement the delicate play of the fingers, the ripple of the tendons on the back of the hand. The only sound the soft harshness of charcoal on paper, the sleep-rhythm of his breathing; shallow, unselfconscious, absorbed, like a child. She blinked against the sunlight on her left side. Tullio would be directly overhead. Starting a new canvas. Still he had said nothing. Only that he might be taking one or two more tours.

'How long can you sit?'

'Only until twelve.'

Motes of dust floated in the warm silence; infinitesimal specks and spirals, twisting and turning, adrift in the universe, crossing from sunlight to oblivion. Like a child's, too, the fine eyelashes. The loose shirt emphasising emptiness. The small rip in the thigh. The white movement of muscle. The drawn face. The hands and fingers the only part of him that seemed calm, in control. Somewhere below a door slammed, sending a faint vibration through the Palazzo Lanzi, setting the motes dancing, shaking the kaleidoscope. In the stillness that followed she thought she heard Tullio crossing overhead. Something told her that he would not be painting, that he would be drinking cup after cup of coffee. A word. A word was all it had needed.

'Can you do the same time tomorrow?'

'Yes, if you like.'

She found his profile again in the mirror. The artist himself a painting, framed by a wardrobe door. Speckled. Peeling here and there, where the silvering had worn thin. And what about herself? Why had she not said that she had no intention of posing nude for Giuliano Amedei? To provoke? To precipitate? She moved her arm to the edge of the worktable, its undulating varnish smothered once more in oil paint, the colours of his last work. Herself in a different order. A few part-used tubes of the expensive, Belgian oils.

'Can you take the earrings off?'

She slipped the pins from their studs and found a space on the table. She faced the mirror again, strangely naked.

His eyes were waiting for her in the door of the wardrobe.

'I knew it was you. I knew as soon as you started.'

She attempted to keep her own voice light.

'Did you hear the applause, down in the street?'

'I knew by the way you played.'

She held his look, helped by the doubling of the distance, coping with him at one remove. Gloom had settled into the apartment, rubbing itself into the corners. Outside, the town was getting on with the business of the day.

'The piano's always been in my head. I always played it in my head.'

'Don't tell me it didn't sound a lot better.'

'No. Only in one or two places. It was astonishing. It was like thought becoming real.'

Claudia smiled in the mirror, failing him in her response.

'It's a beautiful piece.'

'It's the opening bars. Just those first twelve notes. They cut your heart in half. Like love at first sight. Every time you hear them the wound opens up. It never heals.'

She smiled again, trying to return him to normality, to the one remove.

'You play it too much. Don't you like any of the others?'

'The D minor.'

'Which is that?'

'I'll play it for you tonight.'

Tullio held the finished board to the window, tilting it to and fro to check that the light fell evenly, perfectly, on the smooth surface of the gesso. He lowered the panel to the wall and brushed the fine white powder from the thighs of his trousers and the hairs of his forearms. In the last hour he had sized and scraped one new canvas, fine-sanded another, and cleaned several brushes, which now lay in a neat row and in numerical order on a paper towel. He had also rolled up a dozen tubes of oil paint, starting with their lead seals, fattening the tubes in a satisfying way. He found a space for the coffee on the worktable and took up a position, feet apart, before the easel. The linen canvas stared back, the light on its slight texture more beautiful than anything he could imagine placing on it. She had said nothing about the new portrait. Only that she was giving him an hour before work. Eventually he dropped the brush on the table, carried the coffee to the open window.

The rooftops of the town were not at their best in the middle of the day. Dirty rather than mellow. Too bright an edge to the blackening reds and oranges. The sky too white. She would be directly below where he was standing. He could speak to her, if the window were open.

He went back to the canvas, faced its blank, inner eye, placed the cup back on the table. Ideas swam nearer, being rejected as they threatened to come within range. Could one, in any case, make oneself a better painter? Or did one paint what one could paint? After a few minutes he turned again to the window. There was no sound at all from below. He leaned out over the street, empty apart from the portinaia chatting with the postman, a van parked outside the ortofrutta, old Gravo wheeling his bike up to the piazza. He turned again to the easel. Did it depend on the unalterable gene pool of talent? Or was it subject to choice, exertion, will? Was it some inner failure of the personality? Were there switches that could be found, effortfully reset, so that with a little less indulgence, less permitted lassitude, the moments could be held on to, perceived more completely, made permanent on the mocking rectangle? The canvas remained blank, the question as unanswerable as that other, wider question that sits on the mind's shoulder. Are you what you are? Or what you make of what you are? Who was that treacherous last-but-one 'you' that made the argument circular? Who was the you that could remake the you? As artist? As man? The brush hung at his side. The canvas waited. The fattened tubes sat smugly in their box. Or did all this introspection simply block the flow of art, of life, turning back the running stream, sullying what might be spontaneous, joyful; muddying waters that should run swift and clear. And what was the alternative? Just to do it? To paint and not to think. He distrusted the naïve and the primitive, the life of sensations rather than of thoughts, Monet's wish to see and not to know. He had still not replied to the offer from 'Arte'.

The telephone rang in the silence. A leap of relief.

'No. Non c'è.'

'Certo.'

'Di niente. Ciao, Guido.'

He wrote down the message for Claudia and sat on the edge of the sofa. He could go down and pass half an hour with Grimaldi, see what he was working on. Or he could finish the biography of Ghiberti. He looked at the lowest shelf of the bookcase. Calvesi on Piero. Baldini on Masaccio. Beck and Amendola on *Ilaria del Carretto*. Perhaps the fault lay deeper. Perhaps the roots lacked depth, reaching into soil that was not aesthetic but merely egotistical; a lust for the bella figura, a route to esteem that would otherwise have to be earned with diligences and abilities that he did not have. An ugly thought, polished to a fineness over the years by the sublime rub of the artist. He sank back into the soft arms of the sofa, staring into the safety of it all, the cowardice, choosing a course where a certain hollow prestige was guaranteed, where evident failure was all but impossible; impossible because of the lack of any measure or proof, because of the permanently hovering possibility that the world was wrong, that the future would think differently, that genius was not recognised. He bowed to those who had been derided, to the painters who had never sold a canvas and were now fawned over as if the genius were obvious, to those who had left the magic legacy that could succour both talented and talentless, who had bequeathed the aura that gilded failure and rejection alike. They were all living now under the protection of Van Gogh, of the examples of the past, of the aesthetic insecurities of the present, of the unknowableness of the future. He existed for a moment without the carapace, exposed by the tradition of those who neither received nor offered such protection, of Giotto and Duccio, of Masaccio and Fra Angelico and Piero della Francesca.

He opened his eyes again. His own work hung around him. By the bedroom door a dusty street in Badia Prataglia, inspired by paintings of drab beauty, of ordinariness made sublime, of Goeneutte's *Boulevard de Clichy under Snow*, of Utrillo's *40 Rue Ravignan*. He knew, had always known, why he had wanted to paint: it was to take part in some indefinable struggle, to hold on to those moments of the inexplicably significant, those fragments of another meaning that so often caught at him, turning him around in the middle of his days, including him for an untenable moment in some all-encompassing unity that could never be revealed. He glanced at the paintings hanging on his walls, and knew that such moments were not represented there. Above the fireplace, the Casentino trilogy: lacking in touch, lacking in life, the hillsides as dull as corpses. In the alcove, a small close up of a tough old vine, heavy with grapes. Competent, at best. Whatever eagernesses had seized him, whatever sense of all-disturbing beauty had driven him to his tubes of colours, had been still-born, dying in labour, in the torn birth canal between the imagination and the fingertips. He turned eventually to the wall between the windows, to the portrait of his wife. Beyond his portion of subtlety, of grace.

Eventually he returned to the easel, unengaged, alone with his own dullness, unbusy, unprotected from himself. The breath in him scarcely stirred. No oxygen found its way into the corpuscles of his blood, the cells of his brain. Blunt of mind. Tired of spirit. Unconfident of heart. He stared at the canvas. But no excitement quickened in him. Only the quiet, discontented breath of middle age. Magnificent Claudia. Brahms, always Brahms. Don't ask me to buy the virtue. He stands with the easel and the sunlight, the curtains stirring, brightness monochroming the studio. The smell of linseed that once called him to the task has a sweet, rancid edge. And he sees only Claudia's nakedness; her fine, private flesh, the light stealing over her thighs, seeking out faint hollows. And had the Bohemian now come to this, the petty, provincial husband?

He began mixing paint, summoning himself, rebellion stirring. He who knew himself to be moved by symbols could allow himself to care about symbols of intimacy, of love and trust, of being to another what one is to no one else. He shook himself free, struggled to the surface of things. What he needed was to work, to find a galvanising idea, to extrovert himself, find something to be excited about, something that would unwind the swaddling of ennui, something that would not take him too long to achieve, so that it could be accomplished before the enthusiasm died and the brush fell. The bowl of fruit on the table caught his eye. A melon in its midst, the thick honey rind, the Islamic patterns of its fossil tracery, the seductive suede-skinned peaches. The hard apples that would crack on biting. The grapes that would resist and then burst on the palate, flooding with sensation rather than thought. He looked from the fruit to the canvas and began to focus, but he could see only Cézanne's fruit, paintings that were not paintings of fruit but of every luscious association of fruit, the fruit that hangs in the collective memory, the mellow weight of fruit, the colour and volume and nature of fruit, the light and the rejoicing of fruit. Paintings of the word fruit, the music of fruit, splitting and spilling through the mind.

He crossed again to the bookcase, his painter's mouth watering for Cézanne. The telephone rang in the corner of the studio.

'Tullio? Gianni.'

Tullio had to think for a moment.

'From the Centro.'

'Oh, ciao, Gianni. So, have you sold all my paintings or don't you have any clients with taste?'

Gianni laughed, but there was no depth in the laughter.

'Actually, it's the paintings I've called about, Tullio. They're all still there. I can't think why no one's bought them.'

'You're not doubling the asking price are you Gianni?'

Gianni laughed again, disproportionately.

'Actually, Tullio, the problem is . . . Tiziana. She's redecorating the place. She wants to have a theme for the restaurant. The whole place in fact.'

'Theme as in park?'

'Tullio, this isn't my idea. She wants to give the whole thing what she calls an Etruscan feel, can you imagine? As far as I can tell it's going to be a lot of burnt pots and muddy drawings on the walls. You know the kind of thing, vases with points that won't stand up on their own. We could put your paintings in the lobby, by the lift to the car park, but it's a bit dim round the back there and I thought I'd better just give you a call.'

'No. Don't worry, Gianni. I'll pick them up tomorrow. I've got an exhibition coming up soon. They'll fill a few gaps.'

12

'Tullio? It's Fabiola.'

It took Tullio a few seconds. His agent had not called in two years.

'Oh, ciao, Fabiola! Come va?'

'Tullio, have you seen the papers?'

'No, why? '

'Go out and get them. All of them. *Corriere della Sera. La Stampa. La Repubblica. L'Unità.* Make sure you get the supplements.'

'Today?'

'And see if you can pick up the new *Quadri e Sculture.*'

'What's this about Fabiola?'

'It's about you, Tullio. I'd like to take the credit but I can't. I didn't know a damn thing about it. Of course I'm always pushing you, but I'd no idea this was coming. Someone must have put it together.'

'These are pieces about me?'

'All the way. Tullio d'Attore twenty years on.'

'Who by?'

He could hear newspapers rustling in Rome.

'There's a big piece in *La Stampa* by Lelli Ugolini. Know anything about him?'

'Yes, I know Lelli.'

'Well, there you are, what are friends for. Then there's a piece by Tommaso Manieri in your local.'

'*La Nazione?*'

'Yes. And Fabrizio Matteini in *Corriere della Sera*. Know either of them?'

'No.'

'Anyway, you'll see.'

'Okay, I'll go get them now. Thanks Fabiola.'

'I was going to call anyway. The Bernard called last night. They've sold four pieces this week.'

'Four of mine?'

'And not all to the same person apparently. It's got to be connected. Someone knew what was coming. Anyway, it means we have to think about repricing. When are you coming to lunch with me?'

'I'll be in Rome next week.'

'Great. Call me ahead of time. We'll go to Il Fiore. Ciao, Tullio.'

Tullio withdrew the brush from the murky liquid and balanced it across the rim. Morning glowed in the room. Claudia was still asleep. He closed the door quietly, standing for a moment at the top of the steps, looking down into the stairwell of the Palazzo Lanzi.

The tables were full outside the Caffè delle Stanze and the Appennino, the shoppers filtering between the market stalls in the Via XX Settembre, the queues gathering outside the bakery, flags flying from the windows of the Albergo Fiorentino, while in the piazza volunteers were erecting scaffolding and planks for the Balestra.

Tullio shuffled newspapers in the sunlight, discarding all but the arts sections onto an empty chair. He pushed the cup aside and began turning the pages of *La Repubblica*. A photograph of himself. A three column title: *D'Attore: in the footsteps of Piero.* He folded the paper in half and sat back.

In a world of so many flashes in so many pans, a steady heat has emanated for twenty years from the studios of Tullio d'Attore.

Even without the by-line he would have recognised Palmiro's long Germanic sentences.

Like Piero della Francesca, in whose birthplace he works and on whose paintings he is a profound authority, and like Cézanne whose work he has admired so intensely and so long, d'Attore has chosen to stand to one side of the intellectual and artistic mainstream of his times. Following almost a decade in the United States, he returned to Italy in the 1980s . . . Scarcely seen in Rome or Milan . . .

There was a poor photograph of a work from a dozen years ago, a carnival scene, the pastel diamonds of pierrot costumes mocked by the motley of the autumn leaves, the painted faces a white agony amid the festivities. He had almost forgotten the piece, but for a suspicion that it was one of those that had gone to the Bernard.

Since his early successes in the 1970s, when he was greeted as one of Italy's most promising new talents, he has – partly in consequence of this self-enforced exile – tended to fall from view, slipping below short term artistic horizons. But in the relative obscurity of the little town of Borgo Sansepolcro in the high Tiber valley, he has quietly, and on his own terms, set about fulfilling that early promise.

Arturo stood with a second caffè lungo, waiting for him to clear a space. Tullio consolidated the newspapers, covering up the photograph of himself.

'Tullio buon giorno!'

'Buon giorno Bruno!'

The ceramicist from the workshop outside the walls patted Tullio's shoulder as he walked past into the bar. Across the street two girls had stopped to admire themselves in the window of the profumeria. Aurelio trickled by on an ancient cycle. Four paintings was more than he'd sold in eighteen months. Lelli's piece was the first item in the supplement.

It is twenty years ago this month that Tullio d'Attore was first discovered by Patrice Vaux in the pages of L'Impression, *and twenty years this month since this newspaper covered his first exhibition at the Galleria Severinas. Twenty years in which fashion's treacherous tides have swirled and pulled in every conceivable direction without diverting the Tuscan from his task.*

He smiled despite himself, imagining the two of them, late at night in the seedy apartment above the Via dei Carbonari, opening another bottle, concocting the twentieth anniversary idea. Feeble. But it would do.

Grabbing the artistic headlines for a week with a work calibrated to that end is one thing; producing work of steady quality over two decades, finding and refining an individual voice, is quite another.

He sipped coffee, shame, relief, reading quickly as the piece wandered into an analysis of another painting from more than a decade ago. A faded chair in a broad shaft of timeless sunlight. A work that Tullio remembered and which might have been another of those held by the Bernard. After describing the painting in detail, Ugolini had used it as the springboard for a peroration:

In this painting, as in almost all d'Attore's work over the last decade, the seriousness is almost palpable. There is weight of contemplation. There is deftness of execution. There is delicacy of feeling. There is a consummate synthesis of the representational and the rhythmically abstract. And there is, also, an unmistakable fin de siècle quality that haunts the edges of his canvas. But these qualities are not sufficient to entirely convince, and the question inevitably arises – is there a place for what one might call the art of the quiet in the late twentieth century? D'Attore clearly believes so. If he were a priest rather than an artist, he would undoubtedly be on the side of the Latin Mass rather than the electric guitar. But ultimately there is a line to be drawn between what is quiet and what is dull, what is subtle and what is enervated, what is restrained and what is energyless – a line that d'Attore has too often fallen foul of. His future reputation will surely rest on what happens over the next year or two in the quiet studio above the sleepy streets of Sansepolcro. The oeuvre is solid. The technique is not in doubt. The talent has been long maturing. Now it needs to emerge from the shadow of its own sober soul, to move out of the backwaters of the pleasing and the vaguely edifying and enter the fray of the twenty-first century, with all its vigour and imagination.

Tullio accepted a millefoglie from a plate that Arturo's wife was offering around the tables. Behind him someone was reading the football reports to a couple of old men. The reviews section of the *Corriere della Sera* also carried a photograph. He had vaguely heard of Fabrizio Matteini.

Over the last twenty years, Tullio d'Attore has stolen almost unnoticed into the pantheon of Italian art. There is a quality

*about his work which ought not to be as rare as it is, and that
quality is — quality.*

Fabiola would already have run her fluorescent pen over the
phrases and half-sentences. He finished the second coffee and
pulled out the arts section of *L'Unità*.

*For five hundred years there has only been one painter in the
small town of Borgo Sansepolcro high in the Tiber valley. But
the day may come, in the perhaps not too far distant future, when
Piero della Francesca may not have to carry the burden of the
town's fame entirely alone.*

He dropped the paper on the table. A party of teenagers with ice
creams wandered by. In the window of the pharmacy, another new
poster had appeared: a seated girl, blonde, naked, slim, twisting
round to look over her shoulder, applying a sun cream, fingertips
caressing the gentle knuckles at the top of the backbone. He turned
towards the commotion as five or six men in costumes of heavy
velvet and old leather were applauded into the Via Maestra,
banners rising to the height of second floor windows, heading
for the rehearsals in the piazza. Tullio screwed up his eyes against
the glare. Another crowd of teenagers drifted by, blocking the
pharmacy window. He reassembled the pages, shaking out the pale
flakes of pastry, beginning again, taking his time, noting the
coherency of the negatives, the notes of reservation playing the
same tune. Lelli had been the most forthright. But Palmiro's piece
had also noted 'a certain passivity', demanded more 'aesthetic
action'. Even the Ercolani piece, after praising the 'near-pious
clarity', ended with a pseudo-populist analogy, noting 'a carefulness, a tendency to play at home, making sure of the draw, stifling
the game'. Matteini had used the adjective 'quiet' four times, and
concluded with his own variation on the theme:

No one risks having their breath taken away by looking at a Tullio d'Attore; no one will feel that chill of manifest brilliance suffusing his veins; he is simply not that kind of painter. But as paintings to live with, paintings to grow old with, paintings to return to at the end of the day, the works of Tullio d'Attore come into their own.

He turned to the last piece, a brief paragraph in *L'Unità* by someone called Aurelio Graziano, hung on the same fragile peg of the twentieth anniversary of his supposed discovery. He read swiftly, elation evaporating. Even the artificial acclaim had found him out. The essence of his work was the dull at heart. The talent toilsome, uninspired. The last article was a rent-a-critic piece. A thin potage of praise. A tired reshuffling of the pack. Sentences that slipped by without snagging the mind. Perceptual sensibility. Overall specificity. Painterly orchestration of elements.

He dropped the newspapers onto the table, his eyes reaching out to the sunlit façades, the abstract composition of overhanging eaves and morning sky, the sharply angled shadows and the plunging darkness of the streets and alleyways that crossed the Via Maestra. The art of the quiet. The backwaters of the pleasing. The shop window confronted him from across the street. The poster-perfect sky. The delicious twist of the naked back.

He was about to take the papers back to the Palazzo Lanzi when Clementine Clarke emerged from the Via Pacioli.

'Buon giorno, Tullio. Grazie.'

She took the seat he had pulled away from the table.

'The Signora at the hotel said you were in all the papers today.'

'Favours from friends, mostly, I think.'

'So why don't you take us all off to see your own paintings?'

'Because they're not exactly late medieval, although some of my critics might not entirely agree.'

'Jamie was asking me yesterday if your work was on show anywhere. Did he ask you about it?'

'No.'

Clementine turned to follow Tullio's look. A balding, over-weight man in an electric blue track suit was approaching. A slight bow to the stranger. A heavily ringed hand on Tullio's shoulder.

'Town's proud, Tullio.'

Tullio nodded, embarrassed, and pursed his lips.

'I've told them a thousand times, we can't be living off Piero for ever. Don't rest on tradition. Build on it. If I've said it once I've said it a thousand times. But some of them . . . well, you know, Pichio's lot. Anyway, Tullio, town's proud.'

When he had gone, Tullio looked up again, shaking his head.

'What was that all about?'

'The Mayor. He's been reading the papers as well.'

'I wish I could read them.'

'I'm quite pleased that you can't.'

'So what's on today?'

Tullio leaned back in his chair, the Tuscan sun on his face, the smell of coffee lingering under awnings. Around him the town flowed on about its business. In the piazza, the banners had begun to rise and fall above the heads of the crowd.

'Just a trip up the road to see another Piero.'

'And tomorrow's Rome, right?'

'For one night.'

'And Orvieto on the way back?'

'Just for a couple of hours. To see the cathedral façade. Maitani's reliefs. The San Brizio chapel. You'll love Orvieto.'

'I hope the cathedral's going to be better than those two in Florence, San Lorenzo and what was that other one?'

'Santo Spirito.'

'Santo Spirito. Not to mention that pigeon loft in the piazza at

Montalcino. Or was it Montepulciano? Really, Tullio, even you have to bow down to the French when it comes to cathedral fronts.'

Tullio smiled and tilted his head back to the sun.

'It'll be about four o'clock in the afternoon. You'll be standing in Orvieto looking up with your mouth wide open. And I'm going to be right there behind you whispering in your ear – "eat your words Clementine Clarke".'

Clementine Clarke laughed, delighted to have provoked, to be going to Rome and Orvieto, to be drinking real cappuccino, to be sitting with Tullio in the Sunday morning sunshine of the Via Maestra. Behind her, the large figure of Sauro Rubellini was bearing down on them from the direction of the piazza, tapping the copy of *La Repubblica* under his arm, eyes enlarged.

'Hail Tullio! Well known boulevardier, bon viveur, and now our new Piero.'

'Shut up and get me another coffee, Sauro.'

'I already called Claudia. We're going to clip all the pieces for Eduardo.'

He threw the newspaper onto the table on top of the rest.

'Seriously, Tullio. I'm delighted.'

'Thanks, Sauro. It's nothing to be excited about. I'll tell you about it later. This is Clementine Clarke from Georgia. Sauro Rubellini.'

'Piacere signora.'

Sauro shook hands with the American, switching into English.

'I 'ave often wanted to meet one of those who 'ave the courage to put themselves in the 'ands of d'Attore. In this town . . . corre voce che . . . there is a story that 'e is paid for this. Please tell me it is not so true.'

'Not only that, Mr Rubellini, but there's a very long queue.'

'This is very strange when everybody 'ere is all the time tryin' very 'ard to avoid 'im.'

'And did you know there's a woman in Boston who's starting

133

some kind of a society for people who've taken Tullio's Tour? They go places together every month, museums, galleries, shows.'

Sauro looked at Clementine Clarke, not quite sure whether he had understood. Tullio, embarrassed, rose to greet two more members of the party who were crossing the street towards the Bar Gerasmo.

The apartment was silent, empty, its tables and chairs darkened by the brightness of the windows. The bedroom door was open, the silk dressing gown across the back of the sofa.

He left the newspapers on the coffee table. The studio quiet, composed, its spirits watching him. The paintings the same as they had always been. The easel under the window unimpressed by the morning's events. He picked up the gown in both hands, lifted it to his face, breathed in the intimacy. The settled quiet of the apartment, the motes of dust in the sunlight, exuding infinite possibility.

When he returned in the afternoon Claudia was back. She came across the room, kissing him, spilling delight.

'It's wonderful. Had you any idea?'

'None at all.'

'Didn't they say anything?'

'Nothing.'

'All the others were Pal and Lelli too?'

'I expect so. Contacts. Friends. People who owe them. I've never heard of most of them. I know they meant well, but I wish they hadn't done it.'

'Tullio, you know how that world works. Besides, you deserve it.'

He kissed her in acquiescence.

'Do I?'

'Have you called either of them yet?'

'No, not yet.'

'Call now. I'll have a word as well.'

Tullio sank back on the sofa and dialled Rome. Claudia paused as she closed the door of the fridge, looked unobserved into Tullio's expectant face. He leaned forward into the phone.

'Lelli? What is all this bullshit? You haven't looked at anything I've painted since the Belle Arti.'

Claudia grinned as she pushed the cork from a bottle of prosecco.

'Yes, even the Mayor stopped me. Seemed to think I was Piero della Francesca.'

She poured two glasses, still smiling, carrying them to the window seat.

'Art of the quiet! How long did you spend thinking that up? And tell Palmiro when he gets back he's full of shit as well.'

He turned to Claudia, silhouetted against the light, glanced at her portrait on the wall.

'Tomorrow. And I suppose you're going to say I owe you dinner.'

The phone rang the instant he replaced the receiver. He switched on the speaker.

'Pronto?'

'Tullio? Maurizio. Listen, Tullio, I told them this afternoon at the meeting. It's time we started honouring our living, I said, starting with Tullio d'Attore. Some of them hadn't even read the papers!'

'Maurizio, was this . . .'

'Anyway the upshot is, they've agreed on a full civic exhibition. Either in the Museo or in the Foundation, whichever . . .'

'Maurizio . . .'

'The thing is, Tullio, we have to do it straightaway. Take advantage of the publicity. I told them things aren't anything today without publicity. Put it on while there's still a buzz. What do you think?'

'An exhibition of my work?'

'Can we do it a week Sunday? We were thinking about an opening night, civic reception, one or two people down from Florence. But it would mean doing it a week Sunday.'

'I could get together fifteen, twenty pieces I suppose.'

'We don't want to let things cool off.'

'No. That's fine. A week Sunday's fine.'

He replaced the receiver and picked up the glass of wine. His picture stared at him from the pages of the *Corriere della Sera*. In the footsteps of Piero. He looked up at Claudia, floating, despite himself, on a floodtide of relief. The easel, the walls, the world, easier to look at.

13

He found what he was searching for high on the wall; a marble relief among the thousand unregarded works of the Vatican collections. The corridor was empty; rhythms of light slanted from the phalanx of windows, setting the polished floor aflame. He held up a hand to the side of his face to reduce the contrast, subduing the violence of the light. The figure had been caught in profile from the left side, gliding gracefully through antiquity, holding her gown from the floor.

A few minutes later he was discovered by a dozen members of his party returning from the Sistine Chapel. By the time he noticed them, they were alongside him in the corridor, searching among sarcophagi and marble busts, the lost capitals and gravestones, trying to locate what he was looking at. He raised a hand.

'Second row from the top, third in.'

There was silence for a few moments, as sixteen pairs of eyes found the marble relief.

'What's special about it Tullio? '

It was the bright woman from Michigan in the yellow halter-top and the long-peaked baseball cap.

'*La Gradiva*. The daughter of a king.'

The group looked harder, studying the flowing figure, held for ever at the exact point of transferring her weight, head slightly bowed, hands holding the flimsy gown from the floor, the slender body revealed rather than covered by the marble robe that flowed with her as she moved. Tullio leaned back against the wall.

'See if you can see it for a moment as if it were completely abstract. Forget that it's a woman or anything at all. Follow its form, its lines, its flow, its balance. As harmony of movement, as gracefulness in complexity, it's masterly. Like a wonderful poem, you couldn't alter a single line.'

One or two tourists on their way to and from the famous chapel had stopped to see what it was that the party of Americans was looking at. From the north door, a guard was keeping an eye on the unusual congregation in the corridor. Tullio waited until a party of schoolchildren had passed.

'Now let the lines, the movement, become a woman again, a woman walking through time. As depiction of grace, of movement as representation, it's unsurpassed.'

Daylight poured in through the tall windows, the floor blazing like the sea, silhouetting the motionless party.

'Now hold on to it for a few seconds as both. As abstract and representation. And now not both, but one . . .'

Another half minute passed. The sun had dipped low over the roofline of the Papal apartments, setting the corridor walls aglow. Tullio spoke softly.

'Alberti said that folds in drapery should give birth to movement, and that movement should be sweet and measured. They all tried for it, Ghiberti, Donatello, della Quercia, Duccio d'Agostino. We'll see them all in Florence. We'll see it on the Baptistry doors. We'll see it beginning in the niches of the Orsanmichele. We'll see it in the Museo dell' Opera del Duomo. And when we're there, remember *La Gradiva* carved over a thousand years before Ghiberti was born.'

After a few seconds the silence was broken by one of those moments that lifted Tullio's life. It was the sombre Virginian, Calvin Reed, who had until now not spoken a word on the tour.

'I don't think I've ever in my life seen anything as beautiful as that.'

Tullio glanced at him in delight, eyes brimming, the love flowing and spilling like panic through his nerves and sinews. Knowing that he had seen it.

❖

He lay on one of the two narrow beds in the hotel watching the light fade.

A different room, the ceiling bowed and dingy; but the same tired paint on the walls, the same smell of disinfectant over age. He closed his eyes and saw the *Gradiva*, its grace undiminished; an unknown Roman, holding in his hands the silver thread. The tour should begin with classical pieces. A glimpse of what had been lost. He had left the letter from 'Arte' open on the table in the apartment, with the handwritten note from Frank Nelson enclosing a few photographs: Frank with Tullio on the steps of the Museo; the whole party in front of Santa Cecilia; Tullio looking over-enthusiastic in front of the St Mark at the Orsanmichele. Deposits would have to be returned. They must know this week or next. In the distance, the car horns, the tidal roar of Roman traffic, the clash of plates from the kitchens.

The clock in the lobby struck a thin half hour. The light was beginning to go, evening rising with a sugary glow. He imagined the excitement of the city painted into the low clouds, reflected in the pavements; Pissarro's *Boulevard de Montparnasse*, the sky crackling with the energy of night. Five more of his paintings had sold, three from the Bernard, two from L'Immagine. On the wall, an old photograph of the flower-sellers and a faded print of shepherds and maids dancing in idealised Roman ruins, a pastoral idyll under an oppressive sky. Fabiola had had no doubts, had advised him to drop the tours he was doing now. Time to consolidate, to make the push for a permanent place in the front rank. Even when he had confessed, told her how it had happened, she had hardly taken it on board. It was to be expected. How soon could he replenish the Bernard's inventory. The décor had been white gothic, the room divided by fluted pillars, pointed arches, like a Pieter Saeredam. The strange ring of the telephone by his ear jolted him. He reassured the front desk that the rooms would be cleared by ten o'clock. By then they would be on their way to Orvieto. Another good group. Already slowing down. Becoming less vibrant. Less grasping. Dwelling more. Beginning to see what all the fuss was about. The data-base woman from Michigan who made quick sketches of everything instead of taking photographs. The daughter with the too-loud voice who had threatened to be sick on the coach. The geneticist from Connecticut who had a way of raising sceptical eyebrows, pretending not to be impressed, so that cries of 'what about it Jim?' were now ending every visit. The rather precious young man whose parents had sent him off to Italy before he went to college. The quiet, serious, deputy director of the US Bureau of the Census who kept a chart pasted on card showing the dates of the artists with arrows to indicate the major schools and influences. The courteous retired naval officer from Annapolis who appeared bemused by all things Italian but pronounced everything 'very pleasant'. The surgeon from Syracuse whose face, rapt, mystic, Tullio sought out whenever they confronted a painting, a sculpture. What about it Jim? Got his dates Paul? Very pleasant indeed. When do we get to see your own stuff, Tullio?

And Calvin Reed, who had loved the daughter of a king.

He sat up against the bolster. Perhaps they were right. The occasion of the pieces was of no importance. The fact of orchestration didn't necessarily make it false. On the bedside table, Fabiola's printed sheets. Tullio d'Attore has stolen almost unnoticed into the pantheon of Italian art . . . paintings to return to at the end of the day . . . one day in the not too distant future . . . He had rushed through the text of the brochure over the bresaola, embarrassed, hurriedly agreeing to an across-the-board increase. Five paintings in a week. Paintings that were no better and no worse than when they were hanging in municipal cellars or on the walls of restaurants, hotels. Paintings he didn't know they had. Paintings from the depths of store rooms. Paintings he only vaguely remembered. Paintings from another lifetime. Even though it was the middle of the day Fabiola had ordered a deep, heavy Brunello which now hung like a lead curtain inside his closed eyes.

The hotel room had turned dark and cold. Claudia would be arriving home. Turning on the landing, continuing on up to the apartment. Or stopping on the second floor. The fine marble gown of the daughter of a king slid over the limbs. The light no longer enough to paint by. They had sent him an invitation for the exhibition.

He forced off his shoes, heard them drop onto the tiled floor. Yesterday had been different, walking his party through the town. Posters in the streets, cuttings from the arts pages pinned up among the municipal notices, his photograph here and there, his step lighter as he had led them through the anterooms towards the Sala della Risurrezione. The paintings sheathed in polystyrene. The geneticist from Connecticut wanting to stop and look. Workmen busy removing the Bassanos and Battista Mercatis. The ceiling of the hotel room stared back at him, touched by the last slant of light, the coving like a moulded frame around a bare canvas. There were almost no nudes that were not anonymous. Form, not character. There had been one or two evening sittings. Perhaps even tonight.

A weed-like determination grew as he lay on the bed. The day after tomorrow he would paint all afternoon; undress himself of doubts, anxieties; get out from under his own shadow; cease the endless, stale questioning. A small panic spread from the base of his spine as he saw the second chance slipping from him as he lay on a bed on a warm evening in Rome. He should be painting now. Not the day after tomorrow. When he picked up the brushes again it would be to do something new; something that would vindicate; something to put substance into the sham; something with vigour and imagination; something that would play away from home; something that would suffuse the veins; something of manifest brilliance. On the bed in the hotel, determination bore itself bravely onwards. On Wednesday there would be no dispiriting comparisons, no tense poising over alternatives, no imagining the insides of doorless corridors. Only painting.

❖

Claudia emptied the contents of two plastic bags, item by item, onto the varnished worktable.

'Can we get started?'

'In a minute.'

'I expect you only have an hour.'

'At the most. And we're going to start with food.'

Giuliano was sifting through brushes and bits of charcoal in the halves of the split plastic bottle.

'Is that supposed to be for me?'

'I'm going to show you what you have to do to stay alive.'

'I've never been more alive.'

Claudia gave him her unimpressed look.

'I'm telling you this once and then it's up to you. You're not a child.'

Giuliano had seated himself on the floor.

'We're all children, except those who've given up.'

'I'm not impressed by your arty little aphorisms either, so you might as well listen.'

She picked up a head of broccoli.

'You buy vegetables from Patrizia, the little shop on the corner. These green things are vegetables. They come in lots of different kinds. They're cheap. You buy them every day. You don't ask her for credit.'

'I don't have time to cook.'

'So you eat them raw. Celery, salad, fennel, carrots, broccoli. Just wash them and eat them. You don't have to think about it.'

Giuliano reached forward and began playing with the foaming heads of broccoli, arranging them to contrast their beaded, light-absorbing green with the dimpled reflectiveness of an orange.

'And you buy fruit. Every day. Whatever's cheapest. It doesn't matter. If you go at the end of the day she sometimes sells what's left cheap. Or if the fruit's very ripe . . .'

'Ripe fruit's no good for painting. You need hard, firm flesh.'

'And there's bread, and rice, and pasta. All cheap. I take it you know how to cook pasta?'

'I eat it raw.'

'Ten minutes in boiling water. Don't bother with sauce. Just olive oil, black pepper, parmesan. And this is tuna. You can open a can?'

'I'm a genius at opening cans.'

'Good. Open some beans. These are cannellini. Just drain them and put them in something. You don't even have to heat them. Just mix in a can of tuna. Some black olives. Chop up a raw onion, the red ones are milder . . .'

Giuliano had seized one of the large onions, holding it to the window, balancing it on the tips of his fingers to watch the light play on its delicate metallic red.

'Tomatoes if you want. Salt. Black pepper. Olive oil.'

'No chocolate?'

'Listen to me, Giuliano. Or you'll be too ill to paint.'

'I paint better when I'm ill.'

'I'm not impressed by stupidity either. Do you like eggs?'

Giuliano put his head on one side.

'Fat, perfect ovals. Not those skinny, pointy ones. And no bulges. I can't bear bulges.'

'And this is olive oil. Toast your old bread. Just rub it with a piece of garlic. Drizzle this on. Salt. Pepper. Something on top. Anything. Tomatoes. Salami. Prosciutto. Cheese. It takes a minute.'

'Okay, I'll eat later. I'll eat it all later. Can we get started?'

Claudia returned the bottle of olive oil to the table and took up her position, sitting straight at ninety degrees to the light, to the artist sitting under the window. The wardrobe had been pushed back to the wall. He was working just forward of profile, already absorbed. She pushed his deathly pallor aside.

'And you can stop looking stern now.'

❖

'You two haven't by any chance been indulging in a little bit of insider dealing?'

Palmiro and Lelli looked away in opposite directions across the crowded restaurant. Around them, the noise of Rome enjoying its dinner, the conversations loud, the wine flowing, the waiters sweating in bow ties and red waistcoats, carrying dishes backwards through the swing doors, queues of anticipation already forming in the small lobby. Lelli pushed a napkin back into the top of his shirt and sighed with satisfaction at the table.

'I suppose we might manage to get up for the show.'

Tullio replaced the bottle of Torgiano in the ice bucket by his chair. Plates of seafood pasta steamed in front of them.

'I was thinking of calling it "The Art of the Quiet".'

Palmiro grinned and sliced into a squid.

'You've always been an ungrateful bastard.'

Lelli raised his glass.

'Yes, you still don't seem to quite grasp that you're dining with two of the most influential voices in the land.'

Tullio lifted the delicate empty shell of a crayfish with his fingers and dropped it onto the devastated rock-pool of his plate to show what he thought of this remark. Palmiro was eyeing two women being shown to a table across the aisle. He returned his gaze reluctantly to the table.

'I imagine your lunch with Fabiola wouldn't be quite up to this standard?'

'The company was better.'

'It's crossed my mind once or twice that I might invite Fabiola Fioravanti to lunch myself.'

'Except it's not lunch that's crossed your mind.'

A self-satisfied, confessional smile appeared at the edges of Palmiro's mouth.

'And what does she think about the great dilemma?'

'She thinks I should give up the tours.'

Palmiro turned his mouth down.

'You could see how it goes for a bit. Sell from stock. What've you got?'

'About twenty from the last year or so. And a lot of old stuff. If I pulled everything in, probably fifty pieces.'

'That should keep you going for a bit.'

Tullio dipped his fingers in the bowl with the lemon and shook his head.

'If I'm going to be in demand for a bit I'd rather it be for something different, something new. Selling old paintings will just put me back where I was before.'

Lelli took another drink and waved a finger across the table.

'Before this magnificent opportunity came along.'

'Try and make it as far as the fish course without falling under the table, Lelli.'

The waiter arrived with dishes of wild boar and polenta. Snatches of German and American filtered through the flow of Italian at nearby tables. In the lobby, new arrivals were being turned away. Lelli waved to a harassed waiter, miming the pulling of a cork. Tullio pushed the serving plate towards Palmiro.

'Anyway, I'm not sure I really want to give them up.'

Palmiro picked up on the small embarrassment.

'You're not telling me you enjoy it?'

Tullio grew defiant.

'They're great you know, most of them.'

'Who are?'

'The parties. The people on the tours. When you see them getting into it.'

Lelli leered.

'Tullio sometimes you don't seem to realise being an artist isn't about painting it's about the figura. Success and suffering are both highly acceptable, but . . . muddling along with tours . . .'

Palmiro ignored him, pouring more wine for himself and Tullio.

'Do you sell them your stuff?'

'No. I've thought about it. It's a bit like taking advantage.'

'Bit scrupulous isn't it?'

'Maybe. Anyway I'm not sure I could bring myself to show them a Fra Angelico in the morning and flog them a d'Attore in the afternoon.'

'They'd know the difference would they?'

❖

The lights on the music system rose and fell to the sound of a cello solo. Lelli slept uncomfortably on the couch. Tullio stood at the window, looking down into the darkness of the Via dei Carbonari. Palmiro waved a finger slowly just above the arm of the chair as the violin came in over the cello.

'You worry too much.'

Tullio began poking through the stack of CDs.

'Not any more. I'm about to enter a worry-free phase.'

'You serious about this new phase thing?'

'Mmm. I'm about to come out from under my own shadow, join the fray.'

'You don't want to believe everything you read in the papers you know, especially if the by-line is Ugolini.'

'What about "passivity", "lack of aesthetic action".'

'Or even if it's Palmiro Quartucci. You've got to find a few critical things to say. Establish a little independence, a little credibility. It's typical of you to memorise all those obligatory little negatives.'

'You've got it wrong as usual. It's not coincidence that you all chose the same negatives. And I happen to agree. It just confirmed things that have been there for years, brought them to the surface. I'm too careful, too quiet – 'quiet' must have been used a dozen times. Stifling the game, backwaters of the pleasing, paintings to grow old with . . .'

'It's obligatory, I told you.'

'It's also coherent. Surely even you can see the irony. The negatives were the only genuine thing about it.'

'Well all right then, there is a point there. You've always hesitated too much. I've been telling you that for years. You have these great ideas and then as soon as you start painting you start worrying, fiddling about with it and fretting away at it until the idea's gone, the spontaneity, the fun of the thing. Don't agonise, paint. Agonising's out in case you hadn't heard.

147

The technique's always been there. A bit of boldness is all you need. Everything else will follow. Style follows where daring leads.'

'Don't start quoting me things you've written.'

'Even if it's what I think?'

'Daring for its own sake?'

'Daring that's . . . unsifted . . . that's not the result of so much worrying, rejection. You've always thought too much about it, Tullio. Let the art do the thinking.'

'I intend to. As soon as I get back. Are you coming up for the exhibition?'

'Has the plumbing improved in the provinces?'

'It smells quite a bit better than Rome if that's what you mean.'

'And are we going to see this new phase?'

'I hope so. A suite of three I hope. I've already got the idea.'

'Then listen to me and just do it.'

Tullio stopped the cello. Lelli opened his eyes.

'I was enjoying that.'

Palmiro lit a cigarette.

'Where to tomorrow?'

'Orvieto for a couple of hours, then home.'

'I haven't been there in years.'

'You haven't been out of Rome in years.'

'Maybe I should get myself a seat on your tour. Lots of attractive single women?'

'A few.'

Tullio slid in a jazz CD and sank into a chair as the piano stepped lightly into the room. Palmiro had produced a frosted bottle of grappa from the fridge.

'I bet they haven't the faintest what they're looking at. I bet it's just so they can say they've seen whatever it is.'

'Some of them, maybe. Not all. They've all got real jobs for

God's sake. What do you want? A certificate from the Belle Arti before you can buy a ticket to the Uffizi?'

'Wouldn't be a bad idea. No, let the dollars roll. But I bet they're a pain all the same.'

'Some of them.'

'Come on, Tullio, they spend five seconds glancing at some painting, ten seconds reading the little brass plate at the side, and then, if it's somebody they've heard of, five minutes fiddling about with a camera. They don't really look at anything. They come because they've been told it's culture, or it's famous, or because it's been on a T-shirt. They go round ticking things off. It's like collecting stamps. It's not about seeing; it's about having seen.'

'Pal, you haven't met any of these people. You're just leaping to superficial conclusions. I suppose that's why you're an art critic.'

'Listen, Tullio, next time you're in Florence take them to see something second rate. Say a Baccio Bandinelli. Say the Hercules and Cacus in the Piazza. Or the Giovanni delle Bande Nere. Tell them it's a masterpiece by Michelangelo. Don't tell me they won't all stand there just as awe-struck. Don't tell me they won't all start clicking anyway.'

'That's not the point. The fact is, they bring their own awe. You might be able to focus it on a lot of things. Because they want a focus . . . for something that's inside them. It's like the wonder, the art, is inside them. Inside them, Palmiro. And yes, you could point them at a lot of different things. But if you point them at something that really is fine, and you help them to see why – why it's so fine, so special – then it's different. There's a different response. Something genuine. It comes out. The art and the wonder that's in them comes out. And when it happens a couple of times a day some of them . . . come to know. They start to see what it's all about. Sometimes, when they see things, really see things, it's like the feeling I get from painting.'

'Christ Tullio! I thought you were doing it for the money.'

'So did I.'

'I think I might do the tour next year. Write a piece about it.'

'It's sold out until the year after next.'

'You're not serious?'

14

Claudia cleared her mind of Giuliano and began work on the new course, projecting ideas onto the blankness of the wall. The Normans in Southern Italy; Robert Guiscard, advancing as far as Salerno; his brother marching south to Palermo. Pale northern faces in the Sicilian sun. Did they get skin cancers? How many generations does it need for the skin to darken? Was it poor health, or was he just eating badly, living in stale air?

'The frown's creeping back.'

The Arabo-Norman style. Romanesque. Byzantine. Moorish. The monk-architects of the Augustinians and the Benedictines. How to structure it all? Sitting here for an hour at a time she ought to be able to think, to step out of the stream that seemed to bundle her along between waking and sleeping.

'I want it softer.'

But thinking without writing, without talking, was almost impossible. Real thinking. Not drifting thoughts. Not feathers to each draught in the mind. Consecutive thoughts. Decisions, Dispensing with alternatives, maintaining a line, arriving somewhere. Tullio had been working since before seven to get started on some new idea. It was years since he'd got up early to paint.

'Good. Softer still.'

The articles had done it. The civic exhibition. Honour in his own country. Divided with himself still. Success proof only of failure. Would the grey silk dress still fit?

'Lips just slightly apart.'

She breathed through her mouth. No one could go on year after year without recognition, a quantum of acknowledgement. Even as he mocked himself you could see the weight lifting from him, the relief of it.

'That's better.'

Happier with the tours as well. Happier to lead his party down the Via Maestra, to be an artist in his own streets. Happier to be at home. To come out of his house within a house. Happier to be with her. Why did he have to have this to be happy with himself, to feel he had substance? A self that would ebb and flow with circumstance. That depended on the external. That could too easily be taken away.

Her eyes crossed the room to the cello. The opening motif that cuts the heart in two. The delicate glances of the piano. The deep drawing out of the music. The subtle beauty of the portrait, the infinite patience of its shadows. Tullio said that all great paintings were really portraits. Landscapes. Still lifes. Boulevards by night. An ordinary street under snow. Portraits of a longing.

'You're letting your head drop.'

He knew it for what it was: a temporary illusion conjured out of nothing by Pal and Lelli. Knew the oblivion to follow. The mote passing through a shaft of artificial light. And something else he had said: about abandoning the art of the quiet, entering the fray.

Maybe it would help if she got involved, offered to do a couple tours herself in the long vacation. Write to 'Arte d'Italia', make a proposal. Bring the Italian Romanesque out from the shadows of the Renaissance. Reclaim the leaning tower, the baptisteries of Pisa and Florence. San Miniato. St Gregory's in Spoleto. Mix the grand and the famous with the humble and the unknown, the pievi of Romena and Gropina. A day's walking in the middle, say from Montepulciano to Sant'Antimo. She stretched her eyes without moving her head, watched the back of the hand as it drew, the delicate tendons of the fingers rising and falling. The last time they had been to Sant'Antimo there had been just three monks to sing the office. Two young men, tall and straight, looking every inch athletes of God; and one who might have been eighty or more. Tullio had noted the kindness in the ritual, the loose white robe and scapular disguising differences in physique and posture; the restrained, dignified, monastic procession enabling the old man to proceed side by side with the others, to kneel with them, slowly, to one side of the altar; the ancient stones of the choir leaning down to cup the frail, cracked voice, drawing it up into the darkness of the vaults, lending volume and fineness, finding an echo of heaven so that it sounded no more weakly the voice of the spirit than the voices of the young men at his side.

'How long have you been with your husband?'

She resisted the urge to turn her head towards him.

'Thirteen years. Ever since he came here. Why?'

Giuliano tore the page from the sketch pad, placed it carefully with the others on the floor beside him.

'Does he make a living from painting?'

'He's got the tours as well.'

'The Americans?'

'Yes.'

'You've forgotten about the earrings.'

She removed the gold half-circles from her ears and found a place for them between the broccoli and the onions. Out of the corner of her eye she could see the dark head alternating with the white face as he looked from subject to sketch. Another minute passed. To her left the fireplace boarded up with plywood, the grain darkened by a peninsula of damp. Once there must have been fine furniture, paintings in gilded frames, servants carrying braziers of coal. But the work on the walls now was finer than anything that would ever have hung here before. The sensuous beauty of the piano; the astonishing subtlety of the waxed floor; the glorious vibration of colour and sound. The cool geometry of the staircase, transforming the brutally physical into a refined abstraction. One day there would be a plaque on the outside wall of the Palazzo Lanzi, underneath the worn-out coat-of-arms.

'I want to do the throat, the neck. Can you take that necklace off.'

She struggled with the clasp of the narrow chain, dropping it in a heap next to the earrings.

'Open the collar up too.'

She unfastened the top buttons of the shirt, pulling the collar wide of her throat.

'It would be easier if you'd take it off.'

A second's thought. She stood and unbuttoned the shirt, pulling it out of the skirt, slipping it over the back of the chair. She adjusted the strap of the low-cut bra as she resumed her position.

She focused on the wall, clearing her mind, facing forward again, concentrating on calm and breathing, determined to think nothing about it, going back to the intricacies of her course.

He began sketching an outline in long, separate, strokes. Soft against the page. She breathed in once deeply, aware of the rise and fall of her breasts.

'How many tours does he do?'

A flash of resentment at the turmoil, the jolting.

'Only four. He might take another couple next year.'

The skin of her shoulders, arms, waist, cold in the warmth of the morning.

'How can he paint and do that?'

Absurd, to be sitting in her bra. Absurd to give it a second's thought. Absurd, the silly urge to take it off. She stared harder at the wall, unable to understand herself.

'He works around it. He's painting now.'

'You've closed your lips.'

She opened her mouth slightly; ran her tongue over her lips.

'Does he ever sell anything?'

She tried to swallow without closing her mouth.

'Five or six this month.'

'Who to?'

'Through the galleries. The Bernard mostly.'

Breathing through the mouth made her dry.

'So why does he do tours?'

'They help make ends meet. And he's incredibly good at it.'

She could see just enough of him to know that he was smiling.

'The tour's booked up for about two years. They have to turn people away.'

'Does he have a reputation as a painter as well?'

'Didn't you see the arts sections of the papers at the weekend?'

He selected another twig of the home-made charcoal. Absurd, to be sitting in her underwear defending Tullio to a stranger.

'I don't read the papers.'

He had stopped sketching, the white of his face steady at the corner of her eye. The raw energy of his look. The intensity of the presence coiled on the floorboards.

'You're frowning. Frowning inside. It's just what I don't want. Concentrate. Think of something else. Think about sex or something.'

15

Tullio had been absorbed all day. Oblivious. Aware only of the light and space and silence of the Palazzo Lanzi.

The brush finally fell, the coffee on the worktable cold. An ache in wrist and forearm, but a singing in the veins; an aliveness, a resharpening of the edge of him. He had plunged in as soon as Claudia had left, repelling anxieties, fighting the disease of doubt, resisting complications and alternatives, forbidding himself to spill over the edges of his predefined task, channelling every energy into execution. And it was almost there. He closed his eyes, felt the small breeze from the window on one side of his face. It was his test; to keep the eyes closed for a full minute, gleaning the smallest sounds from the old building, harvesting the darkness, so that he could see his painting anew, compare it with the original vision that took command of the warm spaces inside the eyelids, untroubled by imperfection, by reality.

He opened his eyes. But now he was confronted not by the sickening fist of disparity but by the thrill of the match. It was close, very close. He had got down onto the canvas the last lascivious greenness of the pear, the damp glow of its skin, its smooth grippiness, the almost imperceptible freckles and little cuts that were beginning to turn brown, the colours changing but the texture, the surface, hardly at all. He breathed in hard through his nose, staring at the canvas. The real miracle was the transition, the imperceptible point where the lower half of the pear began gently to swell, became the back of a naked woman, seated, the weight spreading the broad hips, the separation of the buttocks. The glow of the skin. The firm surface that yet would yield to the touch. The pored smoothness of the contour. The sheen on the weight of the curves. The light from an unseen window modelling the subtle knuckles of the lower backbone. Even under the eye prone to despair, an eye that latched obsessively onto every inadequacy, this was a virtuoso performance, a metamorphosis based not only on colour but on the revealed unity; it was skin and form, handled so subtly that there was no point, as the eye travelled over the damp, tactile surface, at which it was possible to say that this is where the change occurred, or even where it was most pronounced.

He raised his face to the ceiling, pushing both thumbs into the small of his back, pressing in the pain. On the table were three or four large green pears and a spread of books: Titian's tender, erotic *Venus of Urbino*; Ingres' subtly distorted *La Grande Odalisque*; Manet's strange, defiant *Olympia*; an open copy of a girlie magazine.

He ripped off the top sheet of the palette and let it fall to the floorboards, squeezing out the new whites – cremnitz, zinc, titanium – knowing that the momentum was with him, that he could do the same again tomorrow, and the next day, and the day after that. All would not be quiet in the Museo. All would not be sober, dull, enervated. It would launch the new phase, his entry into his own times, with all their vigour and imagination. He swilled the brush in clean spirit and began modifying the light on the tablecloth, working quickly, deftly, sure of each brush-stroke. He glanced down at the girl in the magazine.

❖

Claudia raised her eyebrows at seeing him still at the easel. He looked round briefly, still painting. She came up behind him, rested her warm cheek against his back, slipped her hands around his waist.

'I was worried when you weren't in the bar.'

'I've been painting.'

'So I can see.'

She stood on her toes.

'My God, that's amazing.'

Tullio turned to her, holding the brush away to one side.

'No need to sound so astonished.'

'You've never done anything like that before. Is it part of something?'

'Part of a suite, I think.'

'A suite of what?'

He dropped the brush on the worktable, took her hands, pulled her close, spoke over her shoulder.

'Claudia, don't ask. I'm trying to paint. To paint, Claudia. Not to think. To paint like I haven't painted for a long time. Instead of worrying about painting, wondering what I should be painting, or what's wrong with my painting, or whether I should be painting at all. I'm trying to just . . . paint again, Claudia. It's like trying to breathe.'

She pushed him away so that she could see his face, reached up to kiss him on the lips. It was the longest speech he had made about his struggles. A speech from inside the walls.

'I'm glad.'

She tried to pull away.

'Let me go if you want to eat.'

'Do you mind if I carry on this evening?'

'No. I've plenty to do.'

He turned and the painting ducked under his guard, knifed him with doubt. Out in the street the light was falling, silhouetting old brickwork and the tiled spires of churches, the motley of roofs darkening under a deep electric sky. He swirled the brush in the spirit, squeezing it out with his fingers.

❖

He had washed and begun to lay the table for dinner when the cello began to play.

He lit the candle, watched the flame rise into its grace. The cello stopped. He brought glasses to the table. The first few bars again. Then nothing, the music stopping on the brink. He lit the second candle and switched on the picture lights. The portrait examined him from the wall. The face on the right questioning him. Again the first few notes. Slowly. Mournfully. He poured wine, the glasses throwing the candlelight back and forth between them.

In the kitchen Claudia listened to the opening notes of the E minor carving again and again into the evening. Waiting. Waiting for her. She cut the fleshy cores of the peppers onto the marble of the surface, willing him to play on.

Tullio had turned the easel slightly away from the table. He was about to collect the salad when he saw her stop what she was doing, holding herself still, listening to the same few notes. The curve of her breast against the underlights of the kitchen, the lesser swell of the ribs against the straight edges of the cupboards, the windowsill.

They came to the table in silence, as if it were not possible to speak until the cello had made a decision. Eventually, it played on alone, the music punctuated by long silences, fragmenting intimacy.

'I took him some food the other day.'

'Giuliano?'

She nodded, eating salad.

'When I went down to sit. Just to try to get him to feed himself properly. He's making himself ill.'

'Did you cook?'

She shook her head.

'Just showed him what to do. A few basics.'

The cello had given up again, seeming to lose heart. Claudia looked at him, then at the wall.

'I was thinking. You know Vittorio called about the shop?'

'I called him. I'm moving some stuff in next week.'

'Won't you need everything for the exhibition?'

'I've still got things for the shop. The three from Gianni's. Maybe one or two from your mother's. And I could probably get half a dozen more together if I could remember who'd got them. There's still a lot of people in town.'

'I was wondering whether you couldn't give it to Giuliano, the space I mean.'

'The shop?'

'Yes, it would be a start for him.'

'Would he want it?'

The cello struck up again, indifferently, carelessly. A different sonata.

'I don't know. He'd probably be stupid about it. He won't talk about exhibiting, going to the fairs, getting round the galleries, anything. I keep telling myself it's not my problem, but you should see him. There's almost nothing left of him. He's ill. And if you say anything he just snaps.'

Tullio played with his salad.

'Okay, I'll give Vittorio a call tonight.'

'He won't mind?'

'Not if I tell him what it's about.'

'It won't make any difference to you will it?'

'Not with the exhibition on, no.'

'I just thought if we presented him with the opportunity ready

161

made, without having to go through the hoops . . . it might help get him going.'

Tullio filled the glasses, searched into the depths of the colour.

'Has he ever sold anything before?'

'Only to Landini.'

'You'd better tell him what to ask for them.'

'What do you think?'

'For a full-size work, I don't think he should think about less than four, four and a half. Maybe more.'

Claudia bent to kiss him as she passed behind his chair.

'What was that for?'

'It was for you.'

'They're worth more. One day a lot more.'

She looked back from the kitchen.

'And we could tell Pal and Lelli. If they're coming for the exhibition. They could look in at the shop.'

Tullio swayed the wine glass slowly, out of time.

'He's still painting?'

'Yes. He did a drawing first this time. But he's starting to paint now.'

She looked back at Tullio, inviting him to speak, to ask. He looked into the wine glass, closed his lips. She carried pasta to the table.

They listened in silence, until he took the salad bowl over to the kitchen and began to fill the sink. She looked at the easel, the cello playing again fitfully, interrupted by long silences.

'I suppose if you're working I could give him an hour this evening.'

16

'I suppose I could think about it.'

'Giuliano, Tullio's offering you wall and window space right there in the Via Maestra, with hundreds of people coming for his exhibition and thousands coming for the Balestra. You'd think I was asking you to do him a favour.'

'I said I could think about it.'

'Okay. I refuse to do the worrying for you. You're not a child, as I keep trying to convince myself. If you don't take it up I'll just forget about it.'

'You can forget about it now.'

She took up her position on the chair. The earrings and necklace were already on the table. Should she take off the shirt? Giuliano was choosing a brush. She would wait to be asked. He had made his selection, turned towards her.

'Okay, let's go.'

She faced the wall, making another attempt at the new course, going over the structure. Would it make a tour for 'Arte d'Italia'? 'The Norsemen in the South'. Gianfranco already had the south, though he wasn't always full.

'Don't go getting that determined look again please.'

The room darkened as an invisible cloud fell across an invisible sun. Unless it rained there would be the concert in the Bufalini gardens. Maybe she should invite him, get him out of the building. Tullio might not want to go if the painting were still going well. Three canvases in ten days. And she hadn't been allowed to look at the last two; for some reason he wanted her to see them for the first time under the lights of the exhibition.

'Did you get the card?'

He seemed to be painting only from the sketches, ignoring her. Soon he would wander over to the window, or to look at one of his own paintings, without a word, leaving her in her pose.

'The exhibition. Yes.'

'Will you be coming?'

He ignored the question, painted for another minute, an elaborate expression on his face. Eventually he finished whatever he was doing and changed brushes, glancing up.

'It might be a chance to see his work I suppose.'

She shut him out and began work. There was a wood carving in the Museo Civico that might be relevant. Probably one of the things they would move to make way for Tullio. It had been a long time since she'd worn anything with heels. A breeze passed blindly through the apartment, lifting the paint rags on the table. She had shopping to do, phone calls to make. Tullio still hadn't phoned to see if Pal and Lelli were staying the night. Sunlight reappeared for a moment, suffusing the cello against the wall. She would probably go to the Bufalini anyway. Livia would be there. And Sauro, probably. They could have a drink afterwards. Or come back to the apartment.

'You know that I love you, don't you Claudia?'

Giuliano continued his painting. Claudia remained in her pose, the light falling on her left side.

'I don't believe you said what I just heard.'

He leaned closer to the easel, painting something delicate again, his mouth slightly open.

'Don't tell me that you don't know. Don't tell me that you don't love me.'

Her eyes remained on the wall, on the electric socket hanging loosely from the skirting board.

'I don't love you, Giuliano.'

He continued the meticulous task, eyes never leaving the canvas. A knock at the door. The world demanding entry. Giuliano scowled and gestured with hands that were covered in paint.

'Send them away.'

Claudia rose from the chair and crossed the room.

'Buon giorno. ENEL.'

He flashed a plastic card clipped to the pocket of his overalls. She stood to one side, watched him make straight for the meter in the kitchen. Giuliano ignored him, staring hard at his canvas. Claudia waited by the open door.

'Grazie. Buon giorno.'

'Buon giorno.'

She returned slowly to her seat. A broad fall of sunlight reached across the floor, almost to the wardrobe. Outside the window, a pulley creaked. Pigeons chuckled in the eaves. She stared against the wall. Giuliano had begun painting again.

'You loved me when you played the piano.'

'That was a bit of fun, Giuliano. We were having a dinner party.'

Giuliano turned to hold the brush up to the light, removing an undisciplined hair.

'I wasn't having a dinner party. I was down here playing. And you came to me. I know you did.'

Claudia stood up from the chair. He scowled a protest at the breaking of the pose.

'Claudia!'

'Listen to me Giuliano. I'm going back upstairs now. I'm going because you've made it impossible for me to stay. You don't love me Giuliano. You might think you do but you don't. You never see anyone else. You stay in this room, wrapped up in painting and me and me and painting and so you think you've fallen in love because I'm all there is for you and your feelings to reach out and latch on to. That's all it is.'

Giuliano rose in fury from the stool.

'Don't call my love latching on.'

Claudia walked to the door.

'I'm sorry Giuliano. I'm sorry this happened. I can't come down again.'

'You have to finish the portrait.'

'I don't have to do anything.'

She was gone, leaving the door open, crossing the landing, ascending the broad staircase of the Palazzo Lanzi.

17

'People can live without it though, can't they?'

'Without art?'

'Yes, I mean most people do.'

Bel Cohen looked at the backs of her hands. The plain gold ring, the unvarnished nails; early forties, travelling alone. The coach reached out across the road, readying itself for the first of the hairpins, blaring a warning across the hillside.

'It's about quality of life as well though. I mean you could exist on rice and pasta.'

'You're not saying anyone who doesn't like art has, like, a lower quality of life?'

'No-oooo. But I think they're missing something.'

The coach caught second gear and began labouring up into the Apennines. She returned his glance. Deep red hair, lank around a bland, oval face; a Georges de la Tour in front of a dressing-table, needing the flame of a candle to bring her to life. Outside the window the yellow hillside, dry and struggling; here and there an outcrop of rocks, breaking the stretched skin. Down in the valley a haze hung over the beaded towns, Castello, Selci, San Giustino, Sansepolcro. He had left Claudia with a brief kiss outside Giuliano's door. In a couple of hours she would be following him over the pass on her way to work.

'But what about, say, someone with, like, family, friends, enthusiasm. Someone really involved. You can't say they've got less quality of life than someone who's, like, awful lonely but spends a lot of time in museums.'

'No, but it's not an either or is it?'

Tullio looked across the aisle to the other side of the coach, smiling briefly at Edwin and Alice Meeks. A hiss of airbrakes. The seat belt pulling. The bright cleft in the Apennines above. Bel Cohen dropped her hands to her lap.

'No, but what I'm saying is it's, like, trimmings isn't it? Not what really makes the difference. I mean the world probably wouldn't be much different if Fra Angelico had never lived.'

Tullio held onto the arm rest as the coach used the whole of the road to take the next bend, half closing his eyes, trying to imagine a world without the quiet monk in his cell; without his humble, loving attention to perfectibility; a world without that genuine vision of joy in humility, without the splendid colours of his modesty. Bel Cohen had opened the book on her knee and was finding her page. He turned towards her again.

'Sorry, I was thinking.'

She glanced at him sideways, mocking.

'Thinking the world would be different?'

'Thinking it would be the poorer.'

She closed the book on her finger.

'But not so much poorer. I mean ninety nine per cent of people in the world have like never heard of Fra Angelico, and most of them could be said to be surviving couldn't they?'

Tullio frowned.

'I suppose some of them might just be clinging on.'

The road was opening out, breasting the top of the pass. A brief flash of the sun on the Adriatic. Raphael's portrait of Baldassare on the cover of her book, caught by the master in all the intelligent fineness of his self satisfaction. One of the great portraits. Along with the *Juan de Pareja*. The *Doge Loredan*. The *Patience Escalier*. The *Monsieur Bertin*. The *John Minton*. What would the new portrait be like? Had she thought that it would be on display in the Via Maestra?

Bel Cohen leaned forward to see past him.

'That looked like a really great hiking trail.'

They were beginning the descent now, sweeping down an empty road between open hillsides, patient and sparse. His companion leaned back in her seat.

'I mean it's not like science, is it? Scientists touch us all. Twenty-four hours a day. Science, technology, lets us like jet off to Italy, cross the Apennines in an air-conditioned hour, watch TV, listen to music whenever we want, keep our homes warm, stay in touch with the kids on e-mail, wear nice fabrics next to our skin, cook Thai food, take photos of our holidays, live to be ninety. I mean you could go on for hours. It's practically everything we do. It's made the life we're all living.'

'So what are we saying?'

'I'm saying that there's not a lot of doubt which is more important is there?'

Tullio snapped his book shut.

'Right. That's it. I'm going to tell them to be a lot more careful who they let on these tours.'

Bel Cohen smiled, delighted, and offered him a mint. Tullio accepted sullenly. She placed a consoling hand on his arm.

'No, I know, Tullio, it's true, life would be poorer. The fact that I'm sitting here answers my own question really.'

'It's okay, there's no need to feel sorry for me.'

Tullio stretched his neck against the seat back.

'Anyway, why would anyone want to cook Thai food?'

❖

Claudia saw that the door was open on the second landing; open so that he could hear her footsteps. She descended quickly, refusing to tread lightly. She crossed the landing, aware of his presence inside the dark vestibule of the apartment.

'Claudia!'

She carried on down the stairs and out into the street.

❖

Tullio raised the paperback outside the bar in front of the Ducal Palace. A few other tourists lingered, pushing at revolving racks of postcards. From inside the doorway Emily Delaglio was panning across to the brick walls and marble casements of the palace, capturing a few unhurried students crossing the piazza.

'. . . a collection of after-dinner conversations. Like listening in on people talking five hundred years ago. Talking about what it means to be the ideal man or woman of the Renaissance.'

Parnell Wallace licked his finger to glean the last flakes of brioche from his plate.

'Don't sound like a blockbuster to me.'

'But it was. It was the ancestor of all those 'how to' books in airports: how to be smarter, more attractive, more successful. It became the Bible of taste and manners for all Europe. It almost invented the idea of secular self-improvement, of cultivating the mind and the body, of accomplishment lightly worn, ideas that are still influential today.'

Bel Cohen took the book back from him.

'From the bits I've read they just seem like just the most appalling bunch of snobs. It's all about thinking up lots of, like, affectations . . .'

She raised a hand in a gesture of mock elegance.

'. . . social rules, just so's you can look down on all the poor saps who don't know them. It's probably what made Europe so pretentious.'

Tullio smiled at the chorus of new world rebellion outside the Bar Il Cortegiano.

'Has everybody finished?'

A scraping of chairs and a draining of coffee, a gathering up of bags and sun-hats and sunglasses and cameras; seventeen people straggling across the square towards the entrance of the palace, shielding their eyes against the noon-day sun.

❖

'Claudia!'

Claudia stopped on the stairs leading up to her own apartment.

'Claudia, I'm sorry.'

He stood in his doorway, hands grasping the jambs. She turned again, continued on up to the top floor.

'Claudia, please!'

Something in his tone, echoing on the walls, unstitched her determination. She turned again, looking down on him across the stairwell. He had come barefoot to the bottom step, looking up at her, foreshortened, a dreadful, haggard whiteness to his feet and face. A carnival figure.

'It's finished. The portrait. It's finished. Don't you want to see it?'

'Giuliano, I'm not putting up with any nonsense.'

'Nothing. Nothing. Just come and look. Just for a minute.'

She left the bag of shopping on the top step and descended again. Three times in the last week the cello had called to her, playing the first notes of the E minor sonata. She reached the landing. He stood back in an exaggerated way, lifting his arms at his sides to usher her into the apartment.

❖

Tullio allowed himself a few moments alone in the centre of the courtyard, reaching out to the refinement around him, the harmony of sunlit brick and marble that elicited an inner sense. His eyes cut off the two later storeys and followed the cornices of the original skyline. A stone frame holding on to a square of Italian sky that had awaited only this marble, this brick to come into its blue perfection, living on the edge of its colour, the subliminal variations in its flatness that grew in depth and excitement, like a Rothko. One by one the members of his tour were passing through the turnstile: Bee Sullivan with her gondolier's sun-hat; the environmental auditor from Baltimore adjusting his binoculars; the elderly New Yorker in the crumpled cotton suit; the couple from Michigan who kept themselves to themselves. He stopped them for a last look at the courtyard.

'Close your eyes for a second and imagine all those heavy, oppressive medieval buildings. Dark, brutal, overpowering. Designed to make human beings feel crushed, intimidated, unimportant. And then open them to what the Duke created here: an architecture that's open and light and graceful, that appeals to the finer senses, treats you on equal terms; an architecture that's human in its proportions, that makes you feel that to be a human being is to be something worthwhile, to be capable of being noble.'

'You like it do you, Tullio?'

Laughter followed him into the palace.

He waited for them at the top of the stairs, in the corridor outside the Hall of Iole. On the wall to his left, a poster announced details of the Urbino Biennale: ten artists from all over Italy: Sofia Colacchioni and Alessandro Alcini from Florence. Pierantonio Giussani from Pescara. Michaela d'Alema from the Bologna school. Piero Gucciardini from Modena and Andrea Carrello from Ragusa. Several new names. Sandra Trucciardi from Padua. Gina Chiodo from the Veneto. Two more Tuscans he had never heard of. And opposite each name, the real accolade: an assigned room in the Ducal palace. The Hall of the Men at Arms fresco. The Hall of the Alcove. The Hall of Sculpture. Rooms that demanded fineness.

He raised his hand towards the expanses of cool white intonaco on walls and vaults.

'They looted the Duke's treasures, broke up his great library . . . but they couldn't take away this . . .'

He looked from face to face.

'The palace itself touches all that Duke Federico and his court valued. It's not pompous. It's not grandiose. It doesn't shout. It's not forever attracting attention to itself. It watches. It waits. It sets a quiet example. It articulates the life of proportion and balance, of reason and refinement.'

A figure had turned the corner at the far end of the corridor, silhouetted in a blaze of sunlight.

'Bel's right when she says it was snobbish. It was a society that was in the process of defining itself as a self-consciously refined élite. The idea that society was everybody hadn't arrived yet. As a religious ideal, maybe. Not as a political idea. So we have to forgive them something there. There was snobbery, but there was something else as well. Something that the Duke created that made the name of this little town into a byword for civilisation, the place that courtiers and noblemen came to from all over Europe to learn how to be the new men and women of their times. And it wasn't just about manners and trappings and ceremonies. It was about

173

achieving inner dignity, inner worth. It was about nobility of mind, generosity of spirit. It was about beauty, proportion, in life as well as in art. It wasn't just about how to behave, it was about how to be.'

Noticing at last the broad smiles on the faces of his party, he pretended to be offended, turning to lead the way into the apartments of the Ducal Palace.

❖

Claudia stopped in the centre of the room. The same stale, airless smell. The worktable smothered in oil paint. The sleeping bag stuffed down between the bed and wall. The window closed against the street. And the painting, stretchered with its back to her on the easel. She turned to Giuliano. He urged her forward with both hands to the other side of the easel. She moved to his place under the window, aware of his eyes on her face.

Where she had expected to see some version of her own features she saw instead a profile of Giuliano himself, looking directly into her own face less than twenty centimetres away. There was no dividing ribbon of bare canvas, only the suggestion of an indented pillow, uniting the two. She stared at the faces, the eyes looking into each other, threaded on a single beam of light. There was no escape. No emergency exit of doubt. They were looking into each other with an obvious post-coital gaze, lips slightly parted, eyes aching with sated love. Giuliano had lowered himself to the floorboards in the centre of the room, watching her, poised on the edge of himself. She spoke quietly.

'You had no right to paint this.'

The excitement on his face dissolved into contempt.

'No right to paint it!'

He rose to his feet in one movement.

'Claudia, I've painted the truth!'

She looked at him from the ground of her own anger.

'Stop it Giuliano. I won't hear any more.'

She left the easel, making quickly for the door, closing her eyes on tears, shaking her head.

'I'm going to exhibit it, Claudia.'

The sound of footsteps on the stairs, approaching the landing. She closed the door and turned to face him again.

'What do you mean, exhibit it?'

Giuliano strolled round in front of the easel, looking at the canvas.

'I should have thought it was fairly obvious. I'm going to show it with the others. In the shop.'

She took another step back into the room.

'The offer is no longer open.'

He shrugged, hands in pockets, still looking at his work.

'That's a shame. I've just written a little note to Tullio telling him how grateful I am. I asked him if I could borrow the first portrait back as well.'

The coach pulled away from beneath the palace walls, Tullio sitting towards the back, his mind still in the palace, wandering through the ideal city of the mind, poised at the point of balance between order and freedom, calm and alertness, self-awareness and awareness of others; the point that should by now have been arrived at. He forced himself to turn away, look to the outside. He had painted all the previous day; painted with focus, with intensity, immersing himself in the unmeasured hours, absorbed in fine effects, transitions, finishing the third of the canvases. Only at the end of the day had he looked up at the portrait between the windows. He picked up a postcard that had dropped to the floor as the coach hissed and braked over the pass. Isabella Marías thanked him with a smile, adding it to her collection on the tray-table.

'Do you like Bonnard, Vuillard?'

Tullio hauled himself through four centuries.

'The interiors, yes. It took me a while. But some of them have got that special quality. I suppose it's a combination of ordinariness and poignancy. Something quiet, philosophical. You're a fan of the Nabis?'

Isabella Marías smiled and looked away out of the window.

'Not particularly. I just wondered what the difference was between someone painting an interior scene and someone actually doing an interior. Their own living room, say.'

Tullio raised his eyebrows. She leaned back, tilting her face back to receive the flow of the air conditioning, the light unforgiving on her throat.

'I mean you get to choose all the colours, tones, textures. You get to decide on proportions, shapes . . . You get to compose everything, get things into balance. So if it all comes together, why can't that be art too?'

Tullio picked up a few of the postcards. A corner of the Duke's courtyard, the warm brick absorbing the afternoon light, measuring time differently. The famous portrait of the Duke. The marble bust of Battista, smoothed by the hand of Luciano's brother. The subtly simplified modelling. The imperceptible transitions of contour, surface, volume. Marble sculpted by light, creating the irresistible urge to touch.

'I think it can.'

She looked at him, surprised.

'It's not just decoration?'

'I think arranging their own surroundings is the way most people participate in art: arranging colour, texture, form, for a particular effect on the senses, on their state of mind. They're expressing their own artistic judgements. Those who can afford it, that is.'

The coach braked into the next bend. Below them the Metauro valley, floating in light. He saw the three paintings one after the other in the plastic moulding of the seat-back, each canvas a close up of a contour, an area of volume, that could be peach or pear or nectarine but could equally well be the slow swell of thigh or breast or arm, the one becoming the other without change of line or form, only of surface, of nuance and colour and texture and the way the light fell. In the window he saw Isabella Marías put her head on one side, half closing one eye.

'But you could say they're just putting together things that are already there, things they buy in the store.'

Tullio returned the postcard to the tray.

'But think of the choice. All those materials, colours, textures, lighting effects, shapes.'

'And in a way the inside thing, the three dimensional thing, makes it tougher doesn't it? To do the room rather than paint the Vuillard?'

Tullio frowned.

'But what you said before is probably right. The room gets assembled out of fixed things. And it has to meet a lot of practical criteria. Only the artist faces infinity in both directions.'

'Have you been in the Japanese room in the Met? Or that room in the Islamic section? I'm sure they're there as art. Arrangements of surroundings for their effect on the senses, the state of mind. Like Urbino.'

Tullio closed his eyes.

'I loved the Japanese room. It's physically austere, but the mind feels comfortable.'

'Perhaps you should have been a monk.'

'Much too difficult.'

'I'm trying to do something like that with my living room in Plymouth.'

18

Tullio stood with the mayor and a group of late arrivals at the top of the stairs of the Museo Civico. Most of the leading citizens of Sansepolcro were already crowded into the first three rooms, the Sala del Camino, the Sala Giovan' Battista Mercati, the smaller room where the *San Ludovico* was being restored. His eyes wandered past the Mayor to his own canvases lining the walls under lights that until last week had lit the permanent collection, the Annunciations and Nativities, the Last Suppers and the Assumptions of the Virgin. More late-comers were mounting the broad staircase from the lights of the Via Niccolò Aggiunti, faces opening in recognition – Tullio, come va? – greeting friends and acquaintances, hands being shaken, faces kissed, glasses accepted, wine and conversation flowing. A civic occasion, the town coming together in celebration – i quadri, Tullio, magnifici! – a queue gathering to speak to the artist, to claim him for their own, press photographers moving among the guests, sophisticated poses with glasses raised and smiles and jewels, and in the corner, by the books and catalogues, the cameras of RAI Tre shooting cut-aways.

Tullio sipped his wine and chatted with the director of the Gallery of Modern Art and her husband, down from Florence for the evening. Claudia was wearing a dress he had forgotten, her hair up, revealing the slender neck, the bevelled gold at her throat, the subtle silk sliding over her limbs as she moved, voices coming at him from all sides, his hand being shaken by people he vaguely knew, faces half recognised from the Via Maestra, fellow citizens passed by a thousand times – Bravissimo Tullio! – Maurizio in a dark suit to show off the chain of office, steering him away by the arm, building on tradition, laughter gusting from the group that had formed around what was usually the ticket counter where damask tablecloths showed off plates of prosciutto and melon, pecorino and salamis, ranks of wine glasses and opened bottles of Chianti Aretini. Ciao, Tullio, complimenti! His own paintings glowing over the bobbing sea of dark heads, Piero's masterpieces only three rooms away in the darkness – Tullio, che bel successo! – a kiss from the overglamorous woman in a strapless red dress who after a few seconds became Serena from the ticket desk who wore brown cardigans and was ten centimetres shorter, and from Gianni's wife, who had no doubt already noticed the canvases that had hung on the walls of her restaurant for the last three years, and a bear-hug from Stefano, the lawyer from the second floor of the Palazzo Lanzi, escorting a young woman half his age who may or may not have been his niece from Milan, and from Landini, who had driven over from Arezzo to let it be known that he had seen the talent from the beginning, believed in it through the difficult years, and from Pasquale, who only a month ago had asked him what became of all the paints and canvases – Tullio, quegli ultimi, stupendi! – and from Massimiliano, the museum clerk who had the price list and had been fielding enquires for the last hour, and from Sauro Rubellini, rejoicing for his friend, explaining that Eduardo had meant to come but had been delayed at the last minute by a faculty meeting.

He slipped the mayor's arm, exchanging greetings as he made his way through the exhibition, smiling acknowledgements, carrying his glass before him, walking purposefully to avoid being ambushed, mouthing hellos and excuses until he reached the last room where he found Palmiro and Lelli, standing in front of the new paintings, bottles as well as glasses in hand. He accepted a refill.

'I suppose I've got you two to thank for this.'

Palmiro drank.

'A half-decent wine is the very least we could have expected.'

Lelli ignored him, stooping close to examine the painting of the nude pear.

'So who did you get to paint these for you? I really have to say they're faintly striking.'

'I'm emerging from the shadow of my own soul, remember?'

'Gratitude would be more appropriate than sarcasm at this juncture, I feel.'

Palmiro had moved on to the next in the series. Tullio stood beside him. A moment of alarm as he saw the painting for the first time under the lights of the exhibition. Not his. Nothing to do with him. He looked around the room, at the crowds in the Sala Mercati. Claudia talking to the Florentines. Valentina Mignini reading the catalogue. His eyes returned to the painting. A fine piece. The suggestion of dampness in the texture, the slow swell of the surface of the fruit. Divorced from him only in being devoid of doubt. Palmiro straightened.

'Do you happen to know if that photographer's still here?'

He strode off, leaving Lelli in front of the trilogy.

'Technique was never the problem was it?'

Tullio moved to his side, examining his own work, running his eyes over the finish.

'No, I suppose the technique is sound enough.'

'But what we've got here is a little bit more. What we've got here is a little bit of boldness of conception, a little bit of firepower, I'm telling you . . .'

Tullio sensed someone coming towards him.

'. . . these will do the job for you Tullio. Take it from me, they'll do the job for you. '

'Eccolo!'

He found himself being borne away to be photographed with

181

the Mayor and Sergio Capelletti, the film director from Milan who had grown up in the town. Claudia was in the middle room, surrounded by Landini, Stefano from the first floor, the sindica from Anghiari, Antonio Conti, the reclusive owner of the Palazzo Gherardi. After the photo call he made his way back towards the Sala Giovan' Battista Mercati, pausing to change an empty glass for a full one. No sign of Giuliano.

'Tullio!'

It was Sauro who had placed a hand on his arm, looking round to indicate conspiracy.

'Don't look now. In the corner by the door. Green shirt, blue tie.'

Tullio glanced around the room two or three times in different directions before taking in the group by the door.

'Talking with Chiara Tigni?'

Sauro nodded and sipped his wine.

'Know him?'

'No, should I?'

'Tagliatti. Chairman of the Urbino committee.'

'For the Biennale?'

Sauro nodded and glanced over his shoulder.

'Except that it's a cock-up. You know they picked Pierantonio Giussani from Pescara?'

'Yes. I don't know his stuff.'

'Well neither did they apparently. They've just found out he's completely conceptual. Hasn't done any figurative stuff in years.'

'So?'

'So they're going to rule him out. He's already been told. They might have let it go – the catalogue's done, invitations, posters, the lot – then he got the call from Ballerini.'

'Giussani did? To show in Venice?'

Sauro nodded. Another sip of wine. Another glance over the shoulder.

'So then they'd no choice. You can't set up in opposition and then start picking their players for your team. Very embarrassing.'

Tullio glanced again at the tall figure leaning against the door. Slowly his eyes returned to Rubellini.

'So what are you up to Sauro?'

'Well, I just happened to be talking to Tagliatti in the interval last night. We were at the concert in the Bufalini. The committee had just decided to drop Giussani that afternoon. No one could talk about anything else. You can imagine.'

Tullio nodded, waiting.

'Anyway, just before we went back in, Attilio asked him if they were going to get somebody else. Oh yes, he said. Oh yes. An empty room would just call attention to it. So this morning I sent him a little note with a bunch of press clippings about an artist I know called Tullio d'Attore. I'd just got them back from Eduardo, with an inter-departmental routing slip. No note, mind.'

'Is that why he's here?'

'That, and the fact that I also attached my ticket.'

'Sauro, you're a star.'

'Niente. They should have put you in anyway. Too close to home I expect. Anyway, I only did it to annoy Eduardo. Can you imagine his face if you were in the Biennale?'

Tullio smiled and drank wine.

'I could die happy if a painting of mine had hung in the palace.'

'Well don't die just yet. We don't know what he'll decide.'

'He probably won't be interested.'

'I think he could be, judging by the time he spent with those new paintings in the last room. The fruity nudes. They've got to be new for the Biennale. The last twelve months, I think. Otherwise they could just have dug up some of Giussani's figurative stuff.'

'I suppose I should go over and talk to him.'

'Or you could leave the end-game to me.'

Tullio looked suspiciously at his friend over the rim of his glass.

'And what particular move were you thinking of making?'

'Oh, you know, I thought I'd just introduce him to Claudia.'

❖

Palmiro and Lelli had disappeared from the last room, but there were plenty of others to admire the still lifes, bending forward under the lights to examine the miracle of the transitions.

Tullio edged through the groups of people.

'I must say it's awfully clever. It makes you want to touch.'

'Reminds me a bit of Caravaggio, it's got that kind of lasciviousness. Sensuous, you know, tactile.'

'You can't tell where it begins.'

The handle gave under his hand. He stepped down into the Sala della Risurrezione, closing the heavy door behind him, shutting out the sounds of the party, leaving himself in the semi-darkness.

The plate-glass window allowed the streetlights of the piazza to tinge the room with a weak, monochrome gold. His eyes travelled to the crucifixion, to the magnificent figure of St John. He turned to his right, avoiding the figure rising to meet him on the end wall. In front of him now, the worried, innocent face of *San Giuliano* examined him in all its saintly uncertainty. One by one he brought up Piero's other troubled, twenty-first century faces, struggling for the long-covered figures in Arezzo, the saints and angels of the Montefeltro altarpiece, the *Baptism*, the *Mary Magdalen*, the *Madonna*, feeling the pull of their secular honesty, the refinement of their humility; faces full of doubts, expressions engaged not with some particular trouble but with the greater uncertainty; paintings of the mind, of vulnerabilities; faces that were not humiliated by their doubts, indecisions; for these were qualities that were not to be hidden, not to be covered by masks of resolution, confidence, authority; faces where doubt was not shameful, weak; faces where perplexity had a right to reside, a part of the human condition; faces that said that uncertainty was the only honesty; faces incapable of the intolerance of certainty.

He left his glass on the stone step and turned at last towards the great fresco rising dimly between the vaults of the north wall. Its colours gleaned the light; the soft greens and reds of the soldiers' cloaks; the pink of Christ's mantle; the livid flesh glowing in the plaster. Far off, the static of the party, leaving him utterly alone. He sat on the polished bench in the silence of the council chamber, eyes wandering over the sleeping soldiers, forcing himself in the end to look into the implacable, wide-apart eyes that offered no relief.

❖

It was late when they returned through the empty streets of the town, footsteps ringing on flagstones, the night still warm. They had turned into the deserted square, watched over by the soft medieval sandstone of the Torre Gherardi, the quiet façade of San Giovanni.

Tullio eventually broke the silence.

'So what did you think of the new ones?'

Claudia turned away from him, towards the Cathedral.

'They obviously stole the show. Pal's going to write something about them. Lelli too, I think.'

They turned into the empty Via Maestra, the walls of towers and palazzi still lit by the yellow light.

'I think they might already be sold.'

'Tonight?'

The question more polite than interested.

'To the dealer from Livorno. Linen suit. Pink cravat. You probably didn't meet him.'

'He got very drunk later on. Asked me to dance with him.'

He looked at her, the streetlight catching the gold at her throat. The night was warm and she wore only the silk dress.

'Did you tell him it wasn't a dance?'

'Several times. He said it didn't matter.'

'I hope he wasn't pissed when he spoke to me. He asked me to reserve all three until Thursday mid-day. At eighty per cent of list. And they were in at three million each.'

They had turned into the darkness of the side street, passing darkened windows and shuttered workshops, silence inserting itself between them as they approached the dark mass of the Palazzo Lanzi.

Claudia glanced up at the one light that was burning. The back of the thin figure was clearly silhouetted against a bright canvas, the head slightly to one side, the right shoulder higher than the left.

Tullio let them in to the stony silence of the vestibule. The dim lamp on each landing touched each wall with a quiet glow. Claudia took his arm on the stairs.

'Have you got a tour tomorrow?'

'Just down to Assisi.'

'In the morning?'

'Yes. We'll be back by the middle of the afternoon.'

'Is there a seat? Can I come?'

'Of course. Aren't you sitting?'

'No. And I don't have to go to work either. Teaching's cancelled because of Harding. You hadn't forgotten?'

'I thought it was Thursday.'

'It is. There's no teaching tomorrow either. They're doing something to the lecture theatre.'

They crossed the second landing, passing Giuliano's door in silence.

The walls of their own apartment were bare, windowed white where Tullio's canvases had hung until a few days before. Only the double portrait remained.

'He didn't come, did he?'

'I didn't think for a minute he would.'

Tullio dropped onto the sofa, let his head fall back. His eyes coming to rest again on the painting between the windows.

'What about the shop?'

Claudia looked at him from the kitchen.

'What about it?'

'Does he want it or not?'

'I don't think so. Can you still use it?'

'I suppose I could put a few things up.'

'You'd probably get some spin off. If someone wanted a D'Attore but couldn't afford the ones in the Museo. They might be tempted if they saw something less expensive in Vittorio's.'

'I'd still like him to have it, though. I saw Vittorio tonight by the way. It's fine by him. Do you think you can persuade him?'

'I don't know, I really don't.'

'Does he want to exhibit or not?'

'I don't know what he wants.'

19

'What sort of a price tag would they put on something like that?'

Tullio looked at the postcard of Michelangelo's bust of Brutus being offered to him from the next seat. Another portrait of an ideal. Of republican virtues. Of strength of mind, character. All self-indulgence expunged. Claudia was sitting with a blonde woman somewhere up at the front.

'Something like that would never come onto the market.'

'No, but say it did. Say it came under the hammer in New York.'

'A major piece by Michelangelo? Impossible to say. It would rewrite the book.'

'So what are you saying? Sixty million bucks, like the Cézanne?'

'More. A lot more.'

'So what if you could make a replica?'

'There are thousands of replicas.'

Tullio looked sideways at Mario Stanic from Newport, Rhode Island. The previous evening bustled in his brain, the people and the picture lights. Sauro and Claudia and Tagliatti. The dealer from Livorno who had asked her to dance.

'Yeah, but I'm talking about a real pukka replica. In marble. What if you could do it with computer-guided lasers, reproduce it exactly, right down to the last detail, to the slightest little touch of the chisel? What if you could make it so it was indistinguishable from the original?'

'I doubt if that's possible, Mario.'

'I don't. I bet it could be done now. Or give it a few years and a few million bucks. Anyway, just say you could do it. And say you couldn't tell the difference. And say you could retail for two thousand bucks. So people could have it in the dining-room, or the den.'

'So what are we saying?'

'I'm saying you'd have two pieces of stone that no one could tell apart, except one's worth two thousand dollars and the other maybe a hundred million.'

'One would still be a fifteenth-century piece by Michelangelo Buonarotti.'

'But the difference would be extrinsic. It wouldn't be down to anything you could see or touch. It would only be in what you know about it in your head.'

The lights changed and the coach summoned momentum for the next few hundred metres. He had overcome himself for four new canvases. Suppressed weakness. Found resolution, vigour. Claudia was standing, talking with the driver. She knew. Would always know, all of his own doubts expressed in her silences.

'I see where you're coming from, Mario, but not where you're going.'

'Where I'm headin' is, would the two-grand copy be any less wonderful? I'm trying to see how much of the value is down to external things, reverence for age, snobbery, exclusivity – the fact that the world famous Michelangelo touched it with his own hands, or the fact that it stands in the Bargello instead of Bloomingdale's.'

The coach had struggled onto the superstrada and was building up speed for the hour's journey to Assisi. Gillian Fosforo appeared in front of them, kneeling up backwards in her own seat, joining the argument.

'Come on, Mario. You've seen all those replicas in department stores. They're naff, cheap. I can't see Michelangelo's Brutus sitting there in the . . .'

'I can, Gillian. I can see exactly that. The point is, if you didn't know it was Michelangelo's Brutus, if it was just standing there in Bloomingdale's, would you give it a second look?'

❖

Tullio feasted his eyes on the glorious darkness of the crypt, the walls and vaults of nave and chapels and transept glowing with frescoes so that the light he saw and the air he breathed seemed to be the light and air of the trecento. The group was scattered now, exploring the side chapels in twos and threes, descending to visit the tomb, or sitting, heads back, on the pews below the apse. Claudia was leaving Sandra Stevenson, slipping towards him through the gloom.

For a few moments more, he lost himself in Lorenzetti's *Madonna and Child*, feeling its glow, the intense absorption of the mother in the child, the moment that had lasted for almost seven hundred years, the respect in the faces of St Francis and St John, the purity of the intention burning through the centuries. Its steadfastness. Its focus. Its lost innocence. Its love.

'That's always been special for you hasn't it?'

Claudia had slid into the pew, taken his hand.

'It's just so serious, so beautiful, so . . . uncorrupted. There are better paintings I suppose. But somehow I love this more than almost anything else.'

'So does he by the look of it. He's been there ever since you finished.'

Claudia inclined her head towards the elderly man standing in the dimness to one side of the Lorenzetti. Tullio turned to look at the frail figure absorbed in a quiet corner of the fourteenth century.

'I've never known anyone look at things so long. It was the

same in Florence. We lost him in the piazza so I walked back along the Calzaioli and there he was, still looking up at the Donatello.'

'The St George?'

'The St Mark. And then we nearly lost him again in Siena. He was still with the Maestà when everyone else was in the Duomo.'

Claudia smiled at two of the party who had wandered into the south transept, faces glowing with the school of Lorenzetti. She slid a hand over his on top of the polished wood.

'They loved it you know.'

'I was only a little bit inhibited.'

'By me?'

Tullio pulled a face and looked around the transept.

'Well I thought it was wonderful as well. It felt like I was seeing them for the first time. And they were knocked out, I could tell.'

Tullio looked down the nave, picking out the members of his party among the crowds.

'They're good aren't they? Who were you sitting with?'

'Sue Curtis, the blonde from Buffalo. She was telling me how wonderful you were all the way down the autostrada. Sickening it was.'

'In the land of the blind.'

'Or the land of the blonde.'

Claudia was looking at him sarcastically, teasing. He looked up into the vaulting, at the hexagonal room of the last supper with its attempt at a single light source, the intimate domestic scene beside the momentous moment. His neck ached. He shifted sideways in the pew, turning again to face the south and east walls: Lorenzetti's *Deposition*, triumphing over the awkward shape of the vault, bringing down the weight of its composition on the grieving figures below. Claudia followed his look, her eyes coming to rest on the faces of Mary and Christ, staring into each other, eyes threaded together on a single beam of light. She turned again to Tullio, looking at him until his eyes returned to her.

'I was looking at them, Tullio, at their faces. You can see it. You can see them realising these are the moments they came for.'

Tullio moved to get up. Claudia pulled him down again gently, beside her in the pew.

'Tullio, don't run away from it.'

'You're biased Claudia.'

'No, Tullio. Don't you see why the tour's always booked?'

Tullio looked down at the old tiles of the crypt in the darkness between the pews.

'There are lots of good guides, Claudia.'

'It's more than that and you know it, Tullio. You should hear them on the coach. Why do you always run away from it?'

She stilled his hand with hers, insisting that he look at her. He held her eyes for a moment and turned away.

The party was assembling near the exit, some of them already halfway up the stone staircase, examining the flight into Egypt, the slaughter of the innocents, the temptation in the wilderness. Claudia turned eventually to look at the old man still spellbound before the *Madonna and Child*.

'He's on his own isn't he? I'm going to sit with him on the way back.'

Tullio shook his head.

'I don't think he's strong enough to fight off the competition. My money's on the big guy from Michigan with the nice line in shorts.'

❖

It had rained during the hour in the basilica, the cobbles of the Piazza del Comune wet-bright in the emerging sunlight. Tullio returned with the newspapers to where Claudia had found seats under the shade. Most of the party were still struggling up the Via Portica, running the gauntlet of the souvenir shops, taking photos of each other, buying postcards and ceramics, licking ice creams that wilted in the returning sun. He dropped the business sections onto a damp chair and passed the arts pages over to Claudia. Tourists studied the prices under the awnings and umbrellas of the Trovellesi and the Quinquatrus, watching the old men gathering under the staircase of the Pinacoteca Comunale, the groups of students sitting out on the steps of the fountain, the occasional Franciscan crossing the square. Claudia read swiftly, her coffee going cold. Tullio pushed the cup towards her. The air cooler after the rain. A delicacy about the town.

'So what does Lelli have to say?'

'He says the new paintings mark a significant turning point in the artist's career — "*With these works, Tullio d'Attore has got up from the comfortable settee of habit and poised himself, tense and straight-backed, on the hard edge of the unfamiliar*".'

Tullio made a slight motion of being sick in the street.

'He loves it, loves it, riding about on his analogies. Makes him sound profound without having to know what he means. Saves him having to think.'

He returned to the article as Claudia looked up across the square. More of the party were arriving around them, collapsing into chairs, removing sun-hats, ordering drinks. Tullio tossed his newspaper on the table.

'Pal's piece is all about the new ones as well.'

He drank his coffee. Claudia in profile as she looked out across the square. A moment of clarity. A falling away. A waiter appeared to collect the cups. An ambulance of the Misericordia drove slowly through the piazza.

'Another?'

'Please.'

Their eyes met. He looked away towards the Temple of

Minerva. A silence between them in the piazza. A small boy chased pigeons over the drying cobbles. Tullio picked up the newspaper again.

'I think I can probably turn "Arte" down now.'

Claudia looked down at her coffee cup. It was the first time he had referred to the letter.

'Are you going to give it up altogether?'

'I should. An artist would.'

Tullio's mobile rang.

'Pronto.'

'Yes of course, last night.'

Claudia looked around at the adjoining tables where most of the party had now tactfully assembled themselves, seeing that their guide and his wife were in conversation with each other.

Tullio returned the phone to his pocket.

'Sold. All three.'

'To the dancing drunk?'

'To the distinguished art dealer from Livorno.'

Claudia sat at the dining table, making notes for a lecture. Occasionally she scribbled something in an exercise book. On the sofa in front of the fireplace, Tullio was giving an interview to a young woman from one of the art magazines; a tall, anorexic girl, her head almost shaven so that there was little to soften the clownish line of white where the face make-up ended. Claudia gave up the attempt not to listen.

'So, how would you describe the departures implicit in your latest work? Would you say, for example, that they represent a kind of synthesis of terms, a transition between two different modes of seeing, or, for that matter, two different modes of the experiential?'

Claudia closed her eyes.

'Yes, I suppose you could say they're transitional works, in a sense, though obviously there's a sense in which all works, in fact each individual work, is always transitional.'

'That all art necessarily reflects a temporary vision?'

'If you want to see it like that. I suppose that the art of the permanent is something we said goodbye to in the nineteenth century.'

The girl scribbled frantically.

'And will the direction itself be temporary, or do you see yourself developing this particular genre of exploring common-alities?'

'I'd probably like to take it further. But you know that I . . . that this kind of thing can't be decided cold, in the abstract. It has to be decided not just in the brain but in the brush.'

The girl was writing madly, her thighs twisted towards Tullio on the sofa. At the table, Claudia closed the file with a snap.

'And would you also say that your latest work has its own specific iconography, or would you say it was less . . . less specific than that?'

'Well, to the extent that there's an iconography I think you'd have to say it was less specific. Obviously it isn't an iconography in a settled, medieval sense.'

Claudia slipped out of the room, unnoticed.

When she returned an hour later Tullio was working at the easel.

'Carry on, if you're going.'

'No, I was just about to start. She's only just left.'

'The clown?'

'Yes, she was a bit odd, wasn't she? Kept leading me by the hand to places I didn't really want to go. And then I could only seem to get halfway back.'

'You could have tried playing it straight, contradicting her a bit more, asking her what the fuck she was talking about.'

Tullio looked up to see her expression, gauging whether this was an irritation of the moment.

'I thought you must be downstairs.'

'No, I went to the bookshop. Then I had a coffee with Valentina.'

'The cello's been playing. Just those same few bars. I wish he wouldn't do that. You find yourself listening, waiting. Why doesn't he play like he used to?'

Claudia began clearing books and files from the table. Tullio let the brush fall. He had sketched out the idea in watery umber. Three pale lines, like receding horizons. The lowest just recognisable as the stretched edge of a cello; the second a gentler profile of distant hills; the third a long, subtle line suggesting a reclining figure. He watched her flowing to and fro from the bookcase, bending and straightening, like the girl in the window.

'How's the new portrait going?'

'I don't know. I haven't been down.'

'You haven't asked him about the shop?'

'No. I think we'd better forget about it.'

He squeezed the brush out with the tips of his fingers, and bent again to the canvas.

'If you haven't been sitting, he's probably just been finishing off.'

'Probably.'

'Would he want the first portrait as well, if he takes the shop?'

'Has he asked you for it?'

'No.'

'Well then.'

'He must have some more, apart from the ones on the walls?'

'How should I know? I suppose he could get a couple back from Landini.'

'But he'd need both the portraits?'

'I don't know, I suppose so.'

'You don't seem as concerned about him.'

Claudia crossed to the kitchen.

'I'm trying not to be. He won't look after himself and he won't listen. I don't see why I should get drawn in.'

Tullio took a speck off the canvas with a dry brush.

'No. Anyway, I suppose it might be a little bit embarrassing. Having the portrait, the new one I mean, in the Via Maestra.'

Claudia stared into the marble of the kitchen surface, rebellion rising.

'It's nothing to do with that, Tullio. We've offered him the shop and it's up to him, that's all.'

'I agree. It's just that it's not like you to see it like that.'

'Well that's because for once I'm trying not to be like me. Valentina was just saying she didn't see why women always had to live their lives in the turbulence of men's passing, and I thought that's just what I'd be doing if I start getting drawn into being concerned about Giuliano as well.'

Tullio raised the brush, surprised at the sudden vehemence, unable to leave the subject alone.

'Still, getting him to show the paintings wouldn't really be getting drawn in. It's more like a way out. Helping him stand on his own feet.'

Claudia slammed a cupboard door. Tullio replaced the brush in the tray.

'Ask him again. I'd like him to have the shop.'

Claudia almost snapped.

'All right I'll ask him.'

The telephone rang in the corner of the apartment. Claudia took the call.

'It's for you.'

She left the phone in his hand and crossed to the easel, examining the lines meandering across the canvas.

When Tullio returned to the window his eyes were bright.

'Tagliatti.'

The anger vanished from Claudia's face.

'The Biennale?'

Tullio nodded.

'Five paintings. The Hall of Sculpture.'

'Tullio that's fantastic!'

'I can't believe it.'

Her arms were round him.

❖

He had stayed up late to paint but by eleven o'clock he was out in the Via Maestra, walking the streets of the town, absorbing the news, imagining his paintings in the Duke's palace, moving through its corridors, its staircases, its rooms, feeling its fineness. He cut through into the Via Niccolò Aggiunti, pausing under the dark leaves, glancing up at the statue standing watch through the night. The Hall of Sculpture: a room in which art and history were not external things but something lived, breathed, moved within, expressed in the crossing of a floor, the fall of light through a window; a room as calm and well-proportioned as the mind should be. Turning into the Piazza Garibaldi he noticed the dark figure at the top of the stone stairs. The elderly man from his tour party; the one who always lingered and who lingered now, at half past eleven at night, staring through the plate glass at the dimly lit fresco of *The Resurrection of Christ*.

199

Tullio made sure his footsteps were heard as he took the stone steps.

'A last look?'

The elderly American turned, surprised.

'Yes. I couldn't sleep. The window's a good idea, though of course you can't really see.'

'They put it in a couple of years ago.'

Side by side they looked down the Sala della Risurrezione to where the last reach of the streetlights illuminated the sleeping soldiers, the banner and the face of the risen Christ.

'I want to thank you for this tour Mr d'Attore.'

'Niente. It was good to see you enjoying it all.'

The old man had not moved. Thirty metres away the eyes of Christ confronted him. He turned into the comforting darkness of the square.

20

Claudia drank her coffee alone on the sofa. Tullio had left two hours earlier for Siena. For once the apartment was tidy, the furniture dusted, the almost empty walls calm in the morning light. On the easel, hidden by dust-sheets, his latest canvas. And almost directly below, in another apartment, another painting, an image that refused to go away. She returned the coffee cup to the table. The apartment had always felt secure, solid in its age; not this hollow, precarious, uncomfortable place. The window was open but no air stirred. The smell of oil paint stifled, the coffee touched with linseed. She got up and walked to the window.

The street below was deserted apart from the two elderly women chatting outside the church. In the palazzo opposite, most of the shutters were closed. She turned to face into the room, stood for a moment in front of the easel where Tullio had sketched out a new painting that appeared to be a sun rising over the horizon. Only she could already see that the undulating landscape would be ambiguous, half hillside, half stretched-out human figure. The brain fell into neutral, going nowhere, thoughts dying in the stillness of the morning. She turned again to the window. Two men were negotiating a refectory table into Tersilio's workshop. The women were still there. It was her only free morning of the week.

She moved into the bedroom and looked around aimlessly at the bed, the wardrobes, the window. Why was it that she fell into the interstices of men's lives, living between the bulkheads of their self-preoccupations? Why did they assume they had the right to do this, to be wrapped up in themselves, the energy of their self-absorption creating invisible energy fields that distorted women's lives so that they were almost unconsciously living according to male needs, physical and emotional, perpetually aware of their self-awareness, their potential prides and hurts, their thirsts and hungers, perpetually adapting to life in the male greenhouse, to its soil and climate, its permitted light and water and sunshine? Why must she bear the burden of unburdening. Why could he not ask her, speak to her? Why did she always have to interpret his silences. And it was tiring, resisting the orbital pull, insisting on two equal bodies under the heavens. Sometimes it was as if the words must travel light years to reach him.

The coffee was finished. The morning empty. She was carrying the cup through to the kitchen when the cello began to play, the deep notes penetrating the apartment, pressing their case through the floorboards and beams of the Palazzo Lanzi. The first few bars. And then nothing. She turned to look at the sketch on the easel, the long drawn out horizon, deciding to answer the call.

'Enter!'

Giuliano called aggressively above the cello, continuing to play as she walked into the middle of the room. His eyes were closed.

She stopped a few feet from the easel. The dining chair had gone. He looked at her now through half closed eyes as he played, head pressed against the neck of the instrument, his expression yearning with the music. She met his look without embarrassment, waiting for him to stop playing. He closed his eyes again, drawing sound from the depths of the instrument, moving his eyebrows melodramatically, frowning as he listened, imagining the piano.

'Giuliano.'

He began again, shushing her gently with his lips. She spoke over the top of the music.

'Giuliano, I've come to ask you to give me the painting.'

He played on softly, more carelessly now, looking at her.

'You want me to give it to you?'

'I want you to destroy it.'

The cello stopped, the vibrations dying into silence. A life ending. He smiled.

'Don't be ridiculous.'

'You had no right to paint it.'

'I have a right to paint anything.'

'You don't have a right to take away my rights.'

'Don't be pompous with me Claudia. I paint what I paint.'

'You violated my trust.'

He began playing again, loudly, edgily. Claudia clenched her teeth for a moment.

'Will you stop that please?'

He finished the note, drawing it out long, holding the pose for a second or two before opening his eyes. He leaned the cello against the wall, propping the bow against it, folding his arms, looking at her, confident of the upper hand. The sleeping bag had slipped to the floor.

'Giuliano, why do you want to hurt me?'

'Claudia, I've painted it and I'm going to show it. I want it out in the open.'

'Precisely what do you want out in the open?'

His arms performed loose circles in the air.

'An artist doesn't have a choice about these things. He has to express what he feels. And you won't let me express it any other way.'

Claudia moved a step nearer to him.

'Giuliano, don't give me all this artist bullshit. You're a fine artist, maybe even a great artist, but that doesn't give you the right . . . it's not an excuse to ditch every other responsibility as a human being . . .'

'Claudia, I love you. That and painting are the only responsibilities I have. And this is the only way I have to show it. Believe me. You're only fooling yourself. You don't love Tullio. He can't see you. He can't paint you. He can't paint anything. And he can't possibly love you like I love you, surely you must be able to see that yourself?'

Claudia lowered her eyes to the floorboards, gathering herself, biting on tears of anger. She turned to the easel, moved around to look at the portrait of Giuliano and herself. He watched her, excited, from the bed.

'Look at it Claudia. Look at it. It's the truth.'

She picked up the nearest brush from the tray and stabbed the sharp end through the top left hand corner of the canvas, ripping it diagonally down through the painting, stabbing it again into the opposite corner, dragging it towards the loose centre. Giuliano remained on the bed, as white as the linen that now hung in tattered triangles from the back of the wooden stretcher, revealing the paint-splashed supports of the easel.

21

Tullio stepped back, the brush swinging thoughtfully at his side, transferring touches of lead white to the raised seams of his chinos as he counted the tolling of the bell across the rooftops of the town. Five unbroken hours, suppressing anxieties, doubts, hearing the dry, nasal voice of Lelli Ugolini, steering the painting towards its finish, holding its eye, minute by minute, the apartment dying of quietness around him. He raised his chin, easing the muscles of his neck, oil glistening on linen, the linseed tang of victory in his nostrils, exulting. He opened his eyes, sure of what he would find. The landscape began conventionally enough with distant hills and folds, based loosely on a photograph of the soft-wooded hills behind Cortona. His eyes travelled down the land, observing the hills and valleys as they became the folds and volutes of cotton, of loose sheets on a bed, greens and yellows disappearing into shadowed whites and blues. He dropped the brush on the work-table and turned from the easel, surrounded suddenly by unmanageable space. The dark furniture of the room had assumed an extraordinary weight, the floorboards an unfamiliar sense of distance, the sofa a deeper pile. Around him the four walls shone evenly in the last of the daylight, dimly perceived, unexplored.

He set water to boil and began to carve bread, still absorbed in his surfaces, in dalliance with the outer edges of his craft. Next up would be the triptych of the crucifixion, set in the ornate frame he had discovered in three separate pieces at the back of Grimaldi's workshop, the gilding mostly gone but the wood still sound. A few days to paint the hallowed old men of the Via Maestra into the side panels, in their jeans and felt hats and sneakers; perhaps two more to finish the middle aged woman in the central panel, hanging from the cross, well-dressed, ordinary, twisted at the waist, left leg slightly over the right, the posture of the trecento, the suffering modern. He looked down at the breadboard; instead of two slices he had carved to the end of the loaf. He needed tinfoil, or a plastic box. Or perhaps he would try a new version of the view from the window over the rooftops of the town, a view apparently broken into four by the window frame but in fact each pane a separate painting, continuing the view from a slightly different perspective, so that the town would not quite fit together, producing a disturbing effect. He opened and closed doors looking for tinfoil. There were things he was supposed to have done: sorting out packing materials for Urbino; banking the cheque from the Bernard; calling the dealer in Livorno; dropping an order in to Pasquale; writing to 'Arte'. He found the roll of foil and began ripping off jagged pieces to smother around the slices of bread. The last tour of the year coming to an end. A good group. The two Californians were plainly bored. But the sisters from Toronto were enjoying themselves. And the widowed teacher who had found consolation. And the elderly man in the crumpled cotton suit who lingered longer than everyone else. And the asthmatic woman from Brooklyn who was really on a pilgrimage and had spent most of the time praying and crossing herself before the dubious relics of saints. And the dentist from Colorado and the research chemist from Idaho who had complained about the lights going off in the basilica, dimming only slightly the Byzantine glow of Lorenzetti's *Madonna and Child*. The tender love for the child, the fragile moment, caught in a wall six hundred years ago and still as alive as today, as this moment here, now. He was still staring through the steam into the boiling water when Claudia came in. She turned the gas off on her way through to the bedroom.

'No time. We'll get something on the way.'

'On the way where?'

'I don't believe you've forgotten.'

'Oh God, the lecture.'

'We have to set off straightaway. Aren't you going to change?'

'If you like.'

She glanced up at him.

'Tullio, look at you.'

Through the doorway he could see her undressing. Swiftly, easily. Dropping the clothes on the bed.

He was standing by the easel, staring through the window, when she came out of the bedroom.

'Tullio, we'll be late. And I'm on the platform.'

'Come and look.'

She crossed quickly to the easel. He stood behind her, hooked his fingers over the tops of her shoulders, sliding his thumbs in circles over the fine cotton between the shoulder blades.

'How do you do that?'

'I don't know. Don't ask.'

'Is it for the Palace?'

'Yes.'

She picked up the car keys from the table.

'What happened to the loaf?'

22

They drove quickly through the light industrial estates and retail parks on the outskirts of Sansepolcro.

'Did you bank the cheque?'

'I didn't have time.'

'And you didn't call the travel agent?'

'No, I could do it now.'

Tullio reached down for the bag between his feet.

'Do it tomorrow.'

She turned just outside the town and began the long winding climb along the edge of Umbria to Le Marche. Tullio yawned. Construction sites had also begun to climb the slopes; concrete, earthquake-proof limbs rising from soft fields. He settled back into the seat as the car pulled out past a trailer of limp tobacco leaves.

'Do we know what he's lecturing about?'

'No idea. I think they just wanted him to talk about whatever he wants.'

They were leaving the dusk lights of the Tiber valley behind them now, the view opening out below, climbing through pastured hillsides broken with olive groves and dark lines of vines. Tullio stared into the hesitant gloom, the ghosts of white Chianina cattle rising behind dark hedgerows.

'Where shall we stop?'

'We'll get something in Angelo if we have time.'

'Or pick up a sandwich in the bar across the street.'

'You're going to sit in the lecture eating sandwiches?'

Claudia drove on in silence as the road wound into the Apennines, the striped snow poles standing in the late heat, a jaundiced sky turning to magenta as the day died.

After twenty minutes the Fiat broke the top of the pass and began the descent towards the Metauro, passing between loose walls and stubbled fields. In the distance, the lights of Mercatello. Tullio went back to his paintings, wondering if he might be ready to attempt a portrait. When he awoke they were climbing again, San Angelo and Urbania behind them.

'Sorry.'

Claudia smiled in the darkness.

'Painting all afternoon?'

'Five hours straight. The time flew.'

'That's good.'

'What did you do?'

'Anghiari. A restoration class. Had a drink with Sauro.'

'Is he coming tonight?'

'I expect he'll be there. And Eduardo, of course. He asked me to pass on his congratulations by the way, on the Biennale. Didn't think he could make it to the opening night.'

To the left the lights of the new university buildings were spread like a raptor's claw down the dark, dry hillside.

'Will you be coming straight from work?'

'I'll have to. I've got classes all afternoon and a faculty meeting at six. Are all the artists going to be there?'

'I expect so.'

'Do we know any of them?'

'No. I said hello to Alcini once but he wouldn't remember.'

The car plunged into a dark cradle of trees. When they emerged, a few spots of rain had appeared on the windscreen.

'I got a swap letter this morning.'

Claudia smiled.

'What were they offering this time?'

'A week at their summer place up in Consuma for a portrait of his wife.'

'Obviously he hasn't been reading the papers.'

'No, I suppose not.'

Claudia concentrated for a minute on bends that were becoming greasy.

'Have you decided which ones you're putting in? For the Biennale?'

'No, what do you think?'

'I don't know. Do they have to be new?'

'Recent, yes.'

Below them, to the right, the hills stretched out towards Pesaro the Adriatic. Ahead, the first glimpse of the town. Tullio looked down into the well at his feet.

'You don't seem very keen on the new paintings.'

Claudia glanced in the mirror. An oil light flashed intermittently on the dashboard.

'I'm probably just too used to the old ones.'

He raised a hand to his forehead.

'I'm trying to do something a bit different. Join the fray, as Lelli would say. Do you think I shouldn't bother?'

Claudia remained silent in the darkness, following a cyclist through the tight turns into the town.

'It depends what the fray is for, I suppose.'

He clicked his tongue in a first casual shot of annoyance.

'What has it ever been for?'

'I thought I knew.'

'And now you don't?'

Claudia adjusted her line to avoid a car straying over the centre line.

'I don't know what's going on at all with you at the moment.'

Tullio folded his arms.

211

'Why don't you just come out with it and say you don't like them?'

She leaned forward to see further into the bend. Houses had appeared on the left, the land dropping away to the right. A first glimpse of the palace.

'I think you need your wipers.'

She flicked at the stalk.

'Well?'

'Well what?'

'Do you think they're any good or not?'

'I told you. I don't know what's going on with you at the moment.'

'That could be because you're not often there.'

'What's that supposed to mean? You're the one who's always away.'

'And you're always downstairs.'

'So that's what this is about, is it? Is that what it's about? Giuliano?'

'No, it's not about Giuliano.'

The dark suburbs saluted them, pollarded trees lining the entrance to the town. Tullio pushed a sweet-paper into the ashtray, prodding at its edges with a spotted fingernail, turned to see his own face in the window, watched himself speaking.

'How is the new portrait by the way? You haven't said much about it.'

'Tullio, you're the one who needs to say what you're thinking. If you don't like me posing for Giuliano then say so. I've had enough of your bloody silences.'

Tullio drew a deep breath and looked at her in the darkness. Tears in her eyes, caught by the gaudy lights of a bar. They came into the last corner before the road opened out below the palace.

'Claudia . . .'

She swerved suddenly left into a tree-lined residential street.

'We'll be late.'

'I don't care.'

She turned uphill again, following the one way system around the town walls.

'I thought you were supposed to be on the platform.'

She brought the car to a stop at the side of the road, overlooking the town. A picnic spot by day; a lovers' lane by night. She pulled on the handbrake, turned off the engine, staring straight ahead, biting her lip.

'Why don't you tell me when things are on your mind Tullio? Why must I always be tip-toeing around you?'

Tullio bit at a thumbnail, looking down on the pink glow of the palace walls a few hundred metres below. Between the slim minarets, the balcony; the marble details quiet against the pink brick; the ideal rooms and corridors of the mind. Under the dark pines two elderly men were walking slowly towards them. One of them took a cigarette from his mouth. An arc of red in the darkness.

'I don't know. It's probably because I'm ashamed of most of the things that are on my mind.'

Claudia reached out a hand. He took it in both of his. She leaned across and kissed him on the cheek. He felt the cool of her tears. The engine cracked and twisted in the silence.

'I should have told you. I haven't been sitting for Giuliano for a week. And I haven't posed for him nude at all.'

He turned to her, all of his silences in his eyes. She touched his face again.

'It's all right. I knew how you felt about it.'

'Claudia, whatever I felt, there was no reason . . .'

'There doesn't need to be. I know you, Tullio. I know when things matter to you. I know how you invest things. If it means something to you, that's enough for me.'

'Claudia . . .'

'Besides, I had a suspicion right from the start that he might be falling for me . . .'

She reached up for the interior light.

'. . . and I worked it out that spending hours alone with him stark naked might not be the best way of discouraging him. I should never have played that duet on the piano either.'

Tullio's eyes were closed.

'And is he . . . in love with you?'

'So he says. But he's not really.'

'He's told you? '

'That's why I stopped going.'

Tullio stared down at the palace.

'So there isn't a painting?'

'Oh yes, there is. Or rather there was. It started off as a portrait, a head and shoulders, in profile. Then when I went down to see what he'd painted . . .'

She glanced at his face.

'And?'

'And he'd painted us both. Facing each other. It was a portrait of a couple who'd just made love. There wasn't any other way to see it.'

Tullio looked at her face tilted towards the light. She glanced in the mirror. A second car had pulled up under the trees behind them.

'Then he said he was going to exhibit it. In Vittorio's shop, if you please. Said he wanted it all out in the open. With you, with everybody.'

'That's why you went cold on letting him have the shop?'

'You noticed.'

'I thought it was because you didn't want a nude portrait hanging in a shop window in the Via Maestra.'

'This would have been ten times worse.'

'What did you say?'

214

'Well, if you want to know I went down there yesterday and put the sharp end of a size eight Windsor and Newton right through it. Ripped it corner to corner. And a couple of big stabs in what was left.'

'You destroyed it?'

'Comprehensively.'

Another car cruised by, illuminating the interior of the Fiat. Claudia searched in her bag, handed him a tissue. He turned away into the darkness. Mists of rain moved over the minarets of the palace and descended on the town. One or two of the lights were still on in the Duke's apartments.

'Claudia my silences. He's an artist, I know . . . that I know . . .'

She smiled at his reflection in the rain.

'And you thought my love for you would probably just change, as soon as a better artist came along?'

He lifted his head and turned to her, looking into her eyes for the first time in weeks.

'Claudia, I'm sorry.'

A more insistent rain fingered the roof of the car, running down the windows in channels of its own making.

'Don't build walls, Tullio. Don't build your own house in our house.'

Tullio stared out down the hillside. The car behind had doused its lights. The palace glowed again, dominating the town. Behind the buildings, the courtyard.

'You don't think I should give up the tours do you?'

He had turned away. Claudia touched his face, turning him towards her again.

'No, I don't. I don't think you've any idea how special they are, what they give to people.'

'I've told you, you're biased.'

The windscreen wipers shuddered back and forth against the rain.

'Tell me what you think about the paintings.'

'The new ones? You're right. I don't like them.'

'None of them?'

'None of them.'

She sat with her hands in her lap. Tullio let his head fall back. He had expected to feel disappointment, bitterness, not relief.

'I know you're trying to get out of yourself, out of a rut, do something different, but it's just . . . effects . . . for their own sake. That's the fray you've joined. It might be brilliant but it's not . . . anything to do with you . . .'

He took her hand again.

'. . . and I'm torn because I'm thrilled for you. The Biennale, the sales. But underneath . . . it's because I love you.'

He blocked his breath, feeling his chest expand.

'You've never been pretentious about painting, Tullio. Yours or anybody else's. But you've been letting them pull you in.'

He turned away, released his breath, misting up the window.

'Look at the interview you gave that girl yesterday. It's not iconography, Tullio, it's just pears and bums.'

His head fell to his chest, the distant streetlight orange on the back of his neck. She caught her own sudden reflection in his window, looked through it to the dark tangle of hawthorns of the hillside, the palace below, wondering what she had done. She reached across to touch his face, felt the wetness of his tears, the shuddering of his laughter.

23

'. . . Knight of the Crown of Italy, a Knight Officer of the Order of Merit of the Italian Republic, an Honorary Citizen of Florence, and an honorary academician of the Academy of the Arts of Design in Florence, whose founder members included Michelangelo and Duke Cosimo de Medici.'

One or two of the students, recognising Claudia, moved along the wall to make space on the back wall of the lecture theatre.

'His many papers and books on Medieval and Renaissance art have earned him a reputation that is given to very few scholars in their own lifetime and are of course well known to most of us here tonight. So you may imagine how delighted my colleagues and I were when he accepted our invitation . . . and this despite a recent illness which makes us all the more grateful for his presence among us.'

The vice-chancellor looked up from his notes and turned momentarily to the seats behind the platform.

'. . . with great pleasure and pride that I welcome Professor Robert Harding back to Urbino.'

The applause died away. Tullio found Claudia's hand in the darkness.

Several seconds passed before the audience realised that Harding had begun to speak, provoking a commotion on the platform as gowned figures stepped forward to adjust the microphone. He thanked them with a smile and turned again to his audience.

'Dear friends . . . Dear friends, I was trying to thank the vice-chancellor for his kind words of welcome.'

He turned to glance again at the platform and a few words were lost.

'. . . that I don't really give lectures any more. In fact I don't really do anything any more . . .'

Tullio placed his bag at his feet and straightened to peer down over dark heads to the light of the lectern and behind it the frail, familiar figure in the crumpled cotton suit.

'. . . but I accepted your vice-chancellor's very kind invitation to be here with you tonight . . . accepted partly because I have the fondest memories of the time I spent here as a young man almost six decades ago. And partly . . . because I couldn't quite accept that I had made my last visit to my beloved Italy.'

A sympathetic murmur from the audience, the vice-chancellor nodding. Claudia gripping Tullio's hand.

'. . . just remarked, I have not been too well of late. Rather a severe bout of old age I'm afraid. And it crossed my mind in my more maudlin moments . . .

'So when the invitation came I'm afraid I took it as a sign. And so here I am. Here I am. My forty second visit. Partly to be with you tonight. Partly to see perhaps one more time the things I've loved most in all the years that I've been privileged . . . privileged to spend studying and teaching and writing about the art of the early Renaissance.'

The microphone caught the turning of a page. A few embarrassed coughs rang out in the silence of the lecture theatre.

'However, I've had to accept that my days . . . my days of driving automobiles . . . are over. And I'm afraid I couldn't quite sustain the notion of getting on and off the Pullman. Or working through those books of rail schedules that I couldn't understand even as a young man. Let alone cycling, which of course is how I first got to see so many wonderful things all those years ago. And as some of you may know, my companion of so many previous visits . . . my companion, Geraldine Howard of Yale, passed away in Florence just over two years ago.'

Behind the speaker, several of the faculty were nodding sympathetically, unaware that the Professor was now smiling at his audience.

'And so I eventually had the rather extraordinary idea of booking myself . . . booking myself onto a package tour.'

A stir of laughter arose from the banked seats, rippling up towards the back of the hall.

'I have to admit that I didn't . . . quite know how to proceed. Luckily, a former student of mine helped me to surf the net. And after a week or so of surfing I eventually found . . . found a tour that seemed to touch base with almost all the things I most wanted to see again. So I took my courage in both hands and put in a call. But they told me that the particular tour I was enquiring about . . . that particular tour . . . was sold out for the next two years.

'I told them I didn't think . . . that I couldn't possibly wait two years. And when they understood that I'd be travelling alone, it turned out that they might be able to find one single seat. Apparently the last single seat is sometimes quite difficult to sell.'

He paused again, eyes darting up and down the theatre.

'The brochure that came also informed me that the price included the services of an accompanying expert, to help us understand what we were going to see.'

Another wave of laughter pushed through the auditorium. Harding waited for it to die away, taking a sip from the glass.

'But I confess . . . I confess I was a little concerned at the thought of my travelling companions. I'm sure we've all seen them in the Uffizi and the Pitti, and here in the Palazzo Ducale . . . people with little popping cameras and yellow pants and white legs, telling each other which pictures they've done puzzles of.'

The laughter in the hall was followed now by scattered applause. The audience had not expected to be entertained. Harding beamed out over the packed theatre.

'In my own particular party, I discovered there were to be two businessmen and their spouses, a research chemist from Idaho, and a man who'd spent most of his life with the old Nantucket fishing fleet. We also had a writer of software, an electrical goods retailer, a dentist from Colorado, a hospital administrator from Bismarck, North Dakota, and a professional dog-walker from Brooklyn.'

Laughter was greeting every sentence now. Behind the lectern, the vice-chancellor was smiling down at his hands.

'Our appointed hotel in my beloved Sansepolcro was, I must say, extremely congenial. And on our first morning . . .'

Harding paused for effect, looking out over the sea of faces.

'. . . I learnt that the first visit would be to see a fresco by someone called Piero della Francesca.'

The roar rose to the ceiling. On the platform the vice-chancellor was smiling. Eduardo Mignini rocked to and fro in his seat.

'Well, we trooped through the familiar streets in the sunshine, stopping for a while in the garden for a little talk on the painter's life . . .'

He held up his hand, asking to be allowed to continue.

'And as we were standing there in the garden, the door of Piero's house opened and who should I see stepping out into the street but Gentile Brachelente.'

He raised a hand to turn the microphone, ignoring the small commotion behind him.

'He even gave a little nod to our guide and ran his eyes over our rather brightly dressed little group.

'Well of course I've had the pleasure of meeting the distinguished Director the . . . distinguished Director of the Fondazione Piero della Francesca . . . many times. And I don't doubt he would have recognised me had we met 'most anywhere else. As it was, he just stared at me for a moment . . . and walked right on by. You see – and this is a fundamental lesson for all of you who are studying the history of art – his eyes were deceived by context.'

Harding turned to acknowledge Gentile Brachelente, who was sitting on the platform, attempting to cover his face with his hand.

'But back to my coach tour. And I must tell you . . . it was quite an extraordinary experience . . . walking through those rather dull first few rooms of the Museo Civico with fifteen holidaymakers, stepping down into the Sala della Risurrezione, Christ staring down at us all from the end wall, St Giuliano watching me in astonishment. I can only compare it . . . only compare it to showing a prospective purchaser round a house you've lived in for many years. You can't help seeing things anew, seeing things through their eyes. Seeing things as they are, almost. As if all the years you have known them have been peeled away.'

On the platform behind, guests and faculty members wore permanent half-smiles, caught up in the unexpected turn of the lecture.

'Well so it was, that first morning, about two weeks ago now, that I saw *The Resurrection of Christ* through the eyes of the social worker and the dentist, the businesswoman from Newport, Rhode Island, and the medical man from Toulane.'

He paused, lifting the glass of water under the lectern light.

'And what I saw on the north wall was a large, rather dull, not terribly attractive picture pushed in rather awkwardly between the ribs of the vaulting. Obviously old. But rather muddy and forbidding. Certainly from the point of view of my companions it was hard to believe that it was something worth crossing the Atlantic Ocean to see. A strange sensation – to see such a familiar image as if I had never seen it before, as if I had known it in another life. And in the event I couldn't help looking at the faces of my companions . . . couldn't help listening to our guide, to see what they'd make of it all.'

Harding turned away from the microphone to blow his nose on a cotton handkerchief. Blinking, unhurried, he glanced at his notes and faced his audience again.

'Our guide didn't go in for a deal of detail. No discussion at all of the vexed problem of dating *The Resurrection*. Not even the obvious comparison with the younger Christ in *The Baptism*. No mention, either . . . no mention either of the iconographical ties with Nicola di Segna's polyptych of St. Clare. Nothing at all on solar mythology or fertility cults, or the light on the trabeation.'

Harding put the handkerchief away, looking up at the sloping ceiling of the theatre.

'Instead he addressed himself to what it is that makes *The Resurrection of Christ* one of the greatest works of the quattrocento . . . what it is that makes it one of the greatest frescoes ever painted.'

He allowed a full five seconds to pass, eyes riding over the silence of his audience.

'He spoke of the composition, the technique, only to focus their eyes . . . our eyes . . . on the power of the thing. On what Piero had done with his commission. On what he'd made of it. What he'd made of the soldiers' falling asleep, of the rising from the tomb. And at this point, I must say, I took my eyes off the fresco and stole a look at my companions. One or two of them were still fidgeting, perhaps impatient to move on, tick off more works of art. But most of them were . . . experiencing the painting . . . looking at it as if at something they had always known was there . . . in themselves, in the world they lived in . . . confronting it directly, there in the little museum of Sansepolcro, in front of a dull, rather muddy painting of yet another biblical scene. And at the end of five minutes I don't think there was a person in the room who didn't know, see, feel . . . why *The Resurrection of Christ* was worth travelling so far to see.'

Another pause, holding the audience with his eyes.

'One after the other we visited almost all the things I had hoped

for. The Pisano pulpits in Siena and Pistoia, though not unfortu-
nately in Pisa. Only one day, sadly, in Rome. But we were able to
take in Orvieto for the San Brizio and those wonderful Maitani
reliefs. And of course we came here, to the Palazzo Ducale, to the
most gracious building in the western world. To see the finest
courtyard in Italy. To see the rooms and staircases of the palace.
To see the Pieros and the Raphael.

'Obviously we couldn't visit the upper Basilica in Assisi, but we
did of course see the real Giottos in the Arena Chapel.'

Harding turned slightly to the faculty members behind him, all
of them smiling at this reference to an old controversy, one or two
of them shaking their heads.

'It saddened me particularly . . . saddened me particularly not
to be able to see the two wonderful panels of the Isaac Master. But
we saw the Simone Martinis in the crypt and I was able to spend
some time with Lorenzetti's *Madonna and Child*, still, for me, the
heart and soul of the trecento. And then it was on to Siena and the
Maestà. And in the afternoon, the ruins of the Fonte Gaia, and the
great font in the Baptistry with my favourite della Quercias. To my
great delight, we even made an unscheduled dash to Lucca to see
the restored Ilaria del Carretto. Not ruined . . . not ruined at all in
my view. And that same evening there was a special showing of the
most underrated fresco cycle in the world, there in the church of
the Collegiata in San Gimignano. And then of course there were
the Pieros in Sansepolcro and Monterchi, and the restored half of
The Legend of the True Cross in Arezzo where I am informed that
the scaffolding is about to be declared of historic interest.'

Laughter ran along the platform at the reference to the
protracted restoration of the Arezzo cycle.

'In our two trips to Florence we were able to spend time at the
Bargello and the Museo dell'Opera del Duomo, and at Santa
Croce. And of course in those extraordinary first few rooms of the
Galleria degli Uffizi . . . where I could have easily spent the whole

day. We toured the cells of San Marco and spent twice our allotted time in the Brancacci Chapel. And when everything was closed we studied all three Baptistry doors, and every niche of the Orsan-michele. We even saw the Pietà by Giovanni da Milano in the Accademia, where our guide informed us that he himself had ignored this powerful piece until his attention had been drawn to it by a mention . . . a mention in . . . Harding's *Art of the Early Renaissance.*'

Laughter stirred again in the auditorium.

'I cannot reiterate . . . cannot reiterate here tonight all that was said as we stood before the *St. Mark*, the *Maestá*, the frescoes of the Collegiata. But in all of these places our accompanying expert drew upon our discipline . . . drew upon the history of art . . . not to build barriers but to dismantle the fortifications of time, not to distance or exclude the uninitiated but to include us all in his own joy in what he saw, to bring us intellectually and emotionally closer to what was before us . . . to feel the power of it upon our pulses.

'In our ten days together we saw many of the greatest works of art that have ever been created. And long before the end almost everybody . . . almost everybody in the party . . . was able to see what all the fuss was about. They were able to recognise and respond . . . to the enduring longing for beauty and fineness, for grace and proportion, to the long, heroic striving to make permanent the fleeting moment, to hold on to the fragments of unknown significances, to know the need to represent visions and ideals, the never-ending struggle to rescue some meaning.'

Harding paused to sip water.

'Of course most of the conversation . . . on the coach, in the cafés and restaurants . . . was about the food and the wine and the weather. About what they had seen in the shops. About how many different kinds of ice cream you can get at Vivoli. About what presents they were taking. About their lives . . . their lives back home in Boston or Philadelphia. Or about the plumbing in the hotel. Or about what their children and grandchildren were doing.'

Another sip of water. A cough in the auditorium.

'But I also heard their silence in front of the great works. And I saw their faces as they were confronted with the highest achievements of art. And I saw them responding as the days went by . . . saw them responding to beauty, to the striving to represent belief and perfection and ideal and aspiration, to the representation of states of mind and of being, to perceptions of what it is to be a human being in this world. Day after day I saw them . . . saw them directed towards the immaterial possibilities of delight, towards images and creations of man that ennoble rather than demean. Saw them directed towards the past, to a touching of hands across the centuries, seeing the world and its possibilities for a moment through the hearts and the minds, the beliefs and the hopes, of generations that had gone before . . . breaking down our isolation in time, allowing us all to touch each other in the loneliness of our individual cells. And in a world where the spiritual has retreated, I heard the human spirit sigh.'

He looked long at his audience, the delivery defiant.

'And I learned something else in my ten days.'

A longer pause, the notes no longer needed.

'Too many of us have spent too much of our lives laboriously arriving at new complexities and learned novelties whose importance we exaggerate in order to justify the time we have spent in arriving at them. We have created a profession whose audience and purpose is very largely . . . itself. We have set ourselves apart, our studying and teaching driven and directed more by the internal demands of our own professional culture than by service to a wider, more public culture. We study and teach about the parts, breaking them down into ever smaller pieces for ever closer scrutiny. And as we have become more confident about the parts, so we have become more afraid . . . more afraid of the whole. For what is there to say about the whole work? We have become afraid of it because we fear that it is too big to contemplate, that our intellectual and emotional responses might be inadequate, carrying us into the terrifying world of the unevidenced and the unresearchable, the naïve and the emotional, the world we are afraid of because in it we are only human beings, not experts and professionals. Too often we teach people to break down and analyse and subdue and tame; to make art bearable and graspable again when it should be unbearable and ungraspable. We have become specialists in cutting culture off, preserving it as a thing unto itself.'

A pause. A smile.

'I can say all this tonight because I am an old man with a certain reputation, and no longer fear . . . no longer fear being thought naïve or unscholarly. But I do not claim to be immune from the follies of my profession. Nor do I denigrate the patient scholarship to which many of us have devoted our working lives, the scholarship without which so much of our artistic heritage would be lost, physically or intellectually. But the time has come to use that knowledge not to serve the culture of our own profession but to serve the culture in which we live. I do not pretend to know how that might be done. But I know that it must begin by seeing things whole again, finding again what it was that once so moved and inspired us to spend our lives in the study and service of art.'

Harding folded up his notes and faced his audience.

'This is what I have been doing in my ten days. This is what I have been doing on my package tour. And I needed an expert to help me.'

Harding turned carefully to step down from the lectern, the faculty rising uncertainly to its feet, those nearest to him shaking his hand, welcoming him back to his chair as the applause arose in the auditorium. The vice-chancellor had stepped forward to claim the lectern, smiling indulgently at the stamping of feet, turning

occasionally to the platform where his guest was pushing his notes into the pocket of the crumpled suit.

Against the wall of the auditorium, Tullio floated on the sea of noise, hearing Claudia joining in the unacademic cheers. Her arm slid around his waist, her lips at his ear.

'Biased am I?'

24

Tullio was about to leave the apartment when the clumsy shape of the easel caught his eye, gaunt-limbed against the early morning light. From the doorway he examined the drapery of the landscape, the folds of hills, of sheets.

He left his wallet on the table and returned to the painting. Out in the street the day was just beginning, vans arriving from all over the high Tiber valley, market stalls being erected on both sides of the piazza. Bottom left to top right, top left to bottom right, stroking the dripping brush across the canvas, watching the spirit dissolve the miraculous transition.

The Bar Gerasmo not yet open. He wiped the dampness from the chair, hoping Arturo would bring coffee anyway. He sat outside looking down the Via Maestra, the lightness of the sun's first touch on his face, his eyes following the light over the brickwork of the walls to the church of Sant'Agostino where the *San Giuliano* had stood unnoticed for almost a century.

Coffee appeared, wordlessly, Arturo still asleep. Tullio drank half of it, caffeine waking every cell to the morning, the events of the evening before hanging in his mind like a great painting seen for the first time. He returned the cup to the table and entered the turbulent air of memory, weighing the mass and the colour, determining far or near, establishing the perspective. All down the street the surface of the morning was scribbled over with Harding's words; but they were the notes of the piano, advancing the day, playing over the slower sound of the cello, the deep chords of Claudia in the darkness above the palace. He turned from the piazza to look towards the Porta Fiorentina, seeing her face asleep at his side; the vanishing point to which all other lines were drawn; the point from which to see things whole, judge what must be judged, decide what must be decided. He relaxed the muscles of his face, breathed again, drained his cup. The overnight rain drying rapidly on the flagstones of the Via Maestra. The smell of coffee under the awning. The whole world made new.

Claudia was up and about in the silk gown when he let himself back into the apartment with the morning papers. They kissed for a long time. He spoke over her head, holding her.

'I don't think I'm going to work today.'

'We could go for a walk, get up into the Casentino?'

She lifted her face to him, happy, expectant. He kissed her again.

'What are you going to do? About your young man?'

'Nothing. He'll probably come up and apologise. Some time when he knows you're not in. He's done it before.'

'And tell you he still loves you?'

She turned her head sideways against his chest, holding him snugly.

'He doesn't love me. It could have been anyone.'

He swayed with her in the middle of the room.

'Tell me again about the painting. I wish I'd seen it.'

'It was the same size and shape as the other one, but it was all light Sunday morning tones . . .'

'Not the painting, about putting the brush through it.'

He felt Claudia's laughter against his chest. She looked up into his face.

'What if someone had done that to the Mona Lisa?'

'Good as that was it?'

'Better.'

They swayed in front of the window for a minute, listening to the street coming awake below.

'Coffee?'

'You've just had one.'

'So I'm having another. Are you going to forgive him?'

'I suppose so. He'll probably apologise.'

Tullio pulled a face, weighing the possibilities.

'There's still the shop.'

'I thought you were going to use it?'

'I don't really need it. I've got the new ones for Urbino. And the Bernard's pressing me. And L'Immagine.'

'I suppose I could ask him again.'

Tullio walked back to the window, glancing only briefly at the ruin on the easel, resting both hands on the iron railing. The sun had cleared the roofs opposite, letting the long door of light into the floorboards.

'Why don't I ask him myself?'

Claudia was pressing coffee into the machine.

'Go down there?'

'Mmm. See what he has to say.'

'Why don't you? If I went down I'd only get involved.'

'I think I might go now.'

'Have your coffee first. You won't get any down there.'

'I'd better not have any more. Do you think I should I take the portrait?'

Claudia replaced one of the cups in the cupboard.

'He did say he was going to ask you about it.'

Tullio slipped off his shoes and stepped up on the chair to remove the canvas from the wall. Claudia called from the kitchen.

'I think I like the room better without it.'

Tullio stepped down, surveying four bare walls.

'I'm not sure I don't like it better without any of them. We could get a few prints. They've got some at the supermarket already framed. There's one of a kitten with a ball of wool that I quite fancied.'

'And there's that "Baywatch" one.'

'And those white horses coming out of the sea.'

'Okay, I think I'll get dressed.'

'While I call on your lover.'

Claudia turned into the bedroom door, coyly slipping off the shoulder of her dressing-gown.

'I don't suppose I need to go down right now.'

She pulled the gown on again and turned into the bedroom, closing the door.

'Don't forget the portrait.'

The alarm on Giuliano's face had metamorphosed into a youthful surliness as he led the way into the apartment. He ignored his visitor, seating himself back in front of the easel, making it clear he was being interrupted. Tullio stood the portrait on the floorboards, leaned it gently against the wall. He looked around the room. The untidy bed. The wardrobe door hanging open. The shock of recognition as he glanced at the paintings.

'I've come to talk about the shop.'

Giuliano stared intently at the easel. Tullio ignored the pretence of being absorbed in his work.

'It's still yours if you want it.'

'You know I'm in love with your wife?'

'I know.'

'She's not in love with me.'

'I know that too.'

Giuliano was still looking at whatever it was on the easel, but blankly now, dejected. Tullio walked over to the window, standing opposite the thin figure, facing into the light. The younger man's shoulders had fallen. He looked up at Tullio.

'Did she tell you about the picture?'

'I heard.'

'Do you think she should have done it?'

'Yes.'

A long silence settled over the studio. Outside in the street, a Saturday morning was passing by. The market would be in full flow, people going about their business, getting ready for the weekend, for trips to the hills and Sunday lunch.

'So do I, now.'

Tullio bent to look at a line of panels and bare canvases standing against the wall.

'It doesn't seem to me that there's very much else to say about it.'

'I suppose not.'

'May I?'

Giuliano nodded slowly. Tullio picked up one of the canvases.

'Belgian?'

'Irish.'

Giuliano came over from the easel, picking up one of the smaller canvases, revealing a pair of canvas pliers and a staple gun. Tullio tilted the canvas against the light.

'What ground are you using?'

'Just rabbit glue. I tried some stuff from the local tannery but it was too salty. It wouldn't stay on five minutes.'

'Do you put anything in it?'

'Zinc white, chalk. A drop of honey.'

'Like Van Dyck?'

Giuliano nodded, growing interested.

'It's probably only superstition.'

Tullio smiled and picked up one of the larger boards.

'It puts a sort of responsibility on her, you know, knowing that you're making yourself ill.'

A touch of the old scorn passed over Giuliano's face. Tullio ignored it.

'And knowing that you have an extraordinary talent.'

The face tightened, resisting, yielding. Tullio ran a finger lightly over the gesso, returning the canvas to the floor, selecting one of the wooden panels. Giuliano came closer, examining the surface as Tullio held it towards the window.

'Bologna chalk. Useless for canvas, all right for wood.'

'Do you know Grimaldi? The restorer?'

'No.'

'He uses Bologna chalk for gilding. Still swears by Cennini.'

'I tried marble dust once. It's supposed to make canvas look like a fresco.'

Tullio smiled and lowered the panel to the floor, placing it to one side of the patch of sun.

'If you took the shop you might do well enough to keep going for another year. And it would start getting you known. I've got a couple of friends in Rome. They review for the nationals. Some of the art magazines. I think they might help. In fact I'm sure they would.'

Giuliano stared at the canvas on the easel.

'I haven't got very much to show.'

'I've brought you the portrait back. Landini would let you have whatever he's got.'

'He might I suppose.'

'It's to his advantage as well. I'll be in Arezzo tomorrow if you'd like me to bring them back.'

Giuliano had begun scraping dried paint from the varnished end of a brush with his fingernail. Tullio dropped to his haunches to examine one of the smaller canvases.

'Cambric?'

He looked up from the brush.

'For pencil.'

'What oils do you use?'

'New Holland. Scheveningen.'

'The best.'

'If they didn't grind them too fine.'

'Yes, they can strike through a bit.'

Giuliano dropped the brush into the tray below the easel and wiped his hands on his trousers.

'Where is this shop?'

'In the Via Maestra, opposite Sant'Agostino.'

Giuliano was at the window now, looking down into the street.

'Would I have to be there?'

'It would help. But I suppose you could put your telephone number in the window.'

'I don't have a telephone.'

'You can use our number if you want. One of us is usually there.'

'I'll think about it. Would you like coffee?'

25

Claudia hurried across the Piazza Puccinotti from the darkened faculty building, pushing papers into her briefcase. Ahead of her the walls of the palace, the windows brilliantly lit, a few students still sitting on the warm stones of the steps. In a moment she had passed through into the silent courtyard, the brickwork lost in darkness, the marble columns and capitals hardened by moonlight. She smiled as she entered the vestibule, slowing her pace, beginning the ascent of the staircase towards the voices and lights of the piano nobile.

The Hall of Iole was almost empty, the white cloths of the tables tinged blue against the intonaco of walls and vaults. She paused to pick up a mineral water, a shovel of ice. A bald man with a wispy pony-tail raised his glass by the fireplace.

'The party's moved on I'm afraid. Just the hardened drinkers left in here. Are you sure you won't have some wine?'

'No thanks, this is fine. I think I'll follow the crowd.'

She passed quickly through the second room that had been allocated to Alessandro Alcini; dull, muddy creations of dark, peasant kitchens, lamp-reddened faces, deliberately unrefined faces, vaguely reminiscent of *The Potato Eaters*, totally at odds with the palace, with her mood. In the Hall of the Alcove a dozen people were still admiring the work of Sofia Colacchioni, the young artist from Rome who had been featured in the supplements. She hurried on through the Melaranci apartments, catching up with the first-night crowd that had been moving through the palace for the last hour, intending to come back to look at the modern canvases that hung in place of altarpiece and crucifix, making her way through to the Hall of Sculpture.

The intarsia doors were folded back, the opening partly blocked by the broad back of Sauro Rubellini. She took his free arm as she walked in, leading him towards a space in the centre of Tullio's room.

'Meeting run on?'

'And on and on. Where's Tullio?'

'I've no idea. You could have brought me a drink.'

'You've got a drink.'

She glanced around the crowded room, catching a first glimpse of herself on the far wall.

The image under the picture light disappeared immediately behind dark backs and heads. She remained fixed on the wall until the crowd moved and she saw her portrait, portraits, brilliantly lit on the inside wall of the palace. She turned to look into Rubellini's face. He breathed in hard through his nose, disclaiming responsibility. Handing him the glass she excused her way through the crowds until she came face to face with the painting, newly framed in gold. On the wall, a transparent plastic square embossed with the Montefeltro crest and printed in black: '*Claudia*, Giuliano Amedei, 1975–'.

She moved on to the left of the inlaid doors, coming to the painting of the piano, magnificent in its new frame, its trembling quality more splendid than ever under the palace lights. She turned to find Sauro. He was nowhere to be seen. She pushed on towards the window, catching a glimpse of the cello. Directly ahead were two works whose style she would have recognised anywhere: the one a study of a worn oriental carpet on the floorboards of a decaying palazzo; the other of a man sunk into a tired armchair under a tall window, absorbing the last of the day's light into his thoughts. She began making her way back towards the far door, looking for Tullio. On her left now the familiar portrait of the staircase, and in front of it Giuliano himself, in black shirt and jeans, the feet in thonged sandals, glass in hand, smiling enigmatically, absorbing the attention of a dozen people, including Guido Tagliatti, the vice chancellor, Fabiola Fioravanti, Lelli Ugolini, Palmiro Quartucci.

'Positively basking isn't he?'

Sauro had reappeared at her side.

'Where's Tullio, Sauro?'

'I haven't seen him for about half an hour. But if I had to put money on it, I'd say he was with his Pieros.'

She reached up and kissed his cheek, taking back the glass.

She passed quickly through the last of the guest rooms. The door to the Duke's apartments was closed and locked. She worked her way back through the crowd to the first of the Melaranci apartments, unhooking the cordon that barred the way. Turning along the north corridor she hurried through its rhythms of moonlight and darkness, the quiet courtyard below. The Hall of Angels, also locked. There was no guard to watch her as she unhooked a rope across the entrance to the Hall of Honour, passing through the darkness under its silent tapestries. A painted sign – Galleries closed for the Night – stood across the second doorway to the Hall of Angels. She entered the Duke's apartments, hurrying through the studiolo into the reception hall.

Tullio stood alone in front of the painting, arms folded, head bent forward, examining some detail. He turned to see who had entered, returning his eyes to the *Senigàllia Madonna* as she came towards him.

For a few moments they looked in silence at the living deadness of Piero's faces, the subdued harmony of the unnatural skin-tones, the ultimate steadiness, the tonal finality of the *Senigàllia Madonna*. Tullio raised a hand towards the top right hand corner of the painting.

'All these times and I've never noticed that little wicker basket with the crumpled cloth up there on the shelf. It's perfect isn't it?'

She took his arm, leaned her face against his shoulder.

'Why did you do it Tullio?'

'Oh, I don't know. I thought perhaps the Duke would have liked it.'

26

The light had begun to mellow, the heat to turn the corner of the day. Wine appeared at his side. A saucer of stuffed olives. The early evening passeggiata about to begin.

A young girl came in under the Porta Fiorentina, head lowered, steps awkward and pinched, long hair falling in dark curtains around eyes that darted quick glances in all directions from under a powdery forehead; shyness locked in with a wish to be noticed, self consciousness accompanying her all the way to the piazza. Four more followed some distance behind, desperately nonchalant, striving for that air of uninterested provocativeness, glancing at themselves in the plate glass windows of the optician's, trying out their sexuality on the street where they had tried out their first steps. Tullio lifted his wine and followed their progress down the Via Maestra, fascinated by the attempt to cope with high heels while walking arm-in-arm, their sways and rhythms conflicting so that they stumbled where they would have slinked. He had already finished the painting in his head: the girl seen in a narrow full length mirror as she prepared herself for the passeggiata; the eager anxiety of the glance into the glass; the scattered make-up reflected on the dresser; the rejected clothes on the bed behind; the trying on of womanhood; readying herself for the breathless step through the mirror. Arturo had reappeared, idly scratching his crotch in the doorway.

To his left now an office worker was leaving the Palazzo Gucciardi, pausing under the heavy arch, dropping the keys into her bag. He watched her turn towards the piazza, a woman of about forty, walking neither too quickly nor too slowly, exchanging a buona sera here and there with smiles that brought lines to the corners of her eyes, her mouth, and a welling up of warmth in Tullio's life, a desire to know, a desire for a hundred lifetimes. He reached for his sketchbook. How much more beautiful in middle-age, how much rarer the individual beauty of her years than the masked and unformed beauty of the young.

❖

The coach was waiting outside the Porta Fiorentina, its engine running, the driver reading the sports pages propped against the wheel. Tullio hauled himself up the metal stairs, making his way back between the seats to ironic cheers. He had been stopped three times in the Via Maestra by friends, neighbours, people who wanted to talk.

'Posso?'

He sat down next to the ascetic looking banker from Vermont with whom he had not yet spoken.

'Mr Yardley isn't it?'

'Evander, yes. Not too far to go I take it?'

'Just up the road.'

'Another small-town masterpiece?'

'Another Piero.'

The coach pulled out into the traffic, hauling itself slowly past the tree-lined car park. Across the aisle, the woman from Concorde, Massachusetts, who spoke a little Italian was trying to read a newspaper. Tullio looked past her to where the new hotel was being built near the exit road from the superstrada, at the plastic-wrapped palettes of bricks and tiles standing between cranes and bulldozers, dust swirling from the site-traffic. In a few minutes they had broken through the crust of light industry into the open countryside, heading across the plain of Leonardo's battle, Anghiari on the hill to the right. Maybe he would begin again with the girl in the window, try to come nearer to the edge of his subject, paint her shop-window separateness from the mute companions of her existence, working at the long drawn out loneliness of it all, attempting the moment, the ordinary, poignant, time-standing-still, Edward Hopper moment.

'You were saying that Piero was more-or-less ignored until just recently?'

'Until the late nineteenth century, yes. A bit like Vermeer.'

Tullio looked past Evander Yardley at the fertile fields of the Tiber valley where a dozen pumps were sending great arcs of groundwater across the low sun.

'So will things change again? All these things we ignore now, will people be queuing to see them in a hundred years' time?'

'I don't know that the swings will be quite as extreme. Old paintings get a lot more attention now. Part of the reason for the obscurity of some of these things was just ... obscurity. Not too many people looked at all those gloomy altarpieces in old churches.'

Evander Yardley nodded slowly. Tullio looked at fields of sunflowers turned towards the sun; crude, unashamed, seed-heads bursting with their own vigour, struggling for a share of the sun's subsidy.

'So why does everyone go on about Piero now?'

'I think a big part of it's his faces. There's a lot of uncertainty there, a lot of unresolved perplexity. As if they're caught in a moment of thinking the kind of significant, unresolved thoughts that we all think from time to time. It probably didn't appeal in more confident times, but I think it might be part of what appeals now. His faces can seem so psychologically contemporary. It's as if five centuries were nothing at all. They could be us. And so it makes you believe in them. Makes you believe in the past. Connects you with it in a different way. A lot of old paintings say how different people were. Piero's seem to say how like us they were.'

The banker was looking at a guidebook, open at the Arezzo cycle.

'Vermeer was ignored as well?'

'For a couple of hundred years.'

'You've mentioned him a couple of times already.'

'I seem to think of him in the same breath as Piero.'

'I went to see the Vermeers when they came to Washington. They're very different though aren't they?'

'They are. But there's something there. That sense of a moment that so many great paintings have. An ordinary moment made significant, universal, timeless. Impossible to say what it is. They're both painters of light and silence and stillness, and virtue.'

Tullio paused, summoning up images of Vermeer's women under the light of their windows, of the *Madonna* that was now only minutes away.

The coach turned across the narrow bridge under the walls of Monterchi, hissing to a stop outside the monastery, the party reaching for sun-hats, handbags, wallets, cameras, guidebooks; the line starting to move, filtering down the metal steps, gathering out on the still warm tarmac. Tullio led them into the old schoolroom. Bare arms brushed past him. Bare necks. Hats being swept off. Perfumes scraping by. A close up of human bodies, a Degas composition from a jostled camera. He directed them into the first room on the right.

A few seconds later silence had descended. The rest of the walls were bare apart from a few concert notices. Tullio moved down the side wall, looking over silhouetted heads to the fresco glowing in its air-conditioned prison. He stopped at the front. The building had no history, had only ever been a schoolroom, a municipal store, a council office; yet all who entered responded in the same way, as if it were a holy of holies, an inner sanctum, almost as if they were in the presence not of a painting but of the pregnant Madonna herself, in her swollen gown. He looked up at the fresco, paying it the unstinted respect that was its due, certain again of the invisible thread that ran through time, linking them all, the artists and sculptors, the writers and musicians, the ones he loved, the ones who had felt the fineness of life upon the pulse, the ones who had stood on the edge and not been afraid, the ones who had remained poised there long enough to share the incomplete, everlasting moment. He stood to one side of the group, still looking at the *Madonna*, letting quiet come, sinking into a stillness that grew deeper as the minutes passed, with only the faint, timeless hum from the current that controlled temperature and humidity inside the glass cage.

In the long pause one or two of the party looked round to find him. Eventually he moved to the front, staying to one side of the painting.

'The angels of course are wonderfully done. The pose, the modelling of the heads, the unwanting expressions, the satisfying fall of the robes. The same drawing reversed, as you can see. The same colours reversed as well. The soft reds and greens of the robes. Not to save effort, but for symmetry. And not symmetry for its own sake, but symmetry because differences, individuality, would have drawn attention away, pulling the eye to the sides.'

One or two of the group had crouched down on the coir matting and were looking up at the fresco from below.

'When we come to the Madonna herself, well, there's nothing special about most of it. Nine tenths of it's just the gown. And that isn't Piero at his best. In fact it's probably not Piero at all . . .'

The custodian of the *Madonna del Parto* had slipped into the back of the room. The middle-aged man from Charleston was fiddling with a camera. The lady from Westchester was comparing the original to the picture in her book. A dog barked centuries away in the village. Slowly he raised his left hand to the *Madonna*.

'But the face, the face.'

The reflected light of the Madonna glowed gently on the sixteen Americans.

'You remember in Rome, when you insisted on going to see the Moses? Well, it's very different. But there's something in common. Michelangelo's Moses seems to embody in marble all that the Old Testament stands for, all its grandeur and majesty and authority. And Piero's Madonna catches in a few square centimetres of painted plaster all that the Virgin stood for, all that she has meant to all those millions over all those centuries, all that she still means for millions even today.'

Tullio continued to look at the face.

'How on earth was it done? How in those few square centimetres of pigment could he create acceptance, humility, reticence, resignation, meekness. How could he touch so surely the essence of responsibility, create this portrait of selflessness, of ultimate modesty, ultimate humanity. Behold the handmaid of the Lord. Be it unto me according to thy word.'

Half a dozen more people had begun filtering into the room, forming a second layer behind the Americans. A child ran shouting down the stairs into the garden behind.

'And it's all in the elusive. In the subtle and the delicate, in the precarious life at the finest edges of the painter's art, in the things you'd think least likely to survive for five hundred years. Is it in the heavy eyelids? Or in the almost bare head with its modest adornment? Or in the purity of line of the face and profile? Or the way the light falls so chastely on the bones of the cheeks? Or is it also in the pose, the stout delicacy of the pregnancy, the concern in the placing of the hand, the strain you can almost feel beginning in the lower back? We were talking about realism yesterday; well look at the neck, especially on the left side. Like the neck of Michelangelo's Brutus, it's not realistic. Realism has been put second to something more important; only here it's to show the meaning of that perfect face, to leave it exposed, poised, separate, pure.'

Most of the Americans had entered into the painting now, slipping the ropes of where they were, who they were with, where they would be having lunch.

'And yet the miracle is that all this is done without adding up to insipidity, weakness. Modest, reticent, the Madonna may be. But not weak. There's an extraordinary strength and seriousness in that delicacy, enormous capacity under the submissiveness. It's the face of the Virgin Mary. But it's also the face of a woman . . . a woman capable of carrying the responsibility placed upon her. A face to which you would indeed entrust the future of the world.'

Tullio told himself to stop. There was silence in the room. Like an audience chamber.

❖

The group waited in the piazza, reluctant to board the coach. Tullio moved from room to room, looking for Angelo to discuss the new programme. The biglietteria was empty. He checked the exhibition rooms and glanced down into the garden where a piano was being installed for the evening recital. He scribbled a note and left it on the desk, looking out through the door at his party waiting in the strip of shade under the monastery wall. Instead of joining them in the last of the sunlight he turned left again into the old schoolroom. He was alone with the *Madonna*.

Intimacy slowed him, quietened his breathing. A moment, separate, distinct, the silence singing all around him. He looked at the painting and held his breath. A moment of nearness. A life of such moments. He saw it whole, but could not hold on. He saw the troubled face, heard the sacred, eloquent silence, devoid of frivolity. Obvious now. Obvious that this was not an ideal to consign to another time. Obvious that in this face was written a virtue still to be aspired to. Obvious that this was not womanly virtue but just virtue. He stood before the *Madonna*, having come full circle, looking at the face as it might have been looked at in its own time, as an exemplar, a model. The Tuscan Master, with his troubled, thinking, twenty-first century faces, was still ahead of the game. He raised his head to look again into the cage of light, seeing straightaway the truth of what was represented in those few square centimetres, seeing for the first time what the fresco was all about, beyond what could be named, beyond those resigned, heavy-lidded eyes, the portrait of responsibility, to something more essential still; to that final depth of virtue, that most elusive of qualities that was to do with the right degree of self-awareness, the subtlest quality of them all.

Vanetti dropped the newspaper at his feet and pulled the lever that operated the automatic doors as Tullio boarded the coach, taking the empty seat next to Evelyn Williams from Vermont.

'So what did you think?'

'I thought that face alone was worth crossing the Atlantic to see.'

The author would like to thank Paul Howlett, Pierantonio Tanzola, Giuliano Grasselini, and Mario Matteini for their help in the preparation of this book.

A selection of other books from Sceptre

Facing Out to Sea	Peter Adamson	0 340 69565 X	£6.99 ☐
Echoes of War	William Rivière	0 340 69607 9	£6.99 ☐
The Tempest	Juan Manuel de Prada	0 340 75023 5	£6.99 ☐
Ingenious Pain	Andrew Miller	0 340 68208 6	£6.99 ☐
Confessions of a Lapsed Standard-Bearer	Andreï Makine	0 340 72809 4	£6.99 ☐

All Hodder & Stoughton books are available at your local bookshop or newsagent, or can be ordered direct from the publisher. Just tick the titles you want and fill in the form below. Prices and availability subject to change without notice.

Hodder & Stoughton Books, Cash Sales Department, Bookpoint, 39 Milton Park, Abingdon, OXON, OX14 4TD, UK. E-mail address: orders@bookpoint.co.uk. If you have a credit card you may order by telephone – (01235) 400414.

Please enclose a cheque or postal order made payable to Bookpoint Ltd to the value of the cover price and allow the following for postage and packing:
UK & BFPO: £1.00 for the first book, 50p for the second book and 30p for each additional book ordered up to a maximum charge of £3.00.
OVERSEAS & EIRE: £2.00 for the first book, £1.00 for the second book and 50p for each additional book.

Name . . . .

Address . . . .

. . . .

. . . .

If you would prefer to pay by credit card, please complete:
Please debit my Visa / Access / Diner's Club / American Express (delete as applicable) card no:

Signature . . . .

Expiry Date . . . .

If you would <u>NOT</u> like to receive further information on our products please tick the box. ☐